Craig Rice (1908-1957), creator of madcap murder mavens Jake and Helene Justus and John J. Malone, was Georgiana Ann Randolph Walker Craig Lipton DeMott Bishop in private life. The first mystery writer to grace the cover of *Time*, she was hailed by the issue of Jan, 24 1946 as virtually the only "woman" of what the magazine deemed a distinctively American genre, "apt to mix the pleasures of the wake and the moment in a combination of hard drink, hilarity and homicide." This Rice did in high-spirited, Chicago-based spoofs like *8 Faces at 3* (1939), the *Big Midget Murders* (1942) and *Knocked for a Loop* (1957).

Her life was less a laughing matter, The Dorothy Parker of detective fiction, Rice wrote the binge but lived the hangover. Rice's father was a painter, her mother a "cosmopolite;" while her parents sojourned in Europe, divorced, married and remarried, Georgiana was raised by and aunt and uncle. She ran away from Miss Ransome's School in Piedmont, California, to become a "Bohemienne" in Chicago. There she went through a succession of five marriages of her own, providing two daughters and a son.

When *Time* got hold of her, Rice was living in Santa Monica and had written 15 books, including mysteries under the pseudonyms Michael Venning and Daphne Sanders. She would ghostwrite for stripper Gypsy Rose Lee and actor George Sanders. She scripted two entries in the "Falcon" film series and other creditable B movies.

She was deaf in one ear, blind in one eye and threatened with glaucoma in the other, In 1949 she was committed to Camarillo State Hospital for chronic alcoholism. Rice twice threatened suicide.

She was found dead in her Los Angeles apartment Aug. 28, 1957, "apparently," reported *Newsweek*, "from natural causes." Rice was 49.

—William Ruehlmann
Series Consultant

CRAIG RICE
TRIAL BY FURY

LIBRARY OF CRIME CLASSICS

MISTER E'S™

INTERNATIONAL POLYGONICS, LTD.
NEW YORK CITY

The characters and situations in this work are wholly
fictional and imaginative; do not portray, and are not
intended to portray, any actual persons or parties.
Any resemblance to anyone living or dead is purely
coincidental, and just the rarest good luck.

Library of Congress Card Catalog No. 91-70603
ISBN 1-55882-091-4

Printed and manufactured in the United States of
America.
First IPL printing June 1991.
10 9 8 7 6 5 4 3 2 1

Chapter One

THE LONG, dark corridor of the Jackson County Courthouse was as still as a grave, and almost as airless. Along the edges of the high ceiling, the shadows gathered into darkness, smoky and impenetrable; in the vast space below there was only a strange, murky half-light, more blue than gray, a light that seemed to be of its own making. Outside the great double doors it was blazing noon, but in this corridor it was dusk.

Even on that day, the hottest of the summer, there was a faint and uncomfortable chill in the motionless air.

Harvey Button, the janitor, paused in the act of picking up an infinitesimal scrap of wastepaper from the tile floor, and stood listening, almost as though he hoped to hear some reassuring sound.

Later, of course, he claimed to have had a premonition. It had, he said, wakened with him early in the morning. Not exactly a premonition, either, but a kind of vaguely unpleasant feeling. Yes, it could have been the weather, or even the last night's beer, but, he pointed out triumphantly, it was something much more fateful.

One of the massive doors suddenly swung open, and the blast of sunlight made him blink. A rush of hot air came in with it as though from a furnace.

Above the trees outside he could see a great dark streak in the sky, beginning to blot out the blazing glare. Every leaf on every tree was perfectly motionless.

"Going to storm," Harvey Button said amiably to the couple who had just come in. He slammed the door shut.

"Cool in here, anyway," the man said, mopping his brow.

The little janitor looked at them curiously. The man was tall, red-haired, and very thin; his perspiring face was a mass of tiny freckles. The girl with him was, Harvey said later, a whooperdoo.

Even on this day of almost incredible heat, she appeared cool. Every strand of shining ash-blonde hair was exquisitely in place, her pale, delicate, patrician face was made up to perfection. Harvey Button knew nothing of dress designers and Michigan Avenue shops, but he enjoyed looking at the lines of her perfectly plain gray linen suit.

"Where the hell is the county clerk?" the girl asked pleasantly.

"You mean, where's the county clerk," her companion said severely. "You're in a respectable community now."

Harvey Button grinned. "Who the hell wants to know where the county clerk is?"

"You get the idea right away," the girl said, grinning back at him.

"He's upstairs in the courtroom," the little janitor told her. "Today's the county board meeting." He might have been speaking of a convocation of the angels, from the tone of his voice. "But his deputy can take care of you, if you're looking for a marriage license."

"We've already got one of those," the red-haired man said. "This time we want a fishing license."

"Though," the girl added, "if you have a special on today, we might consider something snappy in a this year's model."

Buttonholes thought the whole thing over for a minute. "You'd better see the county clerk's deputy," he said at last. "First door to your left, down the corridor."

The couple thanked him and went away. He was sweeping up a microscopic bit of ash that had fallen from the blonde girl's cigarette when a tremendous clatter of footsteps began to sound on the stairs. The janitor stood aside and watched as forty-two members of the county board poured out through the corridor, then he began to clean up the small litter they had made on the floor.

It was a wonderful courthouse, if only people would keep it neat. He looked around admiringly. Back in 1882, they knew how to build courthouses. Big, paneled doors, high ceilings, fancy tile floors, and elegant millwork everywhere.

He walked to the end of the corridor, opened the door, and glanced out. In these few minutes, the sky had become entirely dark, immense black clouds pressed down over the trees like a gigantic cover. Not a single breath of air stirred anywhere, every bird in the courthouse square was silent.

"She's going to be a whopper when she hits," the janitor remarked to the world in general.

He shut the door and switched on the electric light in the cavernous hallway. It didn't help much.

A tallish, well-dressed woman with short gray hair came hurrying into the courthouse, slamming the door behind her. The janitor nodded to her.

"Is Mr. Skindingsrude still here, Buttonholes?"

"Yep, Miss McGowan. He's up in the courthouse."

A moment later the door opened again. The little janitor hurried to close it after a portly, red-faced, white-haired man.

" 'Afternoon, Senator."

Ex-Senator Peveley nodded gruffly and began puffing up the steep flight of stairs to the second floor. Harvey Button, otherwise known as Buttonholes, sighed wearily, finished sweeping up the last bits of wastepaper and ashes, and deposited them in a metal box on which he had painstakingly lettered HELP KEEP OUR COURTHOUSE CLEAN.

By the time he had finished, the young couple had returned from the county clerk's office. Buttonholes grinned widely and opened the door for them. The blonde girl looked at the threatening sky and frowned.

"I'm not sure I want to go out in that."

"Are you driving?" Buttonholes asked.

She nodded and pointed to a rakish robin's-egg-blue convertible parked near the courthouse.

"Then you'd better wait till she blows over," the janitor said. "These summer storms never last long."

The red-haired man shrugged his shoulders. "O.K., wheel out a waiting room."

"We haven't got one of those," Buttonholes said regretfully. He scratched his head thoughtfully. "I'll be glad to show you around the courthouse while you're waiting, though." He might, from his manner, have been offering to show them the Taj Mahal.

"Come on, Jake," the girl said. "It's a noble offer. You've never seen a courthouse like this one."

Jake hesitated. "I've seen so much of a courthouse exactly like this one, I bet I could find the men's toilet, blindfolded. Back in Grove County—"

A light came into Buttonholes' eyes. "Grove County, Iowa? I've got kinfolk there. Visited there back in '32. But say, the courthouse in Grove Falls can't touch this one."

"You tell him," the girl said warmly. "Jake's just a helpless provincial. A courthouse would have to go some to beat this."

"You've got to show me," Jake said. He looked at his wrist watch. "Hell, we've got nothing in the world but time. "Come on, Helene, let's see the sights."

"I'm Harvey Button," the janitor said.

"I'm Jake Justus," the red-haired man told him. "This is my wife, Mrs. Justus."

"Pleased to meet you both," Buttonholes said, rattling an enormous bunch of keys. "Well, you've seen the county clerk's office. The highway office is just like it, so's the clerk of the court's. All pretty elegant, too. This here's the county treasurer's office."

He opened a door with a proud gesture.

As far as they could see, it was exactly like the office they had just left, save that this one had windows on two sides. It was a large, high-ceilinged room in which a shining, new mahogany desk stood next to an immense, scarred, roll-top model. Despite its size, the room was crowded from wall to wall with tables, chairs, desks, stools, filing cabinets, and office machines.

Sitting at the old roll-top desk was the most completely hairless man Jake and Helene had ever seen.

He was thin, and even sitting in a swivel chair he appeared tall, but his only other mark of distinction was his nude, polished head. Helene commented later that even his eyelids were bald.

At one end of the office a huge iron door leading to the vault stood ajar. Next to it, in the corner, was an ancient black marble fireplace in which a small steam radiator had been installed.

" 'Course, we don't use the fireplaces any more," Buttonholes said proudly. "They're just for show."

"I'm glad to hear it," Helene said.

Above the fireplace was a framed yellow group photograph marked COURTHOUSE STAFF, 1902. Beyond it a black-framed, hand-lettered sign proclaimed AN HONEST MAN IS THE NOBLEST WORK OF GOD.

"In the treasurer's office of the Grove Falls Courthouse," Jake said, "the sign read 'Honesty is the best policy.' "

The bald-headed man looked up from his ledger. "This one," he said rather coldly, "is the slogan of the Jackson businessmen's association." He added, as though to be agreeable to a visitor, "However, honesty *is* the best policy."

"I've heard it spoken of very highly," Jake said politely.

"That was Mr. Goudge," Buttonholes said, out in the hall. "Alvin Goudge."

He opened the next door down the hall. It disclosed an office similar to the one occupied by Mr. Goudge, save that two plumpish girls were working furiously at a pair of adding machines, and that a row of ten-cent-store toy trucks decorated the top of the carved marble mantelpiece. A wide mustached man with a felt hat pulled down over his eyes was sleeping noisily in the swivel chair in the corner.

"This is the highway department," Jake declared.

Buttonholes stared at him admiringly. "How did you know?"

Jake said cryptically, "This is old home week." He whistled a bar of *Highways Are Happy Ways*. "Back in Grove County they picked the highway commissioner in a numbers game. Let's shove on."

Buttonholes grinned knowingly, nudged Jake in the ribs, and said, "Chet Feeny, our highway commissioner, owns a half-dozen farms up near Mills Center." He stopped suddenly, looked stern, and added in a virtuous whisper, "He *drinks*."

"Maybe he has a secret sorrow," Helene said sadly.

The little janitor led them on down the cavernous hall, opening a succession of doors marked COUNTY NURSE, OUTDOOR RELIEF, and SANITATION. He passed by an ornate pair of double doors on which a gold-lettered sign proclaimed COUNTY COURT.

"It's locked up," he explained. "Judge Foote is away on a fishing trip."

He opened a door disclosing a long, narrow, and extremely steep staircase, and led the way up. Near the top of it was a sharp and perilous curve.

"These are only the back stairs," he explained.

"Two sets of stairs," the blonde girl said. "Sheer swank."

At the top of the stairs were two large, dreary rooms and a tiny hall. One was the jury room and the other was for consultations, Buttonholes explained. The door off the hall led into a broom closet. They went on into the courtroom.

It was an immense, high-ceilinged room, the plaster walls painted in a fair approximation of marble. A dingy mural above the judge's bench appeared to have something to do with justice. It was partly covered with a flag.

"Beautiful room," Buttonholes said proudly.

"I'm glad you like it," Helene said.

Jake looked curiously at the group of people inside the enclosure. There were the two that Buttonholes had seen, Miss McGowan, and ex-Senator Peveley, the latter very red-faced, very perspiring, and apparently very cross. There was a sturdy, middle-aged man with sandy hair; Buttonholes pointed him out as Ed Skindingsrude, chairman of the county board. The tall, handsome man with curly white hair was Phil Smith, the county clerk.

"You'd find it more interesting if a trial was going on," the janitor said apologetically. "Court ain't in session till October."

"I'm sure if you'd known we were coming you'd have made different arrangements," Jake said. "Maybe even a nice juicy murder case."

Buttonholes grinned. "Ain't been a murder in Jackson County in thirty-two years. Fella up in Jay Creek shot his father-in-law over a horse deal, thirty-two years ago. Awful tough bunch of people up in Jay Creek."

"Quick-tempered," Helene said gravely. "Maybe there was more to it than ever got into the papers. Maybe he had a secret sorrow too."

Buttonholes shook his head. "He claimed the old guy stole his horse," he said solemnly.

They trailed slowly across the courtroom. On the

other side, a wide, impressive stairway with a thick, near-mahogany rail led down to the floor below.

"This here's the main stairway," the janitor said. "The little one was put up there just in case of emergencies, but it's so handy it gets used all the time."

"Don't be discouraged," Helene said. "Maybe you'll have an emergency here sometime, and then everybody'll use the main stairway."

Jake had paused on the landing, one hand still clinging to the rail. Through the arched window above the landing he could see that the ominous darkness outside had deepened, the breathless stillness of the air could be seen as much as felt. A faint, ugly, greenish light showed at the very edge of the sky.

"She's going to be a ring-tailed dandy," Buttonhole breathed admiringly, looking up at the window.

"It gives me the horrors," Jake said sharply, reaching for a cigarette. "I usually don't mind storms, but something about this gives me just plain, old-fashioned horrors."

Helene looked at him, opened her mouth to speak, and closed it again.

Buttonholes regarded him thoughtfully. "Are you like that too?"

"Like what?" Jake asked suspiciously. There was a little edge to his voice.

"Second sight. I tend a little that way myself."

"It must be wonderfully useful," Helene said. "How are you on horse races?"

Buttonholes ignored her. "My grandmother was a Welshwoman. She had the gift." He drew a long breath. "Never forget when she met Art Tonny, he was going with my stepsister's oldest girl. She looked right at him and she said, 'Young man, there's the mark of death on you.'" He paused and spat neatly into a sand bucket. "Those are the very words she used."

"I can think of better ones," Jake said admiringly.

"Five years later," Buttonholes said, "he got drunk and drove his car into the river." He added, "Good thing my stepsister's oldest girl hadn't married him."

"Maybe she had the same gift," Helene commented.

They had reached the vast lower hall that stretched from the front of the Jackson County Courthouse to its rear. A sudden breeze arose from nowhere, cutting across the humid warmth like a cold knife, and, as suddenly, died down again.

"Storm or no storm," Jake Justus began firmly, taking Helene by the arm, "we're getting out of here, and—"

That was when they heard the scream.

It came from somewhere over their heads, a strange, half-choked cry. It was followed by another sound, that of a heavy body rolling and bumping down that narrow twisting, back staircase.

The red-haired man reached the bottom of the stairs just as the body of ex-Senator Peveley rolled out onto the corridor floor. Jake bent down for a quick look.

"Well," he said grimly, "there's your second murder in thirty-two years."

Chapter Two

"**B**UT he can't be murdered," one of the plump girls from the highway commissioner's office kept repeating over and over. "He's Senator Peveley."

Jake looked at her. "I'm sorry, but that's one kind of Senatorial immunity I never heard of."

He felt aggrieved, not altogether without cause. "This is the sort of thing we came to the country to get away from," he said to Helene.

She nodded sympathetically. "It's none of our business," she said. "Let's get out of here and go on with our fishing trip, murder or no murder."

"I'm afraid not," Jake said. "Even in the country it isn't considered good form to walk away from a corpse before the police arrive."

Everybody was now looking at the late Senator Peveley but, Jake reminded himself, soon those glances would be directed at them, with a mixture of curiosity and hostility. Helene wouldn't know that. She hadn't spent the first years of her life in Grove Falls.

It was amazing how the courthouse corridor had suddenly filled with people. Only a moment before it had been empty, dark, and cavernous. Now it was crowded with shocked and curious people. He looked up and recognized the gray-haired Miss McGowan, the stocky little Mr. Skindingsrude, the tall, handsome Phil Smith. There were others, strangers to him.

Alvin Goudge, his bald head shining, pushed his way into the center of the group. "Senator Peveley shot! This is terrible! Somebody's got to do something."

"Senator Pevely can't be dead," a thin, spectacled man said wildly. "Why, I was only talking to him five minutes ago."

"What makes you think that's a guarantee?" Jake said irritably. "You figure he's just doing imitations?"

He looked around the group intently. He had been there since the first sound of the scream, and he knew that nobody had gone out through those double doors. Someone, there in that corridor, had murdered Senator Peveley.

A young, brown-suited man Jake had noticed upstairs in the courtroom had pushed his way through the crowd and was standing staring at the body. He was a handsome young man, in a thin, worried way, brown-haired and brown-eyed. There was a lead pencil smudge on one side of his face.

"Jerry Luckstone, the new district attorney," Buttonholes whispered to Jake.

The district attorney's face had turned a sickly white.

"But it's Senator Peveley," he said in a dazed voice.

"Right the first time," Jake said. "Now try for the four-dollar question."

Jerry Luckstone hadn't heard. He was goggling foolishly at the back of the dead man's white linen suit."

"He can't have been murdered," he declared at last. "I'm engaged to marry his daughter."

Jake sighed. "You'll just have to get someone else to give the bride away." He drew a long breath. "Well, what are you going to do about it? A man's been murdered. You can't just stand here looking at him forever."

Jerry Luckstone stared at him, wild-eyed. "Who the hell are you and what are you doing here?" He gasped. "What did you have against Senator Peveley?"

"I never saw Senator Peveley before in my life," Jake said indignantly. "We just happened to be in this damned courthouse getting a fishing license when somebody bumped off your Senator, and that's all I know about it."

"But nobody here could have murdered him," the young district attorney said. He looked around at the circle of faces, his eyes startled. "Why, we all know each other."

Jake saw Helene opening her mouth to speak, and tightened his hand on her arm. That was exactly what he'd been thinking. These people all knew each other. They, he and Helene, were the strangers, the outlanders. He knew that everyone in the corridor was staring at them, with cold, unfriendly eyes, that the two of them had been set apart from the others, standing alone and regarded with suspicion. Even Butttonholes was looking at them dubiously.

"Look here," Jake began firmly. "We were coming down those stairs over there, with this man here, when we heard—" He realized that nobody was listening. "Damn it," he said, "doesn't anybody here know what to do when a murder's been committed?"

Even as he asked the question, he knew the answer. No one did know. Jackson County hadn't had a murder for thirty-two years.

Helene's fingers dug into his arm. "The more I see of this place," she whispered to him, "the better I like any other place we could be." There were tiny beads of perspiration on her upper lip.

"Don't worry," he whispered back, reassuringly. "It'll be all right, soon as they get the idea we're just innocent spectators."

"Just so they get the idea. It may take the best years of our life," she murmured.

A sudden roar of thunder shook the old building to its foundations. Jake could see the lightning flashes through the window in the Highway Department office. Inside the courthouse there was a curious, murky light.

There was something fantastic and incredible about the scene. The circle of motionless people, the white-faced young district attorney, and the late Senator Peveley on the floor, exactly as he had fallen, face down, limp arms and legs sprawled flatly on the floor, a red stain spreading on his white linen coat. It seemed to Jake that he had been standing there for hours, Helene's fingers cold on his arm, until he glanced up at the big hall clock and realized that it had only been three minutes.

"We ought to call up somebody," a man in the group said.

Jake said, "Now you're getting the idea. Who do you know?"

"We've got to let the newspapers know," another man said.

"Somebody has to tell his daughter," Ed Skindingsrude said, with a sidelong glance at the young district attorney.

The handsome, gray-haired Miss McGowan cleared her throat. "Jerry, call the sheriff."

Everyone relaxed. The district attorney blushed faintly, muttered something that sounded like "Of course," and hurried into one of the offices. The group began breaking up into subgroups, two people here, three people there. A subdued murmur of voices began.

"We mustn't move the body until the sheriff gets here," a girl said.

It occurred to Jake that was the first time anyone had mentioned touching the body.

Suddenly everyone in the corridor was staring at Helene. Jake felt the fingers on his arm first become steel pincers, then a deadly weight, then slip away entirely. In the next instant, before he had time to make a move, she was a little crumpled heap on the floor.

It was as though a bell had been rung. Every person sprang into action at the same time. A murdered man on the courthouse floor was something nobody knew how to cope with, a fainting woman was something else again. There were a dozen voices at once, saying "water," "ammonia," "the couch in the clerk of the court's office," "a doctor."

Someone said something about first aid and having been a Boy Scout counselor.

Another person informed them of an Aunt Helen who used to faint at funerals.

People crowded between Jake and Helene. Before he could do anything, a stocky, gray-haired man had picked her up and carried her into the office of the clerk of court. Jake, and most of the spectators in the corridor, were two steps behind.

On the worn leather couch, she looked very small and very pale, one strand of her silvery hair fallen across her colorless cheek. A sudden pang of terror seized Jake. He had never seen Helene faint before. He flung himself down beside the couch and took her cold hand in his.

"It must have been the heat," the man who'd been a Boy Scout counselor said.

"She looks puny," the chairman of the county board commented.

Jake felt the ice-cold fingers tighten on his hand. He looked at her closely. Her white face was motionless, her eyelids closed. Again the fingers tightened, ever so quickly. He gave a faint pressure in return and rose to his feet.

"She'll be all right," Jake said firmly. "Just a touch of the sun." He took out an already damp handkerchief and mopped his brow. "Just let her rest here a minute, and she'll be all right. She has these spells now and then."

To his great relief, the spectators retreated into the hall, leaving him with alone with Helene. He dropped into a chair beside her.

"What the hell's the idea?" he whispered fiercely.

"Jake, I had to get out of that crowd," she whispered back, without opening her eyes. "I had to talk to you."

"Well, go ahead. We are, to coin a phrase, alone at last."

She opened her eyes wide and stared at him. "A man's been murdered, and everybody just stands around and looks silly."

"They're just shocked, so they act natural."

"Jake, let's get out of here. Let's get out quick and get in the car and be halfway to the next town before anyone can say 'Boo.'"

"And have every police car in Jackson County looking for us because we beat it? Besides, we never could get out through that corridor without being stopped. A couple of these boys look as if they could say 'Boo' fast."

"I don't like it here," she said stubbornly.

"Your point is well taken. However, in a little while they'll remember that ex-Senator Peveley was nothing to us. We just happened to be in the building when somebody bumped him off. As soon as that sheriff gets here, we can tell him what we saw, and then go." It was a magnificent performance of whistling in the dark.

She sighed and was silent.

Jake rose, walked to the window, and looked out. There was a broad expanse of bright-green lawn and, beyond it, what he guessed to be the jail. It was an ugly angular building of yellow brick, with barred and recessed windows. Near by a small Civil War cannon stood in front of an indignant and unpleasant-looking cast-iron soldier. Jake wondered if it had been put there to scare people away from the jail.

"It's raining pitchforks and hammer handles," he commented. Just as he spoke, a great branch broke away from one of the immense old elm trees and blew past the window.

"I hope that was only the wind," Helene said faintly.

Across the lawn Jake saw the door to the jail building open, and a stocky, red-faced man come out. He stood there for a moment, looking at the rain, then began running the length of the path that led to the courthouse. Halfway there his hat blew off, he stopped briefly to retrieve it, and went on running.

"Here comes the sheriff," Jake said. "Pretend you're well enough to go back out there." He added, "Thank God somebody's here now who knows what to do—I hope!"

He put an arm around Helene as though supporting her, and led her back into the corridor. The body of ex-Senator Peveley still lay where it had fallen. The spectators were standing around, whispering, in awed little groups. Everyone turned to look curiously at Helene.

Just as Jake and Helene reached the hall, the great door at its east end opened suddenly, letting in a gust of wind and rain and the stocky, red-faced man. The little janitor, Buttonholes, rushed forward to help close the door and looked regretfully at the pool of muddy water on the tile floor.

A new wave of tense expectancy greeted the sheriff's arrival. They watched him with the respect due authority in the situation.

The sheriff walked the length of the corridor on tiptoe, his hat in his hand. No one spoke to him. He bent down for a moment next to the body, looking at the stain on the white linen coat. When he straightened up again, the color was draining from his face.

"He's been murdered!" the sheriff said in a startled voice. He was silent a moment. "That's right, he's been murdered. We've gotta call the police!"

Chapter Three

"IT'S NONE of my business," Jake said, lighting a cigarette, "and I don't know that I care very much, but who might have wanted to murder your ex-Senator?"

Buttonholes scowled at the railing he was dusting. "Senator Peveley wasn't exactly what you'd call a popular man."

"He must have been popular with some people," Helene declared. "He couldn't have bought all those votes."

"Personally popular is what I mean to say," Buttonholes told her.

The three were waiting in the county clerk's office. Sheriff Marvin Kling and the young district attorney were holding a lengthy debate just outside the door. Others in the group of spectators had scattered to various offices in the building. Ex-Senator Peveley still lay on the corridor floor, exactly as he had fallen.

Later, Helene commented that she wouldn't have believed any of it possible, if she hadn't been there. Sheriff Kling's first act, after his belated realization that he was in charge of the situation, was to order both doors to the courthouse locked. The county clerk had objected to this, on the reasonable grounds that people were coming in all the time for fishing licenses. The sheriff had finally compromised by placing a deputy at each of the great double doors, with strict orders to let people in, but not to let anyone out.

"That way," he said grimly, "we'll have the murderer right here in the courthouse, and we won't have to chase him halfway to Illinois, the way we did with those two guys who stole the slot machine from Marty Gill's roadhouse.

"And nobody," he declared, "is allowed to touch the body until the coroner gets here." That was the one thing he was positive about.

"Well, he's sure of something," Helene commented. "I wonder if he knows why."

"I doubt it," Jake said. "He's been reading detective stories and that's the only thing that stuck in his mind."

Unfortunately, Charlie Hausen, Jackson County's coroner, an undertaker by profession, was conducting a funeral in Waterville, nine miles away. He'd drive down to Jackson the minute it was over.

"That's all right," Sheriff Kling announced. "Nobody here is in any hurry."

Someone had suggested placing a sheet over the body, but there appeared to be some doubt as to the legality of the procedure. Besides, there was nothing in the Jackson County Courthouse to serve as a sheet, and Sheriff Kling refused to allow anyone to leave the building to get one. He appointed an uncomfortable, white-faced deputy to stand guard over the remains, and let it go at that, declaring that now there was nothing anybody could do until Coronor Hausen finished with his funeral and arrived.

In the meantime, no one could leave the court-house.

On the whole, no one seemed to object. Phil Smithy did remark, mildly, that no one in the building had been out to lunch. The sheriff pointed out in return that Kline's Grill would send in sandwiches. Miss McGowan glanced at her watch, frowned, and telephoned the Library Guild to apologize for not being present at the afternoon's meeting. The white-faced young district attorney shut himself in his office.

No one in the building made any pretense of continuing work. A group of men gathered in the highway office, around Sheriff Kling. The office girls were a subdued, but still chattering group at the farthest end of the corridor. The deputy sheriffs refused to let anyone up to the second floor.

The thunder had slackened a little, but outside the rain was still falling. Helene glanced longingly toward the door.

"I could kick up a row about being kept here," Jake said. "But somehow I've an idea it wouldn't be tactful. I don't think we move these bodies, either, until the coroner arrives."

"Oh well," Helene said. "Maybe in time we'll get to like it here." She paused in the act of lighting a cigarette. "There's a chance we'll be able to leave after the coroner arrives, isn't there?"

"Don't worry," Jake told her firmly. "If you think I'm going to let any small-town sheriff—"

She interrupted him with a sigh. "That's what you said the time I was arrested for speeding in Evanston. You said no Evanston cop was going to put me in jail—"

"That was different," Jake said virtuously. "That was breaking an Evanston speed law. This is only murder." He took her arm and steered her into the county clerk's office, where Buttonholes was staring longingly at his mop and pail, and at the corridor floor where the body lay. Otherwise, the office was deserted.

"You'll have plenty of time to clean up later," Jake told him consolingly.

Buttonholes sighed, shook his head, and put away the mop.

"Too bad it didn't occur to any of us to make book on your premonition," Helene said.

Buttonholes brightened. "That's right. I'd forgotten. Funny, ain't it. I remember my grandmother, old Mrs. Button—" He paused, scowled, and finally said, "I guess I told you about that."

"How are you fixed for premonitions now?" she wanted to know.

The janitor thought for a minute before he answered. "It isn't exactly a premonition. I just feel like the worst was yet to come."

"If you're right," Jake said, "and I have a nasty suspicion you are, by the time it does come, we'll be halfway into the next state." He had a premonition of his own about that, but he was keeping it to himself.

"What was the corpse like?" Helene asked. "I mean, before he was a corpse?"

"He was a very famous man," Buttonholes said solemnly. "He was a Senator for two terms, and he ran for governor once but he didn't get elected. I guess he was about the most famous man Jackson ever had."

"At least," Helene murmured, "the most famous in the last thirty-two years."

"Outside of being a Senator," the janitor went on, "he owned half the shoe factory here, and he was president of the bank. I guess he owned a lot of real estate and mortgages, too. Ex-Senator Peveley must've been a rich man."

"And who'll get all that now?" Jake asked casually.

"His daughter, I suppose. She's all he had. Her name's Florence. She's engaged to marry Jerry Luckstone. Maybe she won't inherit everything, I don't think she and the old man"—Buttonholes cleared his throat apologetically—"got along any too well. A lot of people didn't get along with him."

"With all that money?" Helene said.

Buttonholes blinked. "He was kind of quick-tempered, and he always had to have his own way. There was plenty of people didn't like him, but that don't mean murder. Folks up here don't go around murdering."

"Somebody up here does," Jake said. "Probably never heard about the rules."

Before Buttonholes could answer, a brown-haired, pretty girl slipped into the office, glanced silently at the trio, went over to the telephone, and called a number.

"I want to speak to Mr. Burrows." Her voice was so low Jake and Helene could barely make out the words. It was even lower when she spoke again.

"This is Arlene, Tom. Yes, I know I wasn't going to call you up again. But I knew you'd want to know. Senator Peveley has been killed. Murdered." There was a longish pause, then, "I don't know. Somebody shot him, and he's dead." Another pause. "On the floor of the corridor. Tom—"

Evidently Tom had hung up. The brown-haired girl jiggled the phone hook once or twice, said, "Oh dear!" and unexpectedly burst into tears. Buttonholes made an impulsive move in her direction, but she ran into a little coat closet and shut the door.

Helene looked after her, shaking her head. "Never a dull moment in Jackson, Wisconsin," she commented.

Buttonholes frowned. "If her father finds out—"

He was interrupted by the arrival of Phil Smith, the county clerk. The handsome, white-haired man smiled politely at Jake and Helene.

"Sorry you've had this interruption of your fishing trip," he said smoothly. "Still, you're better off here in the courthouse than you would have been out in this rain."

"We're not wet," Helene said, "if that's what you mean."

Jake sighed. "Does anyone have any idea who killed him?"

Phil Smith shook his head. "Not an idea in the world. I don't see how it could have happened, myself." He scowled. "Why, we were all right there in the courtroom when we heard the shot, and he fell."

"Someone who was up there must have shot him," Jake said.

The county clerk shook his head. "Impossible. One of those people? Absurd." He looked indignantly at Jake, who shrugged his shoulders and looked away.

"You'll have to admit that somebody shot him," Helene said.

Phil Smith looked at her indulgently. "My dear young lady—"

There was a little commotion in the hall as one of the big doors banged.

"Charlie Hausen's here," Buttonholes announced, with a sigh of relief.

Helene started to follow them into the corridor, but Jake caught her arm.

"Take it easy," he advised. "We'll just sit tight till the coroner gets through."

"And then what, or are you going to make it up as you go along?"

"Then," Jake said firmly, "it'll be time to tell the sheriff he can't keep us here any longer."

"That's wonderful," she said, "if only the sheriff agrees with you."

She was silent for a moment. Jake stared at her admiringly. She looked exactly like what she was, a debutante heiress. Her falling in love and marrying him was still a miracle every time he thought of it.

"It's funny we didn't hear the shot," she said suddenly.

"We were downstairs, and at the other end of the building," he reminded her. "These 1880 walls are thick."

"Where do you suppose the gun is? Do you think we should let the sheriff in on the fact that there must have been a gun?"

Buttonholes appeared in the doorway. "You'd better come out in the hall. Sheriff Kling's making a list of everybody who was in the courthouse."

The west door of the corridor stood open, and through it they could see an ornate and shining hearse standing in the rain.

"Charlie Hausen drove it here from Mrs. Albert's funeral," Buttonholes said.

As he spoke, two young men in dark suits carried a stretcher in from the hearse and began moving the Senator's body, under the supervision of a short, black-clad, anxious little man with a derby hat. Everybody turned to watch. The door suddenly banged shut after the stretcher had been carried out, and everybody jumped.

A small table had been moved into the corridor, and Sheriff Marvin Kling sat at it, making a list. He glared up at Jake and opened his mouth to speak.

Jake decided to beat him to the draw. "How much longer do you think you can detain us illegally?" he said with virtuous indignation. "Do you know who we are?"

"Hell," the sheriff said, "I don't even know what your name is."

"I'm Jake Justus, and this is Mrs. Justus," Jake said. As the sheriff wrote it down he added, "I'll be glad to give you any information I can, but let's make it snappy. I don't want to spend the rest of the summer here."

Sheriff Kling looked up coldly. "Where were you when the shot was fired?"

"I didn't hear the shot. We were just at the foot of that big staircase when we heard him fall down the other stairs."

"That's what you say," Sheriff Kling said.

"We've got a witness," Jake said. His voice was dangerously low. He pointed to Buttonholes. "He was right there with us."

"Sure I was," Buttonholes said helpfully.

The sheriff's eyes narrowed. "Don't mean a thing.

Everybody knows Buttonholes is the worst liar in Jackson County." He wrote something down, Jake couldn't see what it was. "Don't you try to make a break for it. You stay right where I can see you until I get through making my list."

A deputy shoved him away from the table, and Helene caught Jake's arm just in time to save the deputy's front teeth.

"All we need now," she said, under her breath, "is for you to get into a fight."

She led him out of earshot of everyone in the corridor, while he muttered words that had to do with Sheriff Marvin Kling's character, intelligence, origin, and the disgraceful habits of his entire family tree. He wound up by demanding, "who does he think he is, anyway?"

"I don't know for sure," Helene said, "but he acts as if he thought he was sheriff of Jackson County." She frowned. "Jake, what's it all about? They can't seriously think we had anything to do with it. Why is everybody so damned suspicious of us?"

Jake drew a long breath. "It's a little hard to explain to a city girl like you. We're strangers. No one else is. The people here may not all like each other, but they all know each other."

"But they can't do anything to us for being strangers."

"They haven't found that out yet," Jake said grimly, "but I hope to teach them."

Sheriff Kling finished his note-making, rose, and looked around.

"Everybody who doesn't regularly belong in the courthouse come into this office here," he roared.

Jake set his jaw hard and strode down the length of the corridor.

"Now look here," he said. "My wife and I are on a fishing trip. We didn't come up here to spend our vacation in the Jackson County courthouse, and we're not going to hang around any longer."

"You think so, do you?" the sheriff said.

"Ask any questions you want, but ask 'em quick," Jake said. "And then we're getting out of here."

Sheriff Kling glared at him. His face turned two shades nearer purple.

"Oh no you're not," he roared. "You're going to stay right here till I find out who murdered Senator Peveley." He added furiously, "And I don't care if it takes all summer!"

Helene poked Jake in the ribs. "Is he being Donald Duck or General Grant?"

The diversion worked. Jake's shoulders relaxed, he laughed. "Let's hang around and find out," he said.

Chapter Four

JAKE LOOKED at his watch. It had been exactly forty-seven minutes since the murder of Ex-Senator Peveley. At the rate things were going, it would probably be forty-seven years before Sheriff Kling found out who murdered him.

The great door at the west end of the corridor banged open, banged shut again, and a young man pushed his way into the center of the group around Sheriff Kling with the approximate speed and fury of a lightning bolt. He was a short, slight young man with sandy blond hair and a pale face that was liberally sprinkled with light-brown freckles. At the moment he appeared to be trying to strike Sheriff Kling dead with the glance he shot from behind rimless glasses.

"What's the idea? I don't suppose it would occur to you to call me."

The sheriff glared right back at him, wiping the sweat from his forehead with the back of his shirt sleeve. "I've had enough on my mind without bothering about you."

The young man drew a quick breath. "How long ago did it happen? What have you done? Why—" his eyes fell on Jake and Helene. "Who are you?"

"The city slicker," Jake said irritably, "and who are *you?*"

"Tom Burrows, of the *Jackson County Enterprise.* Who—"

"Now look here, Tom," Sheriff Kling began.

The young man turned back to him. "When was he murdered? How did it happen? What have you done with the body? Who killed him?"

"All in good time," the sheriff said.

Tom Burrows muttered something profane, pushed his way into the county clerk's office, and picked up the telephone. "Get me the United Press in Madison and reverse the charges. Tom Burrows calling."

"Now wait a minute," Sheriff Kling said.

"And have every other correspondent in the county beat me to it? Nuts! This is space rates!"

The sheriff turned to the people still standing irresolutely by the door. "Damn it, I thought I told all you to come in here."

"Don't go exceeding your authority, Marv, or you'll get into trouble," Tom Burrows said casually.

"You go to hell," Sheriff Kling roared. He mopped his brow again. "Now, all of you who don't belong in the courthouse, tell me what you were doing here."

Ed Skindingsrude spoke up. "You know what I was doing here, Marv. It's county board meeting. I stayed behind to have a word with Phil Smith."

"What about?"

"About the abominable slot-machine situation in the county, due to the laxity of the sheriff's office."

Sheriff Kling purpled. He swallowed a few words before he turned to the tall, tailored, gray-haired woman.

"How about you, Miss McGowan?"

"I was here to see Mr. Smith, on some bank business. It had to do with the school bonds, but I don't think you need to have all the details." She spoke crisply and very coldly.

There were only three people in the group being questioned, besides Jake and Helene. The third was a pretty, blonde woman with a carelessly made-up face. Sheriff Kling turned to her.

"What were you doing here, Cora Belle?"

"I was waiting to see Jerry Luckstone," she said sullenly.

"What about?"

"None of your business. Ask him, if you have to."

"I will," the sheriff said grimly.

Tom Burrows had been talking into the telephone, finished with, "That's all now, I'll call in later," and hung up.

"Now," the sheriff said, turning his glare on Jake, "What were you doing here?"

"I was getting fishing licenses for my wife and myself," Jake said. He spoke slowly and clearly, as though to someone unfamiliar with the language. "It looked as though it was going to storm, and we decided to wait in the courthouse until it blew over. The janitor very kindly offered to show us around while we were waiting."

"By the way," Tom Burrows said, "while you're finding out what everybody was doing in the courthouse, what was Senator Peveley doing here? Has anyone tried to find that out yet?"

"I can't exactly ask him," Sheriff Kling said snappishly.

"No," the young man agreed, "but someone else might know. And incidentally, where's the gun?"

The sheriff stared at him for a moment, then bellowed at the top of his voice, "Joe! Has anybody left the courthouse?"

"Nobody but Charlie Hausen and his assistants, and the body."

"Then don't let nobody leave without you search 'em first," Sheriff Kling ordered. "And Joe, you and Harry, you search this courthouse from top to bottom. Take Buttonholes with you."

It was a good sixty seconds before the deputy called back, "What'dya want us to look for, Marv?"

"The gun, you damn fools," Sheriff Kling roared.

Jake sighed. If they were going to have to wait until the finding of the gun that had killed Senator Peveley, it looked like a long stay in the Jackson County courthouse. Suddenly a new idea appeared to strike the harassed sheriff, who bolted out of the room. Jake shook his head wearily and lit a cigarette.

He realized that the storm outside was over and that the clouds had disappeared as quickly as they had come. Shafts of sunlight were beginning to stream down through the great green trees and penetrate the rain-washed windows of the Jackson County Courthouse.

"Lovely day for driving," he said wistfully.

"No satisfying you, is there?" Helene said. "And after all the trouble I took to arrange this for you."

Tom Burrows grinned. "Pardon me for making a nuisance of myself," he said, "but just who are you?"

Jake grinned back. "I'm Jake Justus, and this is my wife."

"Well I'm damned!" said Tom Burrows surprisingly.

Jake raised his eyebrows. "Do you want to make an issue of it?"

"Jake Justus of the *Examiner?*" the young man asked. As Jake nodded, he bounded across the room to shake hands. "I guess you wouldn't remember me. I worked for the City News Bureau for a few months."

"That so!" Jake said cordially. "Did you know Walter Ryberg over there?"

"Know him!" Tom Burrows said, "I worked for him! I didn't know many people at the *Examiner*. I did know Charley Blake at the *American,* and I knew John Lally at the *News*. I sold him a short short story once."

Helene said, "I hate to interrupt a reunion, but oughtn't we to be planning an exit line?" She turned to Tom Burrows. "You seem familiar with this so-called sheriff. What's the magic word that gets us out of here?"

"I'll tell him we want to go fishing," Jake told her airily. He turned back to the young man. "What are you doing up here?"

Tom Burrows laughed. "You've heard about the newspaperman who wants to retire and run a country weekly?"

Jake nodded. "That's every newspaperman."

"Well, I'm the one who did. I worked for the United Press for a number of years, and then a great-aunt left me a legacy, and I bought the *Enterprise*."

"Making any money?" Jake asked curiously.

"A little, but I'm making it by being a local correspondent for a Madison paper. Are you still with the *Examiner?*"

Jake shook his head. "I quit years ago. I was a press

agent until last winter. Now I'm running a night club." He slid his long frame onto a desk top. "I won it on a bet."

Tom Burrows' eyes suddenly narrowed. "Wait a minute. I read a newspaper once in a while. Weren't you mixed up in a bunch of murders last winter?"

Sheriff Marvin Kling chose that inopportune moment to come into the office.

"What kind of murders?" he demanded.

"I was only joking, Marv," Tom Burrows said quickly.

Sheriff Kling snorted and looked at Jake and Helene suspiciously.

"Found the gun yet?" Tom Burrows asked, before the sheriff could pursue the subject.

"We're still looking," the sheriff growled. "We'll find it. We're searching the grounds, too, in case the murderer dropped it out of a window. Right now I'm finding out exactly where everybody in the courthouse was when the Senator got shot."

Jerry Luckstone came into the office, still pale, and visibly shaken. He nodded briefly to the young newspaperman.

"Jerry," the sheriff said, "look over this list of who was upstairs when it happened, and see if it looks O. K. to you. You were there." He handed the district attorney a slightly soiled sheet of paper.

"Ed Skindingsrude and Miss McGowan," Jerry Luckstone mumbled, checking off the names as he read, "Jerry Luckstone, Phil Smith, Cora Belle Fromm, Arlene Goudge. Yes, that looks right to me. Marv, whatever could have become of that gun?"

"We'll find it," the sheriff said loudly. He took his list. "Everybody else was downstairs and couldn't have done the shooting except these two, and I'm damned if I know where they were at."

Jake held his breath for ten seconds and then exploded. "You know where we were. We were down at the foot of that big staircase. This guy here—"

"Buttonholes is a liar," the sheriff said. "And nobody asked you anything."

The young district attorney shoved Jake aside. "Listen, Marv," he said desperately, "come out in the hall. I've got to talk to you."

"Wait a minute," Tom Burrows said. "I've got to call the U.P. back. You'd better think of something for me to tell 'em."

Sheriff Marvin Kling scowled at him for a minute. "Tell 'em all Jackson County mourns the death of ex-Senator Peveley. Tell 'em he was a respected citizen and—"

"Hell, they know all that," Tom Burrows said. "You'd better say something about his murder."

"As far as I'm concerned," Jake said coldly, "you can tell them I've taken my hat and gone home."

"You're not going anywhere," the sheriff said.

"Oh yes I am," Jake told him. "I'm not going to let any small-town sheriff push me around any longer. I'm getting out of here." He drew a quick breath, his bright-blue eyes narrowed. "You may be a sheriff, but I'll tell you something. There's such a thing as a warrant, when you want to hold anybody. And there's such a thing as false arrest. You'd better take a correspondence-school course in the law."

The sheriff said, "I'm the law in Jackson County."

In spite of himself, Jake started to laugh. It was the kind of speech that brought down the house at the neighborhood movies. Then the laugh froze on his lips. The little deputy was moving slowly up to him on one side, the big, sloppily dressed deputy was closing in on the other. And Sheriff Kling, two hundred and fifty pounds of sheer brawn, was standing in the doorway, an ugly look on his face.

"Nobody knows where you were when the Senator was shot," the sheriff said, weighing his words, "and I heard Tom here talking about you having been mixed up in a bunch of murders." His little eyes bored into Jake's face. "Maybe I'm a small-town sheriff, but I know how to take care of you Chicago gangsters."

"Lay off the speechmaking," Tom Burrows said, one hand on the phone. "What do I tell the U.P.?"

Sheriff Marvin Kling's lips tightened. "Just say—" he paused, "Jackson county has the situation well in hand. And say I'm holding two material witnesses."

Jake Justus' big, rangy frame tightened for action. One flash of sunlight through the window turned his red hair into a flame. He took one step toward the sheriff.

"And I mean them," the sheriff concluded, pointing to Jake and Helene. He wheeled to face Jake. "I know something about the law too."

"You son of a bitch," Jake said, in the same moment that he moved. Helene screamed.

Tom Burrows grabbed the telephone and yelled, "Get me the United Press in Madison and make it fast—"

Chapter Five

JOHN J MALONE
79 WEST WASHINGTON STREET
CHICAGO ILLINOIS

   JAKE INVOLVED IN MURDER IN JACKSON WISCONSIN CAN
YOU COME

                                        HELENE

JOHN JOSEPH MALONE, Chicago's noisiest and most noted criminal lawyer, stared sourly at the telegram on his desk. It might be a gag, or it might be serious. Whichever it was, he wanted no part of it.

He was a short, pudgy, red-faced man, with a thick shock of damp black hair perpetually in need of combing. His Finchley suit, freshly donned that morning, already looked as though he had been sleeping under the El for six weeks. There was a small spot on his bright plaid three-dollar cravat, and a cascade of cigar ashes on his damp shirt front.

There was nothing about his appearance to indicate his success in his profession, but both his reputation and his clientele were enviable—or unenviable, depending on how one looked at it. His greatest concern was in seeing that none of his clients landed behind the bars, and whenever this couldn't be achieved without actually appearing in court, his manner before a jury was not so much technical as pyrotechnical.

He made a disgusted face at the telegram. "The last time Jake and Helene got mixed up in a murder damned near ruined me," he muttered.

He found pencil and paper under a litter of last week's newspapers on his desk, and began composing a telegram to send in return:

HELENE JUSTUS
JACKSON WISCONSIN

TELL THEM HE DIDN'T DO IT AND STOP BOTHERING ME I'M A BUSY MAN

MALONE

He gave the telegram to his office girl, lit a fresh cigar, and leaned perilously far back in his chair, thinking things over.

There had been the time, back in Jake's press-agent days, when the secret bride of Jake's bandleader client had been accused of murdering her dear old great-aunt. Malone had untangled that one. That case had brought Jake and the North Shore heiress Helene together. Then the radio star Jake was press-agenting had become involved in not one murder, but three, and Malone had not only saved her from the law but brought her through the affair with her reputation unblemished.

Jake and Helene were married now. On his wedding day Jake had rashly bet Mona McClane, one of the world's wealthiest women, that she couldn't commit a murder and get away with it. That casual little bet had caused Malone to run himself ragged solving a murder which turned out to be the wrong one, and finally all but turned his hair white solving what proved the right murder.

Now, he told himself, he was damned and double and triple damned if he was going to get mixed up in any more of Jake and Helene's affairs.

"Jackson, Wisconsin," he snorted. "Who the hell ever heard of Jackson, Wisconsin!"

The fact that he had received scandalously fat fees in all four of the affairs didn't temper his feeling about them in the least. The money was already spent.

"I won't go!" he roared.

The pretty, dark-haired office girl appeared at the door.

"Did you call me, Mr. Malone?"

"No!" he shouted.

She retreated, murmuring, "I'm not deaf!"

In due course of time the second telegram arrived.

JOHN J MALONE
79 WEST WASHINGTON ST
CHICAGO ILLINOIS

   THIS IS SERIOUS WE NEED YOU

                              HELENE

For a few minutes he sat staring at the telegram, his forehead wrinkled.

Jake might be in trouble. Helene might have run over somebody. No, that wouldn't be murder. Although he had a conviction that the way she drove her high-powered cars was a crime worse than murder. Neither Jake nor Helene would actually murder anybody, themselves. Therefore it couldn't be terribly serious.

He looked for the pencil, found it where it had rolled under the desk, and wrote:

HELENE JUSTUS
JACKSON WISCONSIN

MY PRESENT CLIENT'S BUSINESS IS ALSO SERIOUS. HE
NEEDS ME TOO. AND HE PAYS ME. LOVE AND KISSES.

MALONE

His present client was one of his favorites, the
owner of a chain of horse parlors who had somehow
fallen afoul of the law.

"And call Harry's wife," he told the office girl as
he handed her the telegram, "tell her I'll have him
out of jail tomorrow."

She sniffed. "That's what you told her yesterday.
You aren't even working on it."

"I am too," he objected. He pointed to a paper
on his desk.

"What's that?" she demanded.

"It's a list of the people who owe Harry money.
I'd rather have the case against him dropped, it would
save time and trouble."

He spent the next hour poring over the list. At
last he made several telephone calls, to persons rang-
ing from a prominent labor racketeer to a municipal
judge. Finally he called to the office girl.

"Call Harry's wife and tell her everything's O. K.,
the pressure's on. Harry'll be home in time for lunch.
Don't forget to send him a bill in the morning."

He picked his expensive, slightly battered Panama
hat from the top of his desk lamp, put it on, and
added, "I'm going out for a while. If any more tele-
grams come, use 'em for cigarette paper."

He strolled down the street to Joe the Angel's
City Hall Bar, and called for a corned-beef on rye and
two beers. While he waited, he bought a paper from
a passing newsboy.

SENATOR PEVELEY MURDERED

SHOT TO DEATH WHILE
IN JACKSON, WISCONSIN,
COUNTY COURTHOUSE

Two Chicagoans Held
As Material Witnesses

Malone looked at the headline until half the corned-beef sandwich was gone before the name "Jackson, Wisconsin" registered on his consciousness. Then he shoved away his plate, upsetting one of the glasses of beer, and began reading the story.

It was a hasty, sketchy account of the crime, giving only the barest facts. Gerald L. Peveley, one-time Wisconsin Senator, had been shot to death while in the Jackson, Wisconsin, county courthouse. Two Chicagoans, Mr. and Mrs. Jake Justus, allegedly in the building for the purpose of obtaining fishing licenses, were being held as material witnesses. Sheriff Marvin Kling promised an early arrest.

"Damn it, they can't do that!" Malone said loudly.

"I beg your pardon?" the bartender said.

Malone waved him aside, and sat staring at the paper.

Jake and Helene couldn't have had anything to do with the murder of Senator Peveley. Nobody could hold them as material witnesses. It wasn't legal. Malone read the story again.

He wondered how much of a bribe Sheriff Marvin Kling was holding out for.

Oh well, it was Jake's worry, let him look out for it. Still, you never could tell about Jake.

He decided he'd better hurry right back to the office in case there was another telegram, grabbed his hat from where it had fallen to the floor, and dived out into the street.

"Hey, Malone, wait," Joe the Angel shouted after him. "You forgot to pay the check!" But the little lawyer was halfway down the street. Joe the Angel shrugged his shoulders and called to the head bartender, "Put another thirty-five cents down on Mr. Malone's ticket."

By the time he reached his office, Malone had convinced himself there was no need for anxiety. From the looks of things, all Jake needed to get out of this was money, and he had plenty of that. The Casino, which he'd won on that famous bet with Mona McClane, had turned out to be a gold mine among Chicago's night clubs. The sheriff had probably taken a look at Helene's Buick convertible and decided this was a chance to pay off the mortgage on the jail.

"There's another telegram for you, Mr. Malone," the girl announced as he walked in the door.

He fairly tore it from her hand.

JOHN J MALONE
79 WEST WASHINGTON STREET
CHICAGO ILLINOIS

    JAKE IN JAIL FOR KNOCKING OUT DEPUTY SHERIFF WITH
LEFT JAB WHAT DO I DO NOW
                                        HELENE

"I decided to wait till you'd read it before tearing it up for cigarette papers," the black-haired girl said acidly.

Malone didn't appear to have heard her. He relighted his cigar slowly, and with exquisite care, and stood looking at the telegram thoughtfully.

"You said," the girl reminded him, "you weren't going to get mixed up in any more of Jake Justus' affairs. You said life was too short. You said you'd be damned if you'd—"

The little lawyer nodded. "That proves it. You *are* deaf. Now be a good girl, Maggie, call up the station and find out when's the next train for Jackson, Wisconsin."

Chapter Six

JOHN J. MALONE arrived by bus in Jackson, Wisconsin, at nine twenty-three, a tired, hot, rumpled, and very irritated man. It had developed that only one train a day went to Jackson, Wisconsin, and that arrived at six-ten in the morning, and involved three changes, with waits of from ten minutes to an hour on the way. Jackson, Wisconsin, was not much harder to get to than Little America.

All the way he had sustained himself by dreaming of a quiet, peaceful little town, moonlit, with wide, shadowy lawns, and a general air of serenity and calm. He stepped off the bus in front of Gollett's drugstore to find himself in what appeared to be the middle of a circus.

Jackson's main street was three blocks long and almost half a block wide. At the moment it was a blaze of lights that shone from store fronts and street lamps, and every available inch of space was jammed with parked cars.

The afternoon's storm had had no permanent effect on the temperature, but only added a sticky dampness to the air. The blazing lights seemed to have attracted every flying insect within the limits of Jackson County.

There was a little crowd standing on the sidewalk, watching the bus come in. Malone spotted Helene in the center of it, a tall, slender figure in a white linen dress. As he drew closer to her, it seemed to him that her face was a shade more pale than normal. He slapped irritably and inaccurately at a mosquito and said, "Where the hell is the jail?" The mosquito returned and came to a miserable end on the back of Malone's neck. "I'll get Jake out if I have to shoot the sheriff."

"It's not a bad idea," Helene said. "Did you bring along a cannon? It wouldn't take anything less to shoot that sheriff." She caught her breath and said, "I never was so glad to see the marines land before. Another minute, and the hero would be sawed in two. Jake is probably having it out with the justice of the peace right now."

She grabbed his arm and dragged him up Main Street at a breakneck speed. Malone took a firm grip on his handbag and panted along beside her through a kaleidoscope of lights, faces, and windows.

"Slow down," he growled at last. "Remember I'm not the athletic-type marine."

She slowed down to almost an average walking speed, and immediately the sidewalk crowd began to engulf them. Malone pushed a plump woman in a print dress off his stomach and said, "It doesn't seem to be any more crowded than State and Madison Streets at high noon. Where in blazes do all these people come from?"

"Out of the everywhere into the here," Helene said coyly.

Malone put down his handbag, nearly trampling a couple of small boys as he did so, and said, "When is the next bus back to Chicago?"

"There isn't a bus until seven in the morning,"

Helene said. Her hand tightened on his arm. "Besides, we need you."

He allowed himself to be led half a block up the street. "Don't tell me all these people live in Jackson, Wisconsin," he said crossly. "The signboard at the edge of town said population three thousand."

"There's been a murder here," she reminded him. "People have been arriving since four o'clock this afternoon. Most of them brought a picnic lunch. They've been spending the evening walking up and down the street, talking about the late Senator Peveley and his manner of taking off, or rather, being took off." She added, "Half of them have been looking at the front of Charlie Hausen's Undertaking Parlor and the other half have been looking at me."

"There's an interesting distinction there," Malone said, "but I can't just put my finger on what it is."

His nerves were still tingling from the bus ride. Once or twice he had a vague notion that he was standing motionless, and the street was moving past him. He thought of another question to put to Helene, just as an overweight farm family crashed into them at the corner of Main and Second Streets. By the time they were disentangled he had given it up.

There were trees, almost indistinguishable from the darkness, a broad lawn, lighted windows, and a flight of steps. Malone contented himself with still being able to breathe, as Helene hauled him through the door.

He stopped suddenly. There was a long corridor ahead of him, lined with immense, closed doors.

"Where are you taking me?"

"The justice of the peace," Helene said. "He's Phil Smith."

"I'm glad to hear it," Malone said, "and don't be in such a hurry."

Helene lit a cigarette in the most leisurely fashion imaginable. "Phil Smith said he'd be here at nine-thirty and have Jake brought up then. I knew you wouldn't get here before nine-thirty so that was the time set." She took one puff on the cigarette, stamped it out, and said, "Tom Burrows fixed it all up."

Malone sighed, said, "Very nice of him. No, don't bother telling me who he is. I'll try to catch up with the melody as you go along."

She pulled open a heavy door before he could get to it, and led the way into the county clerk's office. A sudden blaze of light made him blink. He heard Helene murmuring, "That's Phil Smith," and managed to focus his tired eyes on the handsome, white-haired man sitting behind his desk.

It was not his idea of a courtroom, Malone thought. Combining the offices of county clerk and justice of the peace had led to a little confusion in the layout of the room. But he didn't take much time to think about it. He was still a bit dazed from the long ride, breathless from the hurried walk up Main Street, and completely in the dark about what had happened and was going to happen. All he knew was that Jake was in jail, and he was supposed to get him out.

The white-haired man Helene had identified as Phil Smith rose to greet him, a cordial hand outstretched. "You must be Mr. Justus' lawyer. I'm delighted to meet you. I hope you had a pleasant trip."

"And this is Tom Burrows," Helene said. "And Mr. Malone."

Malone shook hands with the bouncing, spectacled, little man, murmured, "I'm pleased to meet you," wished he were back in Chicago and that Jake and Helene were in Zanzibar, or possibly Kamchatka.

A door opened suddenly behind him. Malone wheeled around and saw Jake, his red hair mussed, his freckled face pale with not-too-well-repressed fury. The men on either side of him, Malone guessed, were the deputy sheriffs, one a small man with a scar on his upper lip, the other a large, slovenly, and sleepy-looking individual.

"I see you got here," Jake said. "It's about time."

Phil Smith looked at him. "Patience is the best remedy for every trouble," he quoted gently. "Plautus," he added.

Jake glared back, opened his mouth to speak, shut it again, finally drew a long breath, and said " 'Beware the fury of a patient man.' Dryden. Hell, I don't even know what the charge is. This son of a bitch didn't tell me."

"Now, now, now," Malone said, placatingly. He wasn't sure who Dryden was, but he knew all there was to know about justices of the peace.

"The guy knocked me down, Phil," the fat deputy said.

"He kicked me," Jake declared. "And if you think for one minute—"

"Keep your temper," Phil Smith said amiably to Jake. He looked reproachfully at the fat deputy and said, "I didn't ask you anything." Then he looked down at a paper on his desk. "I don't want to bother with taking evidence. An honest man appeals to the understanding, or modestly confides in the internal evidence of his conscience. Junius." He cleared his throat. "According to these charges, Mr. Justus, attempting to exit through the west door of the courthouse, was intercepted by Deputy Sheriff Harry Foote, and thereby called him an objectionable name."

"And I'll tell you what it was, too," Deputy Harry Foote announced. "He said—"

Phil Smith silenced him with a grave look. "At this point the deputy, in the defense of his duty, struck Mr. Justus about his person—"

"In the belly," Jake corrected.

"—whereupon Mr. Justus struck the deputy full on the point of the jaw, causing great damage—" He paused, looked up at the deputy sheriff, and said, "You don't look so bad, Harry." Before anyone could answer he'd looked back at the paper. "The charge is disturbing the peace and resisting an officer in the attempt to do his duty."

"Do your duty and leave the rest to heaven," Helene murmured.

Phil Smith smiled at her. "Corneille," he said approvingly.

Malone interrupted the love feast. He strode up to Phil Smith's desk. "My client pleads guilty," he said. "How much is the fine?"

The handsome, white-haired justice of the peace thought it over for a minute. "Two dollars and costs," he decided. "That comes to three dollars and a half."

"A bargain," Jake said, reaching for his wallet. "Can I hit him again for three dollars and a half?"

Phil Smith took the four one-dollar bills. "He that is slow to anger is better than the mighty," he said softly. He handed back two quarters in change. "And the way of the transgressor is hard. Proverbs Sixteen, and Proverbs Thirteen. The next time, the fine will be twenty-five dollars and costs." He rose, beamed impartially at all of them, said, "I hope you have a pleasant stay in Jackson, Wisconsin," and went out the door.

Malone mopped his brow. "I hope to heaven the rest of the charges against you are nothing serious. If I had to see you through a murder trial up here, I'd have to bone up on *Bartlett's Quotations.*" He paused, saw that Jake and Helene were exchanging their own comments on the case, and turned to the injured deputy. "I'm sure there wasn't any serious damage," he said amiably. He reached for his wallet. "Have a couple of drinks on me."

A moment later, Jake and Helene beside him, he paused on the courthouse steps and sniffed the outdoor air. "I only know one quotation," he said. "Money is the root of all evil. I don't even care where it's from, but deputy sheriffs are no different from city cops, and you owe me ten dollars." He mopped his brow.

"That makes a total of thirteen dollars and a half," Jake said, "but it was still worth it. Now where's a quiet place we can talk without being quoted in court later?"

"We're going to my office," Tom Burrows said. "The *Jackson County Enterprise* is the only place in town that isn't full of newspapermen."

He led the way down the street. The office of the *Jackson County Enterprise* was a small frame building with a false front, halfway down the block between Second and Third. Its windows still faintly showed where a sign HEDBERG'S FEED AND SEED STORE had been inadequately erased. Inside the front room were three immense roll-top desks, only one of them open, and a long, disordered table. The brown-haired Arlene Goudge sat patiently by the telephone.

"There hasn't been so many newspapermen in Jackson in its history," Tom Burrows said. "And they're still arriving, by car, by bus, and even by plane. Photographers, reporters, and one radio newscaster."

Malone took off his tie and unbuttoned his collar. "The Chamber of Commerce must have been busy."

"We've had a murder," Tom Burrows said, "or hadn't you heard? And Senator Peveley was a famous man." He picked up a newspaper from the table. "There's the *Tribune,* just came in on the same bus with you."

Malone glanced through the story. Senator Peveley had, it appeared, done everything a Midwestern Senator could do to make himself newsworthy, climaxing it by being murdered.

"Where's the press now?" he asked.

"Most of them," Tom Burrows said, "are in the hotel bar."

The little lawyer looked wistful. "I've had a long ride, and I'm very tired," he began.

"Not now," Helene said firmly.

Tom Burrows looked at his watch. "They're going to do a news broadcast from Main Street at eleven," he said. "I'd like to watch. That still gives us an hour or so to talk." He picked up a large paper bag from the table. "Follow me."

He led the way out through the composing room and down a flight of stairs.

The Main Street of Jackson County ran parallel to a river, and all the buildings on the west side of

the street were built on its bank. Below the composing room of the *Jackson County Enterprise* was a
storage room which faced the river. Its double doors,
now wide open, were directly over the water.

Malone agreed that it was the coolest place in town.
He located an upturned empty box, sat down, and
fanned himself. It was like being in a little cave, dark
and mysterious, with a stream flowing at its edge.

The paper bag contained cheese and cold beer.
Tom Burrows took out an enormous pocketknife,
first used it to open the bottles, and then began cutting the cheese into generous hunks.

"Now about this murder," he began.

"Who cares?" Malone said dreamily. "Who cares
about the murder of an ex-Senator?" He lifted the
beer bottle to his lips, took it away, and sang a bar of
Kathleen Mavourneen.

"I care," Jake said, "if they're going to hang me
for it."

"They don't hang people for murder in Wisconsin," the lawyer said. "They put you in jail for life.
I checked up on it to make sure." He took another
long, comforting pull at the bottle. "You got me all
the way up here because you'd socked a deputy
sheriff. All right, that's all fixed up. So let's forget the
whole thing and be merry."

"That's only part of it," Jake said. "The smallest
part of it. Are you my lawyer, or aren't you?"

"Sometimes," Malone said mournfully, "I begin
to think I'm your guardian." He lighted a cigar and
stared at the end of it through the darkness. "They
can't keep you here. It's against the law."

"That's what Jake said," Helene told him. "But
the sheriff takes a larger view."

Malone sighed. "All right. Begin at the beginning and don't leave out anything you can remember."

He listened in silence until Jake reached the point where the sheriff had said, "I'm the law in Jackson County." Then he snorted loudly.

"You're making it all up."

"He is not making it up," Helene said. "Nobody would deliberately make up a sheriff like that one."

"I still don't believe it." He puffed hard at the cigar. "They've got nothing against you."

"We're strangers in town," Jake said for the second time that day. As Malone sniffed indignantly, he added, "You and Helene don't know anything about small towns. I lived in one until I was grown up. Any stranger is an object of curiosity and suspicion, even when he doesn't happen along at the time of an important murder."

"There's more to it than that," Tom Burrows said. "Sheriff Kling is up for re-election this fall. He doesn't want to make anybody mad at him and lose a vote. At the same time, he has to give the impression he's doing something about this murder. So he claims these two are material witnesses and diverts attention to them. And I haven't any doubt," he finished, "that if, as time goes along, he doesn't find any other murderer, he'll just pin it on Jake, and be done with it."

There was a little silence.

"Of course," Tom Burrows said, "he may find the real murderer in the meantime."

This time it was Jake who snorted. "As the saying goes, I wouldn't like to hang until he does!"

"It's damned funny," Malone said thoughtfully, "that somebody could walk up to Senator Peveley and shoot him without anybody seeing it, in a public place like the courthouse. Wasn't anyone around? Weren't there any witnesses?"

"There were an even half-dozen witnesses," Helene told him. "But nobody saw the shooting because nobody was looking."

"It was like this," Jake explained. "There's this little flight of stairs leading up to the courtroom and the offices on the west side of the courthouse. The shooting took place right at the head of the stairs. Everybody was milling around, picking up papers, or getting hats, or talking, when suddenly there was a shot, Senator Peveley let out a yell, and rolled down the stairs."

"But," the lawyer said, "somebody must have seen the murderer. A man or woman with a gun doesn't vanish into thin air."

"Everybody was looking at the Senator," Jake said. "Everybody started down that flight of stairs in a rush, nobody paid any attention to anyone else. With the result that none of those six witnesses can swear where any of the others were at the time the shot was fired, or where any of them were immediately after it was fired."

"But the gun," Malone said irritably. "Where the hell did the gun get to?"

"That," Helene said smoothly, "is what's giving Sheriff Marvin Kling a sleepless night, I hope."

"Did they search the courthouse?"

"They did everything but tear it down," Jake said. "And they searched everyone in the courthouse."

"Well," Malone said, "if only six people were upstairs at the time the Senator was shot, one of them must be his murderer. In any case, Jake is no suspect, if he was going down the other staircase at the time."

"Sheriff Kling says he's the law in Jackson County," Jake said quietly. "And he's not trying to be funny. Do you want to see me on trial before a Jackson County jury, with the young D. A. and the sheriff coming up for re-election in the fall?"

"You see?" Helene said. "Viewed from practically any angle, it's a bad spot."

"I've seen worse ones," the little lawyer said reassuringly. "Just leave everything to me. Somebody in Jackson County must have heard of evidence. How about this witness of yours, this Buttonholes?"

Helene snickered. "He's the town liar. Besides, he's got a Welsh grandmother."

"Well," Malone said grimly, "that's one thing they can't get Jake for. We'll produce a birth certificate."

"Wonderful," Jake said. "But I'd feel even easier in my mind if you got to work and produced the murderer."

Chapter Seven

THE RIVER had turned silver gray in the darkness. Malone gazed at it reflectively.

"Tell me about all these people," he said at last, "and begin with the corpse."

Tom Burrows settled himself comfortably on his packing box. "The late Senator Gerald Peveley was born on a farm in Jackson County in 1878. He attended Miller township school at Miller's Creek from 1885—"

"Skip the frills," the little lawyer said wearily, "and get to the facts. His family, his business, his personality, and his women."

"And his enemies," Jake added.

"He had plenty of those," the young newspaperman said. "Enemies, I mean, not women. From all I ever knew, the Senator led a blameless life. Of course you can get away with plenty in a town like this."

"That isn't the way I heard it about small towns," Malone said coyly.

Jake snorted. "That shows what you know about it. Why when I was fifteen—"

"Never mind your private life," Helene said sweetly. "You can write to Dorothy Dix about it. Go on, Tom."

"Well," Burrows said, "Senator Peveley was a prominent citizen. No ex-Senator, with that much dough, could be anything else in a place like Jackson. If he'd been an ordinary guy, everybody would have openly and admittedly hated his guts."

"He didn't look exactly lovable," Helene ventured, "from what I saw of him."

This time it was Malone who asked, "If he was so all-fired unpopular, how in the hell did he get elected Senator?"

"That's an easy one," Tom Burrows told him. "He was popular with the party. He had plenty of money to contribute to campaign expenses, and he contributed with a lavish hand. He was elected county treasurer at a time when the whole ticket slid in, and then when he wanted to make it state treasurer, the party pushed him through. Finally he wanted to run for the Senate, and the party said, 'Oh well, why the hell not,' and there he was.

"Besides," he went on, "he had a certain gift for oratory and for making a public hero of himself. He was a real asset to the party, until he quit."

Jake said, "I suppose eventually he just got tired of making an asset of himself."

"I just wrote a swell rags-to-riches story," Tom Burrows said. "Farm boy to Capitol, in ten easy lessons. It was a lot of baloney. The Senator's old man left half a dozen farms when he kicked off."

Malone blinked. "It still reads like rags to riches to me."

"In this country," the newspaperman said, "half a dozen farms means real dough. He was worth about ten times that when he died, but that was Henry's doing. Henry had the real business head."

"Nice for him," Malone said. "Who's Henry?"

"The Senator's brother. He's rather unusual."

Tom Burrows paused. "Oh well, you'll probably meet him yourself. Henry's a widower, no children. The Senator had one child, Florence. She's engaged to the young D. A."

"Spare me the young love interest," Malone said. "I just want to know who was on the second floor of the courthouse when the Senator got his." He added, "You can call this getting in on murder on the next-to-the-ground floor."

"Never mind how you get in on it," Helene said. "How do we get out of it?"

Tom Burrows' voice was thoughtful when he spoke again. "You'll have to take the town history, I'm afraid. A little town like this is all currents and cross-currents. Everybody is related to everybody else, or entangled with everybody else through birth, church, or business affiliations, hatred, love affairs, or debts. Take that group up in the courthouse today."

He paused to light a cigarette. "Well, starting out with Jerry Luckstone. His father is old Judge Luckstone, of Luckstone and Applebury. Was county judge about fifteen years ago. Jerry's grandfather was a Judge Luckstone here, too. Jerry's a bright, likable young man only recently out of law school."

"How did he get to be district attorney?" Helene asked. "Or do you draw names out of a hat up here?"

"Well, he was appointed assistant because the D. A. was a friend of the family. Then old Judge Luckstone is something of a power in county affairs, and Jerry's a smart young boy and everybody likes him, so a couple of years later he ran for the office after the old D. O. dropped out, and got elected."

"It's as simple as that!" Malone murmured admiringly.

"Jerry and Florence Peveley announced their engagement about a month ago," Tom went on. "I understood the Senator wasn't too pleased, but he didn't come right out and object. Before that Jerry used to run around with Arlene, and I guess he used to go out with Cora Belle once in a while, but so did most of the male population of the county."

"Is this a slight shade of the 'scarlet letter'?" Helene wanted to know.

"Oh no, nothing like that. Cora Belle—she's Mrs. Fromm—is frowned on a little, but everybody is still speaking to her. I understand she was something of a lively girl when she was still in high school. There was a little talk when she quit two months before she was to graduate and ran off to Milwaukee, ostensibly, at least, to take some kind of job. Then sometime later news came that she had married a guy named Fromm. A few years ago she divorced him and came back here, and she's living fairly lavishly on her alimony. Cora Belle's a heluva lot of fun." He said the last in a faintly reminiscent tone.

"I think I'd like to discuss the case with her," Malone said enthusiastically. He added, "Any link between her and the Senator, except possibly a little hanky-panky on some dark country lane?"

"Nothing I know about. But she runs around a lot with Ellen McGowan's younger brother, and I've heard that the old dame doesn't like it a little bit."

The lawyer sighed. "I see what you meant about currents and crosscurrents," he said wearily. "How about this Miss McGowan?"

"Ellen McGowan," the newspaperman said, "is what's popularly known as a remarkable woman. She's cashier of the bank, member of the school board, head of the library committee, and belongs to a couple of women's clubs. A highly respected citizen, and very capable."

"I prefer my women a little more helpless," Malone said, "and not quite so remarkable."

"She must have been very good-looking, in a tall, thin sort of way, about twenty years ago," Helene said. "What ever possessed her to become a lady banker?"

"She sort of inherited it," Tom Burrows explained. "Her father was cashier of the bank, and she wanted to be his assistant when she came out of school. From all I hear, she worshiped him. He was another prominent citizen and held a bunch of county offices. He was county treasurer for years. Something of a gay old boy, if all I hear is correct. Used to back the trotting races at the Jackson County Fair and play the market with his spare change."

Malone clicked his teeth disapprovingly. "He came to a bad end, I presume."

"Some time ago he took sick and retired," Tom Burrows said. "She shipped him off to California to get well and took over his job in the meantime. But he died out there, and she stayed on at the bank."

"A dreary sort of purposeful life," Jake said. "I hope her brother didn't turn out so well."

"He didn't. Oh, I guess he's a pretty good farmer. He's fifteen years younger than she is, and their mother died when he was born, so she brought him up. He's never married, and she's half out of her wits that he'll marry Cora Belle."

"From what I've seen of Jackson, Wisconsin," Jake said, "he could do a lot worse."

"She's admired, but not too popular," Tom Burrows said. "Arlene calls her a cross old cat."

"A kind of misanthropussy," Helene suggested.

"None of this seems to have much to do with the late Senator Peveley," Jake said, yawning. "What about this Goudge girl?" He suddenly remembered the phone call in the county clerk's office and wondered if he should have spoken.

"Arlene's all right," Tom Burrows said, with a sudden forcefulness, as though he'd been called on to defend her. "She's just a plain damn fool." He paused a moment before he went on. "She works for Henry Peveley in his real-estate office. Her father's the county treasurer, also head of the Brotherhood of Churchmen. He makes a public speech on every possible occasion."

"A highly reprehensible type of citizen," Jake said, setting down a beer bottle. "But I don't see much connection between Arlene and the late Senator."

"There isn't," Tom Burrows told him, "unless you count in that Jerry Luckstone is engaged to the late Senator's daughter, and that Arlene used to be crazy about Jerry Luckstone. As a matter of fact, I suspect she still is."

"Well," Helene said, "that leaves us two people who were on the second floor of the courthouse at the time of the crime."

"Ed Skindingsrude might murder somebody," Tom Burrows said, "but he'd do it in a rage, and probably with his bare hands. He's a mild-looking little guy, but he's got the temper of a wild man. Been chairman of the county board for twenty-four years, and a damned good one. In private life, he's a very prosperous farmer, and head of the farmers' co-operative."

"Possible links with the Senator?" Jake asked.

"I don't know," the newspaperman said thoughtfully. "He started to beat him up, right in the lobby of the bank, some two years ago, but somebody stopped him. Claimed the Senator had rooked him on some stock deal. He'd been a director of the bank, but he resigned in a huff. Still, that's hardly enough to bring on a murder in cold blood two years later."

"Well," Helene said, "there's still the handsome county clerk, the quoting genius."

"Phil Smith wouldn't murder a flea," Tom Burrows said forcefully. "He's the gentlest man alive." He paused to open the last bottle of beer. "He used to teach Latin, Greek, and classical history in the high school here, until about twelve years ago when Senator Peveley and the school board decided the classics were wasted on Jackson's youth and that a department of farm management would be more purposeful." He paused again, and then said, "Yes, I know what you're going to say, but that's no motive for murder."

"You'd be surprised," Malone said, "if you knew what trivial things can bring on murders. Is there any other tie between this classical scholar and the late Senator?"

"One," Tom Burrows told him. "The Senator's wife was Phil Smith's sister. But that's all. No one ever heard of Phil even losing his temper with anyone. When he lost his teaching position, old Judge Luckstone had the idea of running him for county clerk, he was elected and he's been re-elected every year since. He's not only every bit as gentle as I said, but everybody in town loves him."

There was a longish silence.

"A lot of very nice people," Helene said at last. "But none of them seems to have murdered Senator Peveley."

"One of them must have," Malone said. "One of those six."

He tossed his cigar out into the river, stood, and stretched like a short, plump cat.

"It's time for that on-the-spot news broadcast," he announced, looking at his watch. "Let's go."

Arlene Goudge was still sitting hopefully by the telephone when they climbed back up to the *Enterprise* office. It developed that the evening's calm had been marred by only two events. Buttonholes had discovered an enterprising citizen showing visitors the scene of the murder in the courthouse for ten cents a head, and had called the police. An hour later the police discovered Buttonholes showing visitors the scene of the crime for twenty-five cents a head, and threw him in the city jail.

Tom Burrows waved to the wistful Arlene to join them and led the way to the intersection of Main and Second Streets. Here the pressure of the crowd reminded Malone of Bathhouse John's on Election Eve, save that this crowd was a little rougher. They managed to shove a path through to the center, where the newscaster, a round-faced, perspiring young man, was talking rapidly into a portable microphone, while his equally perspiring assistant tried to push back the crowd.

"We've missed the overture," Helene whispered.

By the time they were within hearing distance, Mr. Goudge was being interviewed. He declared that he had known Senator Peveley, man and boy, for fifty years, "and a finer, more Christian gentleman you couldn't ask to find. A member of our Brotherhood of Churchmen, and a pillar of the community. His death is a great loss to Jackson County."

The newscaster explained that he only wanted to know if Mr. Goudge had any theories about the murder.

At this point a perspiring third assistant ran up and handed the newscaster a sheet of paper.

"Ladies and gentlemen, we interrupt this interview for an important news bulletin. We have just received the information that Sheriff Marvin Kling has arrested District Attorney Jerry Luckstone and lodged him in the county jail, for the murder of Senator Gerald Peveley—"

Ed Skindingsrude, who had been standing on the platform, forgot the nation-wide radio audience.

"No," he shouted. "No, Jerry didn't kill him."

Chapter Eight

THE CROWD milled around excitedly, their din making it impossible to hear what was being said on the platform.

Arlene Goudge clutched desperately at Tom Burrows' arm and began crying, "He didn't do it, he didn't do it," over and over.

Malone took one look at the girl and said, "Get her out of here. Jake, you edge up there and hear what the old guy has to say. Come along, Helene."

They pushed through the crowd and half dragged the girl back to the office of the *Enterprise*. She was still repeating, "He didn't do it," when Helene kicked the door shut behind them.

Tom Burrows shoved her into a chair, slapped her roughly, and said, "Stop that!" Then as a flood of tears threatened, he whipped out a handkerchief, wiped her eyes, and said, "You poor baby."

She looked up at them, her eyes wild. "You've got to do something! Can't you get Jerry out of jail? Can't you prove he didn't do it, or find out who did, or—something?"

"My dear young lady," Malone began.

This time she really burst into tears, curled up in the chair, buried her face in her arms, and cried like a kitten. It was the last straw for Malone.

"Don't cry," he roared at her. "I'll do something.

I'll do anything. I'll get him out of jail. For the love of Mike, *stop it!*"

She paused long enough to blow her nose on Helene's handkerchief, push back her hair, and say, "Oh, Mr. Malone!"

"Now look here," Malone said, with a vague attempt at sounding stern.

She blew her nose again and looked at him with wide, miserable eyes. "Jerry didn't have anything to do with the murder."

"Womanly intuition isn't enough," Malone said. "Or do you know, for sure?"

She pinned back the last strand of damp hair. "He was trying to make friends with Senator Peveley. Because he was engaged to Florence. And Senator Peveley didn't like him. He told me so."

"Senator Peveley?" Malone asked, trying to keep up.

"No. Jerry. He was engaged to marry Florence, and the Senator didn't like him, and so he was trying to make friends with him, and so of course he wouldn't have murdered him."

"That's perfectly right," Helene said sympathetically. "That isn't the way I make friends with people, either."

It seemed to Malone that there was a grain of logic there somewhere, but he couldn't just put his finger on it. He started to ask another question, when Arlene Goudge rose, tucked her compact in her purse, and opened the door. She was beginning to cry again.

"I'm going to have a baby," she said almost indignantly, and slammed the door on her way out.

For a good thirty seconds nobody said anything. Tom Burrows turned white, then red, then white again. Suddenly he dived out the door, as it slammed they could hear him saying, "Wait, Arlene. But, Arlene—"

Malone stood blinking at the door. "I don't understand," he said.

"You can get books that explain it," Helene said. "It's just like the flowers and the little fish."

"I mean," Malone said patiently, "what does that have to do with the murder of Senator Peveley?" He mopped his brow. "The thing I like about little towns," he said, "is that they're so quiet and peaceful. Nothing ever happens."

"Listen, Malone," Helene said. "I'm trying to figure out whose girl she is. This afternoon when she telephoned Tom Burrows she said something about having promised not to call him up again. And she cried about it. But he looks completely flabbergasted about the whole thing. And here she is all of a flutter to get Jerry Luckstone out of jail, and he's engaged to another girl anyway." She sighed. "They certainly do everything the hard way in Jackson County."

"Don't bother me," Malone growled at her. "I've got enough on my mind without worrying over who's in love with whom, and who is the father of Arlene Goudge's child. All I want to do is get you and Jake out of this mess and get back to Chicago."

"You promised—" Helene began.

"She was hysterical," Malone muttered. "She won't hold me to it. Besides," he paused and added, "I didn't promise to get this guy out of jail. I promised to do something, but I didn't say what it was."

Before Helene could make any comments, Jake arrived, hot and breathless.

Ed Skindingsrude, he explained, had refused to enlarge on his startled and startling statement.

"Probably," Helene said, "he did it himself."

"My money's on Phil Smith," Jake said. "Anybody who has the reputation of being the gentlest soul in town must have the seeds of murder in him somewhere. Besides, losing a job teaching Greek, Latin, and classical history is a swell motive."

Malone frowned. "Motives are bound to pile up, probably suitable for half a dozen murders, as we begin to dig into the private lives of this town," he began.

"We?" Jake demanded.

"A slip of the tongue," the little lawyer said, blushing. "Don't give it another thought. Now that the worthy sheriff has clamped somebody in jail, especially somebody as important as the D. A. himself, he won't want any further truck with you. Tomorrow morning we'll kiss the dust of Jackson County goodby off our heels, and be on our way."

"You mean another heel bites the dust," Helene said.

Suddenly the door of the *Enterprise* office opened, and a red-haired girl strode in, followed by a short, plump little man with a rosy face and curly white hair.

"I thought I'd find you here," the girl said.

Jake stared at her. She wasn't a pretty girl, in fact her dead-white face was definitely on the plain side, but she certainly was a striking one. She was tall, even taller than Helene, and her hair was like a prairie fire. She was dressed in slightly soiled denim slacks.

"Were you looking for us?" Malone asked politely.

"I told her she shouldn't come here," the little man said anxiously. "I told her it didn't look well for her to go wandering all over, especially dressed the way she is." His face wrinkled unhappily.

"You seem to know us," Jake said. "How about a little reciprocity?"

"I'm Florence Peveley," the girl said, "and this is Uncle Henry."

"You see?" Uncle Henry said. "Here her father's only been dead since one-fifteen this afternoon, and she's going all over town, dressed like that." He looked appealingly at Malone. "What will people think?"

"I don't give a good red damn what people think," Florence Peveley said impatiently. "Never have, and I don't intend to start in now. Look here, you"— she was addressing Malone—"I know all about you. One of those reporters told me your life history, practically. Thank God you're here. You've got to do something about this."

Malone blinked. "About what?"

She scowled at him. "That insane sheriff locking Jerry up for murder. It's absurd. Jerry's the damnedest fool I ever knew in my life, but he wouldn't murder anybody, especially Pa."

"That's a fine way to talk about the man you're engaged to," Uncle Henry said disapprovingly.

"The hell with all that," the red-haired girl said. "Are you going to do something, or aren't you?"

"What do you want him to do?" Helene asked helpfully.

"Find out who the hell—pardon me, who killed

Pa, and get Jerry out of jail. I can't have my fiancé in jail, it looks like the devil." She smiled at Helene. "I like you, you look as if you had sense."

"Thanks," Helene said, "I have. I like you, too. I always wished I had red hair."

"Do you? It's a terrible nuisance in weather like this, there's so much of it." She turned back to Malone. "You can practically name your fee, I have plenty of money. At least I hope I have." She looked at the worried Uncle Henry. "Pa never did change his will, did he?"

The white-haired man shook his head speechlessly.

"Thank God. If I'd thought he really meant it, I'd have shot him myself. How much do you think it ought to set me back, Mr. Malone?"

"I am planning to go back to Chicago tomorrow morning," the little lawyer began stiffly.

She interrupted him with two startling syllables, and added, "A thousand, two thousand, whatever it's worth to you. Name it."

"Ten thousand," Malone said recklessly.

"That's pretty steep. How about five?"

"I'll split the difference," he said instinctively.

"O. K. Seventy-five hundred. But start now, and make it snappy. Come on, Uncle Henry." She turned toward the door.

"Wait a minute," Malone said. "I haven't said I'd do anything yet."

"Nonsense, nobody ever turned down seventy-five hundred bucks. Come and see me first thing in the morning, and I'll give you all the dope on Pa."

Helene said, "Wait, Miss Peveley. It isn't settled yet."

"Of course it's settled," the girl told her. "And

I've got to beat it home, or one of those God-damned photographers is liable to catch up with me. I don't want my picture on the back page of the *Tribune* in these pants." She opened the door, said, "See you in the morning, Mr. Malone," and was gone, followed by Uncle Henry.

Jake waited sixty seconds, and said, "Whew!"

"The hell with her," Malone said, "and the hell with her seventy-five hundred bucks. Still," he added after a moment, "that would buy a lot of pork chops."

"What you do is your own business," Jake said firmly. "But we are not staying in Jackson County."

"Now look here," Malone roared. "You got me up here and got me into this."

"I'll give you a reasonable fee for legal advice and your busfare," Jake said, "and for the love of Mike, go back to Chicago and don't mess with small-town murders."

"I guess I know my own business," Malone said angrily, "and seventy-five hundred bucks—"

"Is a lot of money," Tom Burrows said, coming in the door. "For that, you can buy the *Jackson County Enterprise*. Or for half that."

"I don't want it," Malone said. He lighted a cigar. "How's the girl?"

"All right, I guess. She was pretty well calmed down when I left her at the corner near her house. Her old man doesn't approve of boy friends bringing her home. I mean, he just doesn't approve of boy friends." The young man fanned himself with a copy of last week's *Enterprise*. "Look here, I don't quite know what you think. I mean, about—" He stopped and seemed to wonder what to say next.

"Well, *are* you?" Helene asked politely.

He frowned. "I don't think so. I'm pretty sure I'm not. I don't know, though—"

"Make up your mind," Helene told him.

Tom Burrows frowned. "It's a kind of long and complicated story."

He didn't have a chance to tell it. The door opened again and the well-tailored, gray-haired Miss McGowan walked in, accompanied by a gangling, stoop-shouldered deeply sunburned man. Malone guessed this was the farmer brother. Seen at close range Ellen McGowan appeared more marvelously efficient than ever.

"You're Mr. Malone, aren't you?" she said crisply. "I've been hearing about you."

The little lawyer bowed. "I'm Mr. Malone," he said, "and what you've been hearing about me is probably correct. But if you're here to ask me to get Jerry Luckstone out of jail, you're wasting a lovely evening. Because I'm going back to Chicago on the next bus I can get."

She frowned. "I certainly hope you don't mean that," she said. "And if you do, I hope you'll change your mind. Nobody in this county has the sense of a chicken, and Jerry's got to be gotten out of that jail." She set her lips in a firm line.

"Why?" Malone asked politely.

"Because," she said, "he didn't murder Senator Peveley. And what's more, I know it."

Chapter Nine

"THERE SEEMS to be a popular impression in Jackson that I'm omnipotent," Malone said slowly. "It's very flattering except that I'm afraid I can't deliver the goods. Really, there's nothing I can do to free this young man except blow up the jail."

"I hope that won't be necessary." Miss McGowan smiled wanly. "Can't you find out who did murder Senator Peveley?"

"I'm a lawyer, not a detective," Malone said.

She made an impatient gesture. "I've read about you in the papers. And one of those reporters here today told about your exploits in the past. So I know what you can do, and heaven knows, nobody else here can do anything."

"What makes you so sure this young man didn't do the murder?" Jake asked curiously.

"I know he didn't." There was a hard glitter in her gray eyes. "I know, because I was talking with him when I heard the shot."

"Hell," Malone said, "why don't you tell the sheriff that? You're all the alibi this guy needs to get out of jail."

"That isn't enough," Miss McGowan said. She frowned slightly. "That doesn't tell who murdered the Senator."

Malone said casually, "Why do you care? Is it any of your business?"

"Civic affairs should be everybody's business," she said firmly. "If they were, there wouldn't be slot machines, and public graft, and murders." She drew a long breath. "And roadhouses." She spoke of the latter as though they were far, far worse than murder.

"Oh come now," Tom Burrows said pleasantly.

She fixed a cold eye on him. "A disgrace. That's what they are. Senator Peveley's daughter was seen out at the Den last night, the night before her poor father was murdered."

"Well," Helene said mildly, "maybe she doesn't have second sight."

Malone lit a cigar and snapped the match inaccurately toward a cuspidor. "You say you were talking with Jerry Luckstone when the shot was fired. Do you remember where anyone else was at the time?"

She shook her head. "I wasn't noticing. Jerry was by the court reporter's desk in the middle of the room. I was just about to leave when I remembered I wanted to talk to him, so I started over that way. I called to him, but before he could answer, there was the shot."

A nice, concise report, Malone thought approvingly. She'd make a good witness.

"You ought to trot over and tell that to the sheriff," he said quietly. "That's all you need to do."

"He won't believe me. Or if he does, he'll pretend not to believe me, out of pure spite."

The little lawyer raised his eyebrows.

"Miss McGowan and the sheriff have had a mad on for two years," Tom Burrows told him. "She fought him all over the county when he was up for

election, and since then she's had the women's clubs
on his tail."

"Marvin Kling is a vicious character," the woman
said, pressing her lips together. "He and that deputy
of his have handed the office back and forth long
enough."

"Sheriff can't hold office more than two successive
terms," Tom explained. "Marv Kling has a chief
deputy, Joe Ryan. Marv holds the office two terms,
then Joe runs in the next election and he holds office
two terms with Marv as chief deputy. They're in the
tenth year now."

"That's not bad going," Malone said admiringly.

"It's disgraceful," Miss McGowan said. She looked
disapprovingly at Malone.

"Still," the lawyer said hastily, "the sheriff can't
refuse to believe you just because he doesn't like
you."

"He can," she told him, "and he would." She
added, "But you can find out who did murder the
Senator, and prove the sheriff is unfit to hold office."

Jake said, "That holds great appeal to me."

Malone sighed. "I'll think about it overnight. I
need to amble down and see this sheriff tomorrow
morning anyway, to bust this silly material-witness
business for my friends here. Maybe it'll give me some
ideas."

Miss McGowan nodded. "I suppose I'll have to be
satisfied with that." She nodded and left, her silent
brother followed her out of the room.

"Civic virtue is a wonderful thing," Jake said.

Malone mopped his brow. "Let's get out of here
before one more woman comes in and wants me to
spring Jerry Luckstone from the Jackson County can.

It'll only take one more to make it a coincidence."

"I'm going home to bed," Tom Burrows said. "I feel as though I ought to stick around, but the *Enterprise* doesn't go to press till next Thursday, and my career as a county correspondent is temporarily cut off by the visiting press." He began closing the office for the night.

"We reserved a room for you at the hotel," Helene told the lawyer. They said good night to the newspaperman and started down the street. "It's a good thing we did, too. That hotel hasn't had more than five guests at a time since it was built, now all of a sudden it's overflowing."

Main Street of Jackson, Wisconsin, was quieter now, and most of the lights were out. It was past midnight, but a few small groups lingered on the sidewalk talking over the day's events. Halfway down the street Malone stopped suddenly, looking ahead of him.

"You mean to say that's a hotel?"

The General Andrew Jackson House was a four-story frame structure of three or four assorted styles of architecture, each one apparently added at a different period. It stood on the corner of Main and Third Streets, and a small porch ran around two sides of it to form a small balcony on the second floor.

"It needs a paint job," Helene admitted, "but it's home to us."

"Two baths on every floor," Jake added, "and we managed to get you a room with running water."

Malone groaned. "That settles it. I'm having nothing further to do with the murder of Senator Peveley, not for love nor money nor civic virtue."

"You can't leave till tomorrow," Helene said

firmly. "Be brave. Be a pioneer. Think of your grandmother in a covered wagon."

"The nearest my grandmother ever got to a covered wagon," Malone said indignantly, "was my old man's livery stable."

He dubiously inspected the lobby of the General Andrew Jackson House. It was a smallish room, with a staircase running up one side, and a compartment for the clerk in the corner. The few pieces of fumed-oak furniture didn't encourage him much.

The sound of voices and occasional laughter came from a doorway marked BAR with a small neon sign. He looked toward it wistfully.

"Stay away from there," Jake said, "or you'll be all over tomorrow's papers solving the murder of Senator Peveley. It's full of newspapermen."

"Besides," Helene said, "we all need sleep."

Malone sighed. The thin-faced desk clerk who appeared on the verge of complete exhaustion consented to take his name on the register and handed him a key marked 102. With another sigh, Malone picked up his bag and followed Jake and Helene up the turkey-red carpeted stairs.

Finding 102 proved to be a complicated affair. The General Andrew Jackson House had apparently not only been built during several different periods of architecture, but in several different directions and on several different levels. There were a few steps up or a few steps down at every turn of the narrow corridors. By the time the door was located, Malone had abandoned all hope of ever finding his way out again.

"I suppose in case of fire, you just jump," he said mournfully.

"There's a rope coiled up on a hook by the window," Jake said. "Good night and happy dreams."

The little lawyer sat down on the edge of the bed and looked around unhappily. It was a smallish room, with two windows overlooking the balcony, papered with an elaborate design of grass, leaves, and bunches of grapes. The furniture consisted of an iron bedstead, painted white, a brown wooden rocker with a worn leather seat, and a battered imitation-golden-oak dresser. There was a tiny washstand in one corner, and above the bed was a print of *The Lone Wolf*.

It had been hot out on the street, but not with the pressure-cooker quality of this room. Malone decided to telephone down for a cold drink, then discovered there was no telephone in the room. He realized there were probably no bellhops, either.

He went to the window and looked out. At this hour, Jackson, Wisconsin, was quiet and peaceful, even inviting. Down the street he could see an electric sign that proclaimed THE HERMITAGE TAVERN. He grinned at that. Someone in Jackson had studied history.

It couldn't possibly be as hot in the Hermitage Tavern as it was in this room. Nor would the Hermitage be full of newspapermen who would lead him into temptation.

He got lost twice getting to the staircase, left the lobby by the wrong entrance, tried to remember the direction of the electric sign, and got lost again. A half block's walk took him to the riverbank. He tried again in another direction and wound up in front of the post office on Maple Street. The next turn led him to Fourth Street.

The gas-station attendant at the corner of Fourth and Maple told him to go back down Maple Street one block, turn left, and there would be the Hermitage Tavern, right on the corner of Third.

It was a long block between Fourth and Third. Malone was hot, tired, and deep in gloom. In Chicago, now, he told himself, he couldn't walk a block in any direction without finding someone who'd have a drink with him. Here, he got lost looking for a bar.

As he approached the corner of Third Street, he saw the reddish glare cast by the sign he had seen from his window. Suddenly he paused, wondering.

Little, white-haired Henry Peveley was standing at the door marked HERMITAGE LADIES' ENTRANCE, giving it an oddly rhythmic knock. He looked up, saw Malone, smiled, and whispered, "Hello."

Malone decided to play. He whispered a greeting right back.

"Were you looking for a place to get a drink?" Henry Peveley asked.

Malone nodded.

"I'll fix you up," the little man said. He knocked again. This time the door opened a crack. An eye peered out and observed Henry Peveley.

"Friend of mine," the latter said, pointing to Malone.

The door was opened wide by one of the most enormous men Malone had ever seen in his life, a middle-aged, red-faced, waddling giant who wore a bartender's apron tied sloppily about his middle.

"This is Mr. Malone," Henry Peveley said. "He's a friend of mine. You can let him in any time."

"Oh, sure," the bartender said.

Malone, slightly confused, sat down beside his new friend at one of the sticky tables. His confusion grew when the bartender returned with two coffee cups, each containing a man's size drink of cheap whisky.

"This is good stuff," Henry Peveley told him. "You can trust it." He lifted the cup. "Here's looking at you."

"Here's how," Malone said automatically.

Henry Peveley shook his head. "Been an exciting day. Hasn't been so much excitement since somebody stole the skeleton from the high school."

"Odd thing to steal," Malone said.

"It was odd. Nobody ever found it, either. Lots of crimes go unsolved in this world." He lifted his cup again.

"Speaking of crimes," Malone said, "I don't suppose you have any theories about your brother's death?"

Henry Peveley frowned. The effect was rather as though a nicely scrubbed pink baby had decided to look severe. "It must have had something to do with politics, but I don't know just what. Still, he'd retired from politics. It's all rather hard to understand."

"Murder often is," Malone said helpfully.

"It couldn't have been for business reasons," Henry Peveley went on, "Gerald's not been very active in business for a good many years. He was willing to let other people make his money for him. In fact, he'd gotten rather bored with life lately and decided to take a more active part in things." He frowned again. "No, business couldn't have had anything to do with it, and he had no real personal life, so it must have been for political reasons."

"That's very logical," Malone agreed. "Except that he'd retired from politics."

"True." Henry Peveley nodded vigorously. He raised his voice. "Herb!"

The elephantine bartender came into the back room and over to their table.

"Herb," in a very low voice, "have you a bottle of that I can take home?"

"Sure thing," the bartender said, in the same low, almost mysterious voice. He went away, returning in a moment with a flat, dark, unlabeled bottle.

Henry Peveley turned over a bill from a comfortable-looking roll and carefully stowed the bottle in an inside pocket.

"Have one on the house," Herb said, gathering up the cups.

"The world is in a terrible state," Henry Peveley said, shaking his head dolefully and looking at Malone, who nodded in return. After a moment he added, "It's all the fault of the administration."

"Absolutely," Malone agreed. He felt this was no time to get into a discussion of the New Deal.

Herb came back with the two refilled cups. Henry Peveley emptied his in one breath and set it down hard.

"It's all the fault of that man," he said firmly. "That man Hoover."

Malone felt uncomfortably chilly, in spite of the fact that the temperature still stood at about 92°. Could it be that the heat of the day, and the trip to Jackson, Wisconsin, had unsettled his mind? Or had some strange, Wellsian phenomenon taken place while he was trying to find his way from the General Andrew Jackson House to the Hermitage Tavern?

He felt all right, he told himself encouragingly. Yet here he was in the backroom of a speakeasy, from which his new friend was carrying away a pint of

obviously bootleg liquor, and that man Hoover was
still President.

Henry Peveley picked up his change and rose.
"I've got to get along home," he said. "If you want
to come here again, just remind Herb you're a friend
of mine. I'll see you tomorrow."

After he had gone, Malone sat staring at the coffee
cups for a long time. At last the bartender appeared
in the doorway.

"You'd better bring me another one," Malone said
unhappily.

It was brought to him in an ordinary glass. He
stared at it, then at Herb.

"Tell me," he said, "how do I look?"

Herb's moonlike face broke into a wrinkled smile.
He sat down on one of the little wire-back chairs,
spilling rolls of flesh over on both sides of it.

"I guess you ain't never met Henry before," he
said amiably. "The time I have, listening for him to
knock, and washing the labels off a bottle before I
sell it to him!"

Malone downed his drink, fast. "Then *I'm* all
right?"

"Henry's a smart man," Herb said meditatively.
"Was a smart boy, too. Manages his real-estate business well. Never has any trouble. But Henry, he lost
a powerful lot of money, back in '29. It kind of unsettled him."

Malone said, "You could call it that."

"He never got any of it back, either," the bartender
said, wiping off the top of the table. "Not that he
can't get along on what he makes in his real-estate
office. He does real well. Yes, Henry's a smart man."

"But?" Malone said hopefully.

"The only trouble with Henry," Herb said confidentially, "is that he thinks it's still 1929. It don't trouble him much. He gets along fine and tends to his business good, only he thinks it's still 1929. So he thinks Hoover is still President."

Herb rose, gathered up the cups, and started back to the bar. Halfway he paused and heaved another tempestuous sigh.

"The hardest thing in Henry's life," he said sadly, "is that he don't know prohibition's been repealed yet."

Chapter Ten

SOMEONE had stolen the skeleton from the high school and hung it from the electric light in the center of his room. A tall girl with red hair walked in through the window and gave the skeleton a push that sent it swaying and rattling. The sound it made was a loud, raucous, and rhythmic clanging.

Malone turned over, groaned, and woke up for the eleventh time since two o'clock, in time to hear the last notes of the town clock, which seemed to be ringing just outside his window. By now he'd figured out how to tell time by it. Two strokes for the quarter hour, four for the half, six for the three quarter, and eight for the hour itself, plus the number of strokes for the hour.

He had an odd feeling that he'd been bound, hand and foot, while he slept, before he discovered that the sheet, now damp and crumpled, had wrapped itself around him in the fashion of an Indian sari. With a little difficulty he disengaged himself, swung a pair of short, plump, hairy legs over the edge of the bed, and sat there curling and uncurling his toes.

There must have been a time in the winter, he told himself, when white, beautiful snow was banked up high against that window screen, and the pale finger of frost etched delicate designs upon the windowpane. That would have been in February, and here it was only August. It was damned funny that a room could get so warm in just six months.

He glanced at his watch and found that it was nearly five o'clock. It was going to be a long, hard, and probably unhappy day, he reminded himself, what with small-town politics, murdered Senators, unmarried mothers, and white-haired, elfish little men who didn't know that prohibition had been repealed.

"One reason I stay so young for my age," he told himself aloud, "is that whenever I decide to sleep, I sleep. No nonsense about either conscience or insomnia." He drew a long, determined breath. The air carried an odd mixture of sweet clover, fresh earth, and growing things, and the early morning fumes from the Jackson, Wisconsin, tannery. "I just tell myself 'Go to sleep, Malone,' and that's all there is to it."

He bravely ignored the warmth and wrinkles of the bed, and buried his face in the pillows.

It was five minutes before he identified the sound that was keeping him awake. A strange, piping, shrill, and altogether obnoxious sound that came from the birds in the trees just outside his window.

They not only piped, they yelped. With a sigh, he rolled over on his back and lay there wondering what the hell would get the birds up at this hour. Surely the worms could wait. It wouldn't be so bad if they all yelped in the same key.

There was one bird, with a particularly nasty voice, that seemed louder than the rest. That one, Malone decided, was the bird that had waked up all the other birds. Nor was it an ambitious bird who wakened early in order to herald the sun. It was probably a disreputable, disorderly bird who had been out all night, and now had staggered home in the first pale light of day to make the morning hideous.

Suddenly Malone bounded out of bed, grabbed a heavy glass ash tray from the dresser, and hurled it from the window with all his might. It crashed loudly against the tree, and for a moment there was a wild shrieking and yipping as the offended birds circled wildly up toward the graying sky.

In the next moment they had all returned to talk things over, at the top of their voices.

To the east, just across the junction of Main and Third Streets, he could see a mass of faintly pinking clouds piled up over the trees. There were odd-angled roofs half hidden by the foliage, a church tower gilded by the early morning light, the tall cupola of the courthouse where ex-Senator Gerald Peveley had been murdered, a few chimneys, and beyond, low rolling hills, checkered with green and beige fields, reaching out to the horizon. Suddenly he felt deeply sorry for the late ex-Senator Peveley, and hoped that his murderer would be found and punished. Life was just too wonderful to leave.

Everything, he decided, was almost unbearably sad. Life was wonderful, but nobody seemed to know what to do with it, and the world was beautiful, but nobody looked at it except tourists. He felt that he had discovered an important and impressive truth, and felt uncomfortably lonely about it. Here a kind of perfection of existence was always close at hand, and no one reached for it. Instead people hated each other for inadequate reasons, small hotels were built without air-conditioning, and the damned birds woke one up at five in the morning.

A shrill whistle from the street below caught his attention. He looked down and saw Helene, a small, delicate figure in white slacks, her blonde hair pale in the early light.

He hastily pulled the corner of a worn lace curtain over a broad expanse of brown, hairy chest. "You ought to be asleep," he complained.

"I can't sleep. Besides, Jake got up a while ago and he's wandered off somewhere, and I wish you'd come down and help find him."

Malone muttered something about people who could get lost in a town of less than three thousand people, and promised to be right down. A few minutes later he joined Helene on the sidewalk.

"I don't suppose there's a place in town to get a cup of coffee at this hour," she said. "We might as well walk." She thrust her hands into the pockets of her slacks, and strolled down the street, looking like a beautiful and absurd little girl who had decided to play tomboy.

"The only place I'd like to walk is back to Clark Street," Malone growled. "And I don't care how many miles it is."

He had started to ask something more about Jake, when the town clock rang again.

Helene counted on her fingers. "Five-fifteen," she announced.

The little lawyer shied a rock at a sidewalk sparrow. "That damned clock! Ordinarily they go to bed at eight o'clock in this burg. Why do they have to know what time it is all night long?" He yawned. "Where's Jake?"

"Probably a suicide," Helene said. "About the time the birds began to twitter, he got up and dressed, muttered something about the river, and went out."

"Not a bad idea, either, on a day like this," Malone said gloomily.

"Think how nice and cool it will be next winter," Helene said consolingly.

Malone growled something profane under his breath. "I'd give the next ten winters of my life right now to be back in Chicago, in a nice quiet place to sleep."

At the end of Third Street, just before the bridge, a narrow path led off along the riverbank. Helene followed it, the lawyer a few steps behind, complaining loudly about the rocks that got into his shoes. Beyond the shed belonging to the *Jackson County Enterprise* the path curved off to the right following a bend in the river, and just around it they found Jake sitting on the grass, his back against a tree, gazing soulfully out over the water.

Helene and the lawyer sat down beside him.

"Beautiful day," Malone said crossly. He lit a cigar. It tasted terrible.

Jake sighed, and was silent. Across the river a series of smooth green lawns ran up from the water's edge, great, shadowy elm trees bent and swayed over them, and behind their foliage stood small white wooden or yellow brick houses, fringed with beds of orange marigolds, or lavender petunias. It was very peaceful and very still.

"Good God," the little lawyer exploded, "can you imagine people actually living in a place like this!" He groaned loudly.

"People do," Helene said. She drew her knees up to rest her chin. "People like us, and like Arlene

Goudge, and Ellen McGowan, and Cora Belle
Fromm, and the late Senator Peveley."

"The late Senator Peveley lived in a mansion,"
Jake said gloomily. "I've seen it. Dun-colored brick
and decorative woodwork and three porches."

Malone had been staring across the river at the
little houses. "They hold all the potentialities," he
murmured. "The people in them love each other,
and hate each other, and perhaps even murder each
other, though they wait thirty-two years to get around
to it. In a small town like this everything happens that
happens everywhere else, except that it's on a micro-
cosmic scale." He was silent for a moment, scowled
heavily, and said, "Where in the hell is that damned
gun?"

"Lost," Jake told him.

Helene suggested helpfully, "Someone outside the
courthouse shot the Senator through the window."

"Not at that turn of the stairs," Jake reminded
her. "Besides, he was shot at close range."

"The gun's got to be somewhere," Malone said. He
relit his cigar. "Unless somebody could have carried
it out of the courthouse."

Jake shook his head. "You couldn't have carried a
tune out of that courthouse without one of those
deputies stopping you."

"Then it's in the courthouse and nobody's done a
really good job of looking for it."

Jake sighed again. "The courthouse was searched
from top to bottom, crossways and sideways. The only
things that turned up were a quart bottle of bourbon
in the clerk of the court's office and two pairs of
loaded dice in the county judge's desk."

"Interesting," Helene said, "but hardly cause for murder."

Malone looked disgustedly at the cigar. "Loaded dice have caused almost as many murders as women," he said crossly. "And I've seen slaughter over a drink of bourbon, let alone a quart of it." He paused and added wistfully, "Was it good bourbon?"

Jake shook his head. "Very cheap bourbon."

"Well, anyway," the lawyer said, "there wasn't any gun. Damn it, it must have gone somewhere."

"It's none of our business," Helene reminded him, "or are you going to take up Florence Peveley's offer?"

"I'm going back to Chicago," Malone said doggedly. He rose, stretched, and brushed the dry grass off his pants. "But a guy can be curious, can't he?"

They strolled back uptown in search of breakfast. It was still very early but Main Street was open for business, and already crowds were beginning to gather. The dining room of the General Andrew Jackson House looked like a Loop cafeteria at high noon. Malone felt a certain grim satisfaction in observing that the newspapermen had evidently also had a little trouble with the songs of the early birds.

Every chair at every table was occupied, and the nervous and harassed waitresses were racing back and forth to the overworked kitchen, occasionally dropping silverware or china with a horrendous clatter. The proprietor, a short, thin, potbellied man with wispy gray hair, watched from the doorway, his face an engaging combination of cupidity and amazement.

Helene remarked afterward that they could only have made their entrance into the dining room more conspicuous if they had ridden in on giraffes. The hubbub of conversation had stopped entirely by the time they were two feet inside the door, and everyone in the room had put down his knife and fork to stare. The sudden silence seemed to be saying, "Here they are now."

Helene thrust her hands into the pockets of her perfectly fitted white slacks and looked around the room with cool aplomb. She was, Jake observed, attracting the major share of the attention, and no wonder. It took more than the murder of a middle-aged ex-Senator and a sleepless night in a stuffy small-town hotel to impair Helene's appearance. Her carefully made-up face gave the impression of having been freshly washed in the morning dew. In the dim light of the dining room her hair gleamed as though it had just been polished.

She stood there looking as though she confidently expected someone to rise and offer them a table, and inevitably someone did.

The young reporter from the *Milwaukee Journal* shoved back his chair with a loud clatter and signaled to them. "We're just finished."

Helene's grateful smile had made lifelong slaves of better men that he would ever be. Indeed he was half-way to the door before he remembered that his prime purpose in offering up the table had been to get in a few early questions. By that time it was too late.

"Mr. Justus," a young woman from Chicago was asking, "when you saw Senator Peveley there on the floor, how did he look?"

"Dead," Jake told her. He added to the waitress, "Ham and eggs and coffee for three and make it snappy. We're going fishing."

"Oh, but surely," the man from the A. P. said, "you're not going fishing today!"

Jake said pleasantly, "Why not? The fish haven't heard about the murder yet."

Someone murmured something about an inquest, and attention turned to Malone.

"Could you tell me who your client is?"

Malone, his mouth full of coffee, pointed to Jake and Helene.

"How long do you believe they'll be held as material witnesses?"

"Not thirty seconds longer than when I lay my hands on that fathead sheriff," Malone said, sputtering over his coffee, "and if you quote me, I'll call you a liar."

At that moment someone caught sight of Sheriff Kling going down the sidewalk, and the dining room was promptly deserted save for Jake, Helene, and Malone. Later, however, they were met at the door by a photographer for the *Tribune,* and when Malone reached the door of his room he found it barricaded by a plump, pretty little girl from a Madison daily sitting on the floor. She declared that she was not going to move until Malone told her his theory of the murder of Senator Peveley.

"I think it was a *crime passionel,*" he said, leering at her. "And if you'll just step inside my room, I'll show you what I mean—"

She gave a little scream and fled, leaving him in peace. Meanwhile Jake and Helene had reached their door in time to discover an enterprising photographer who had bribed the chambermaid to open it. He was preparing to take a picture of the country hotel room where Chicago's most notable heiress and her night-club-owner husband had spent the night.

The town of Jackson, Wisconsin, had gone completely wild. Farm families were arriving in cars, trucks, and occasional wagons, and an enterprising church organization had already announced that a picnic lunch would be served in Wickett's Grove, just back of the courthouse square, from twelve to three. The town's one traffic cop was riding furiously up and down Main Street on his motorcycle, wondering what to do in case a traffic jam did develop. The son of a local druggist had hastily bought up the town's supply of postcards and set himself up in business on the corner of Main and Third, offering souvenirs. And everyone in town who owned a childhood or early-youth picture of the late Senator was busily engaged in looking for a reporter who might buy it for cash.

Helene announced that she was not going to barricade herself in her hotel room. Everyone who had come to town wanted to get a look at her, she declared, and she intended to make it as easy for the visitors as possible by spending the time before the inquest strolling up and down Main Street. She emerged from her room looking cool and exquisite in an embroidered linen dress the exact shade of the inside of a watermelon rind and carrying an immense pale violet hat which perfectly matched the shade of her small sandals.

"I'm not going to disappoint everyone who wants to see an heiress, and a leading figure in the Senator's murder, by turning up in slacks," she said firmly.

Jake shook his head sadly and agreed to accompany her on her stroll. Malone, meanwhile, donned a white linen suit and a Panama hat for his call on the sheriff. By the time he had pushed his way through the crowd to the courthouse and adjoining jail the suit looked as though it might have been borrowed from a beachcomber, and the hat had been dropped in the dust four times.

He paused on the steps leading to the sheriff's office and looked over the courthouse square. A ring of deputies were protecting it against the curiosity seekers, and it seemed like an island of grass and trees in a sea of people. The courthouse especially fascinated him. Set far back in the square, and surrounded by elms, it managed to appear incredibly large. It was made of soiled and discolored yellow brick, stood three stories high, and was surmounted by a cupola whose pointed roof wore more iron lace than he had ever seen in any one place at any one time. The faded gilt hands of the cupola clock pointed, falsely, to half-past seven. Against the expanse of brick the long, narrow, arched windows were dark, almost sinister. At the top of a long flight of concrete steps were two blank wooden doors, painted gray.

Malone suddenly felt the flesh creep on his bones. The day was hot, yesterday's rainfall had only added dampness to the air instead of cooling it. The sun was already high, but a thin mist darkened the sky. The atmosphere was oppressive, hard to breathe, almost suffocating. There was something about it Malone didn't like.

The door behind him opened and a small, grinning, bald-headed man came out. Malone recognized Buttonholes from Jake's description and introduced himself.

"I'm glad to see you got out of jail."

Buttonholes spat neatly into a bed of geraniums. "Kep' me locked up overnight just for showing a few folks through the courthouse." He spat again. "That ain't all. Son of a bitch made me give him half of what I took in." He didn't offer to identify the son of a bitch, but squinted at the courthouse square, his brow contracted.

"I knew it was going to happen," he volunteered. "I guess Mr. Justus told you. I didn't know what was going to happen, but I felt like something was." He added, "Y'know, my grandmother was a Welshwoman. It was just like she used to say. I didn't know nothing, but I had a kind of a feeling."

"I know what you mean," Malone said. "My grandmother was an Irishwoman."

Buttonholes regarded him thoughtfully. " 'Course, there's nothing can beat the Welsh for being gifted that way," he said mildly. "But I guess you know what I felt." He looked out over the town and frowned again. "I got it again today, too. Something's happening."

This time Malone shivered. "Like what?"

"I don't know," Buttonholes said sadly. "But something. I got exactly the same feeling I had yesterday. Only today, it's worse."

Chapter Eleven

MALONE was disappointed in his first look at Sheriff Marvin Kling. This was his first experience with the small-town forces of law and order, and he had expected something very different. Just what, he wasn't sure. Not quite the old village constable, but something more along that line.

Instead, he found a big, burly, slovenly man seated in a swivel chair, his feet on a table, with a disordered roll-top desk behind him. He wore a cheap, purplish-blue suit with no vest, a striped shirt, and a bright-green tie. A soiled gray felt hat was stuck far back on his head. His big-jowled, ugly face had been reddened by a combination of sun, wind, and whisky, and a heavy lock of greasy dark hair hung over his forehead.

Neither he nor the thin, worried young men who was sitting on one corner of the table made any move, other than to look up, as Malone came in.

"What the hell do you want?" Sheriff Kling demanded.

Malone caught himself on the verge of an appropriate reply and instead said, "I suppose you're the sheriff. I'm John J. Malone."

"Oh," the sheriff said. "You're those folks' lawyer." He lit a cigarette, tossing the match on the floor. "Well, what do you think you're going to do?"

"In about two more minutes," Malone said evenly, "I'm going to give you a bust in the puss."

The sheriff swung his big legs off the table.

"Just a minute, Marv," the young man said anxiously. He turned to Malone. "Mr. Kling isn't feeling particular well. He's had a lot of people bothering him."

"I don't feel particularly well myself," Malone said, "and I didn't come all the way up to this Godforsaken hamlet to get pushed around by a hick sheriff. Who are you?"

"I'm the district attorney," the young man said. "I'm Jerry Luckstone."

Malone looked at him with interest. Any man who had three women trying to get him out of jail was worth a second glance. He wondered how Luckstone did it. The district attorney was a delicate-looking young man, with a narrow, handsome, almost fleshless face, and curly brown hair. Maybe it was that helpless look that turned the trick.

"I thought you were in jail," the lawyer said at last.

"It was a mistake," Jerry Luckstone told him. "Cora Belle came in this morning and told Marv here that she was talking with me, way off in the other corner of the courtroom, when the shot was fired. Marv had just about decided it was a mistake anyway by then."

Malone told himself he hadn't really wanted that fee Florence Peveley had held under his nose. Now he could go back to Chicago without any qualms.

"All right, it was a mistake," the sheriff said angrily. "Everybody makes mistakes. This would be a hell of a world if people didn't make mistakes now and then."

"For you it would be torture," Malone said politely.

The sheriff glared at him. "I found out Jerry here had a fight with the old man over being engaged to Florence, and the old man was threatening to cut her out of his will. That's enough reason for murder. And he was up there where he could have done it."

Malone said nothing. He was trying to decide which woman Jerry Luckstone had really been talking with when the shot was fired; Cora Belle Fromm, or Ellen McGowan. Or if he'd been talking to either of them. He cleared his throat.

"Now about Mr. and Mrs. Justus," he began.

The young district attorney spoke up quickly. "I can see no reason why they shouldn't leave after the inquest. They'll be required to testify there, of course."

"I can see we're going to get along fine," Malone told him. He heard Sheriff Kling muttering under his breath. "It's obvious, of course, neither of them could have committed the murder."

"I ain't so sure," the sheriff growled. "They been mixed up in murders before, and here they are up in the Jackson County Courthouse for the first time, and here we have the first murder in thirty-two years."

"You're talking in allergies," Malone said smoothly. "But a competent officer of the law like yourself wouldn't attempt to introduce that as evidence."

The sheriff looked pleased though confused. "No, I guess you're right there."

Malone lit a cigar. "You've had no more luck finding the gun, I suppose." He drew an indignant glare by way of answer and added, "My only interest in this is idle curiosity, but if it's permitted, I would like to take a look at the scene of the crime."

The sheriff and the district attorney exchanged glances. "Why not?" the latter said. He managed a sick laugh. "Maybe you can give us some ideas."

"It's just possible," Malone said politely.

He followed the two men across the lawn and into the big, shadowy courthouse, more tomblike than ever now with all its typewriters and telephones silenced. Jerry Luckstone informed him that the offices had been closed for the day.

Malone took a quick look at the courtroom, and looked away just as quickly. Buttonholes, busy with a broom and dustpan, looked up to grin at him.

"Now here," Jerry Luckstone said. "Everybody was milling around in here. To be perfectly honest, I don't recall exactly where I was. The Senator came up and told me he wanted to see me. He was sore about something. I told him I was going back in my office and he grunted something about going downstairs to fetch someone—he didn't say who—and started for the stairs. That's the last I saw of him."

Malone nodded. "You didn't notice where anyone else was?"

"No. I have a dim picture of Ed Skindingsrude over there by the jury box talking to somebody— Miss McGowan, I think—but I couldn't swear to it."

Malone walked over to the head of the tiny staircase and peered into the two rooms beyond. "Was anybody in either of these rooms?"

Luckstone shook his head. "Nobody. I'm positive of that."

"Who got to the head of the stairs first?"

"As a matter of fact," the district attorney said, "I did."

The little lawyer sighed. There was a minute hall at the top of the staircase, hardly large enough for a man to turn around in, beyond it a slightly larger hall led to the two rooms. Between them and the courtroom, at the head of the stairs, was a door.

"What's in there?"

"Nothing but a little broom closet," Jerry Luckstone told him. He tried the door, it was locked. "Hey, Buttonholes, come over and unlock this."

"It ain't locked," the janitor called.

"It sure as hell is locked." He rattled it again.

Buttonholes picked up an enormous ring of keys and started over. "It ain't never been locked, and it ain't supposed to be locked," he complained. "I ain't even sure I got keys to fit it."

Malone examined the keyhole. "Try an ordinary dime-store passkey," he suggested.

The janitor found several on his ring, the second one unlocked the door. Malone opened it and peered inside.

It was a tiny closet, dark and dusty. A few old brooms leaned against the wall, a collection of ancient filing cases were stacked at the far end. An old raincoat hung from one hook, a large white dusting cloth from another.

Malone shook the coat and felt of its pockets, kicked the brooms, examined the filing cases, and judged from the dust on them that they hadn't been moved in twenty years.

"I don't know what you expect to find in there," Sheriff Kling complained.

"The gun," Malone said pleasantly. He felt of the dusting cloth, lifted it down from the hook, and carried it into the light. "And there it is."

He shook the cloth gingerly over a table, a small black revolver unrolled itself and dropped to the table top.

There was a long silence. "Either you've got second sight," Sheriff Kling said at last, in a dangerously quiet voice, "or by God, you know more about this murder than you've told anybody."

Malone dropped an inch of cigar ash in the general direction of a cuspidor. Buttonholes looked at him reproachfully and reached for his broom. "It was perfectly simple," the little lawyer said. "It didn't occur to anybody to look in the closet for the gun, because the door was locked. It occurred to me to look there because I had an idea it was the only place the murderer could shoot from without being noticed, and I was right. Obviously the murderer didn't carry the gun away from the scene of the crime, this was the only place that hadn't been searched, so it had to be here."

Jerry Luckstone pointed to the closet. "You mean the murderer was in there?"

"Of course he was," Malone said. He stepped just inside the closet and stood looking out. "Buttonholes says this door isn't usually locked. All right, the murderer brought along a key, an ordinary passkey, and had it probably on the inside of the door. This is a wild guess, but it'll do. He stood right here, with the door open just a crack, when he fired. You see the door protects him from the view of the people in the courtroom."

Sheriff Kling and the young district attorney nodded. The lawyer went on, "He waited until the Senator started alone down the stairs. In passing he had to almost brush against the door of the closet. The murderer fired through the crack. No one would pay any attention to the closet, everybody was interested in the murdered man."

Jerry Luckstone sighed. "That's the trouble with witnesses. They always look at the wrong things." He frowned. "But then what?"

"Then," Malone said, "he hid the gun in the dust-cloth, locked the door behind him, and went downstairs."

"What the hell did he lock the door for?" Sheriff Kling growled.

"So that your deputies would reason that the door had been locked at the time the Senator was killed and wouldn't bother looking in the broom closet for the gun," Malone told him.

"This is all very well," Jerry Luckstone said, "but it doesn't tell who it was." He looked hopefully at Malone.

The little lawyer shook his head. "This is as far as the train of reasoning goes. But you've got a likely bunch of suspects in that collection of people who were up here at the time." He paused suddenly in the act of lighting his cigar, letting the match burn until it all but scorched his fingers. "As a matter of fact—" He stopped himself and paused again. This murder wasn't his affair and he wasn't going to mix up in it. Let the forces of law and order of Jackson County make the same discovery, by the same simple reasoning.

"What?" Jerry Luckstone asked anxiously.

"As a matter of fact," Malone repeated, "you might as well put their names in a hat and draw one out. It would be the easiest way." He finished relighting his cigar. "Well, glad to have been of help. See you at the inquest, gentlemen."

He strolled out of the courthouse, feeling extremely pleased with himself.

Well, as far as he was concerned, that settled everything. Jake and Helene could continue on their fishing trip after the inquest. He privately hoped they would catch nothing but minnows and would never desert Chicago again. The young district attorney was out of the toils of the law, and Arlene Goudge, Miss McGowan, and Florence Peveley would be satisfied. Also Cora Belle Fromm, since she too had taken steps to prove the young man's innocence. There was nothing now for him to do but go back to Chicago and see how big a fee he could squeeze out of Harry for beating that bookie rap.

By nightfall he'd be back in Chicago. The thought revived his spirits. "Oh God," he murmured soulfully, "just to hear one taxi horn again!"

Ellen MacGowan was hurrying up the sidewalk as Malone went down the courthouse steps. He paused to greet her.

"Well, Mr. Luckstone is out of jail, without any help from me," he told her.

She nodded. "I know it."

He looked at her thoughtfully. She was the neatest person he'd ever seen in his life, her trim gray hair might have been parted along a ruler. Her navy-blue print dress had been freshly ironed. It seemed to him that her face had a worried, almost haggard look. Well, you didn't witness a murder every day. It might have accounted for a sleepless night.

"It appears the sheriff made a mistake," Malone said.

She sniffed. "Sheriff Kling is not only dishonest but stupid." She added coldly, "Crime conditions in this county are deplorable."

He was conscious of a strange, dissatisfied feeling as he walked back to the General Andrew Jackson House. It wasn't, he told himself, that he gave a damn who had shot Senator Peveley. Certainly it wasn't that he was trying to promote himself a client out of the affair. But there was no law against a man being curious.

He entered the lobby of the hotel just in time to hear the U. P. reporter calling his office, and paused momentarily to listen.

"Take this, Joe," the reporter was saying into the telephone. "The sheriff up here—Marvin Kling— just called me up and told me he'd found the gun. The gun. G-u-n, gun. O. K.? All right. He found also where the murderer was standing when he fired the shot. He was standing in a closet at the top of those stairs. A closet. No, no, not that kind. A broom closet. Got that? Now. Sheriff Kling says he figured out where the gun was and where the murderer stood by just reasoning that—"

Malone walked on across the lobby, grinning happily. Marvin Kling was a small-town sheriff, but he learned fast!

Chapter Twelve

"YOUR GRANDMOTHER wasn't Welsh," Jake complained, "so don't go around developing second sight. Buttonholes is enough."

Malone looked mournfully down Main Street. "I didn't say it was second sight. I said it was a feeling in my bones. I'm uncomfortable."

"It's your age," Jake said unfeelingly.

Malone sighed deeply. "There's some time to kill before the inquest. I promised that red-haired Peveley girl I'd see her this morning. If I go there I may still be able to send her a bill for advice."

"You're a ruthless moneygrubber," Helene said, "but if you insist, we'll drive you there. I've been dying to show off the convertible to the Jackson sight-seers."

The Peveley house, set on the highest ground in Jackson, was ornate, impressive, and magnificently ugly. It was perfectly square and three long stories high, crowned with a squat, square tower. The yellowish brick was still bright, and the heavy, decorative woodwork had recently been painted a deep, glossy green. As Helene parked her car by the front sidewalk a sudden flash of sunlight caught the immense stained-glass double doors and set them gleaming like ten-cent-store jewelry.

"My," Jake said admiringly. "I bet that cost a pile

of money to build! No wonder he didn't leave any trees in the yard. They might have hidden some of it from sight."

Malone climbed out and slammed the door.

"We're going to drive up and down Main Street," Helene called. "Pick you up later." The blue convertible shot down the street and vanished.

The lawyer knocked lightly on the door; it was partly ajar and swung open under his hand.

"It's none of your business what I do," Florence Peveley was saying at the top of her voice from somewhere inside the house. "I don't care what you or anyone else thinks and I'm going to do as I damned please."

Malone looked anxiously around for the bell. He heard an indistinguishable, low murmur of protest in a masculine voice, and the unmistakable sound of a book being thrown.

"You can go to hell," Florence Peveley yelled.

He found the bell and pushed it hastily. It rang through the house like a fire warning and brought an immediate response from Florence Peveley.

"Well, why don't you come in?" she bellowed.

Malone went in, hoping for the best. In the middle of the room probably called the library Florence Peveley stood, a heroic figure in brief white shorts and a striped sweater. She had good-looking legs and plenty of them, Malone decided at his first glance. Right at the moment she was standing in the midst of a pile of books and furniture, arms akimbo, her red hair flying in every direction, and a black smudge on her nose.

Jerry Luckstone was standing across the room, leaning against a table, looking pale and disturbed.

"Look at him," the girl demanded of Malone. "Did you ever see such a cringing bastard?" She scratched her nose, leaving a smudge on the other side. "Do you blame me for losing my temper with him?"

The young man's face turned faintly pink. "Mr. Malone, she seems to have some respect for you. I wish you'd tell her she can't do this."

"You can't do this," Malone said sternly and automatically. "What the hell are you doing, anyway?"

"I'm getting everything in this house ready to sell," she declared. "I know I can't sell it until the will is read and the property appraised, but at least I can get it ready. And this fool tells me I can't do it now because it isn't respectful to Pa." She made a rude noise.

"Well," Malone said mildly, "after all, he is dead, and the grass hasn't even been planted on his grave."

She plumped herself down on a sofa, her legs sprawled out before her. "All I want is to get out of this place as fast as I can. I want to sell everything and beat it."

"Where are you going?" Malone asked.

"Anywhere, as long as it isn't Jackson, Wisconsin."

Jerry Luckstone frowned. "Now, Florence. I like it here."

She turned on him furiously. "You would. All you want out of life is to loaf around and play golf all day, and lay all the girls you can get after dark, and have a father-in-law who'd fix you up with a soft political job, while—"

That was as far as she got. The young district attorney turned white, moved across the room in a few quick strides, slapped her smartly and resoundingly across the mouth, and was out the front door before she could catch her breath.

"It looks as though you'd have a very happy married life," Malone said.

She didn't hear him. "Son of a bitch!" she breathed, rubbing her lips. It was said admiringly. Then she looked at Malone. "Have a cigarette."

"No, thanks." He began unwrapping a cigar.

"Well, Jerry got out of jail by himself," she said, "but you send me a bill for whatever worrying you did. Do you blame me for not pretending to feel heartbroken that Pa's dead?"

"Of course not," Malone told her.

"I will say it was a shock. I knew a lot of people hated him, but I never expected anybody to murder him. It's a wonder I never thought of it myself. He was an awful stinker, you know."

The little lawyer raised his eyebrows questioningly.

"I mean just plain stinker. He wasn't only an unprincipled businessman and a crooked politican, he was a stinker." She repeated the word as though she enjoyed it. "He practically murdered my mother. Yes he did. He was so mean to her that she took poison. Everybody thought it was heart trouble. She should have given it to him. I never could get Uncle Phil —that's Phil Smith—or Doctor Goudge to admit it to me, but I know it."

"Goudge?" Malone asked. The name was familiar.

"Old Doc Goudge. He's the county treasurer's older brother. He's been in the county insane asylum the last four years." She threw away her half-smoked cigarette and lit another. "What were we talking about? Oh yes, Pa. He did Ed Skindingsrude out of a lot of money two years ago. In fact, he did everybody out of money. He was such a louse even the party wouldn't support him for Senator any more. And he has two illegitimate children that I know of in the county. To say nothing of the way he treated me."

She got up and began pacing the floor. "I've been cooped up in this damned house in this damned town for too many damned years, and it's damned near driven me crazy."

Malone caught himself on the verge of saying, "You're damned right."

"Nothing to do. Not a damned thing to do. That's what made me sore. I've got to get away as fast as I can. I'm neurotic, you know. Very neurotic. I wish I could tell you how much money I've spent on doctors, and they all told me the same thing. Very neurotic. Are you surprised, living in a place like this?"

"Frankly, no," Malone said, thinking of the town clock and the birds.

"Here I was twenty-nine years old, and not getting anywhere. So I decided to marry Jerry Luckstone. I thought he might at least run for the legislature and I'd get as far as Madison. He thought Pa's political drag might do him some good. He really didn't give a damn about me. He'd go out and mess around with all sorts of girls, but he wouldn't lay a finger on me. That's his small-town morality. He was just respecting me because we were engaged. I'm a virgin, you know. And twenty-nine years old. But I've come to the conclusion I ought to do something about it, just to know how it's done."

Malone measured the distance between himself and the door, and said, "Have you any idea who murdered your father?"

She shook her head. "Any one of that crew might

have done it. They're all stinkers, except Uncle Phil.
You'll see, when you've been here awhile."

"I'm not going to be here awhile," Malone said.
"I'm going back to Chicago tonight." A great load
seemed to lift from his mind as he said it.

"Lucky you." She grinned at him. "Well, send me
a bill. And I'll look you up when I get to Chicago."

"Do that," Malone said, putting all the conviction
he could into his voice. "We'll go out and have a
drink or something."

He paused on the sidewalk to mop his brow. Florence Peveley was a little strenuous. Still, she did have
beautiful legs.

A block down the street he found Jerry Luckstone
leaning against a tree, waiting for him. They walked
on toward Main Street together.

"I don't know what you think," the young man
said uncomfortably.

"I think it's a damned hot day," Malone said, loos-
ening his tie, "and I think your girl has a violent
temper and a beautiful figure, which isn't a bad combination when you think it over."

Jerry Luckstone frowned. "That isn't what I mean.
Florence is all right if you understand her. I hope you
didn't believe that crack about my marrying her because of her old man's political drag."

"Not at all," Malone lied.

"I wish you'd stay here," Luckstone said unexpectedly. "I'm terribly mixed up about the whole
thing."

"I know how you feel," the lawyer said sympathetically. "I'm mixed up too. But I'm going to do
something about it. I'm going back to Chicago."

The district attorney seemed to be talking to himself. "I can't understand why she did it."

"Who?"

"Cora Belle."

Malone blinked. "I seem to have missed a couple of pages here. What are you talking about?

"Cora Belle said I was talking to her when the shot was fired. But I wasn't, you see. I wasn't talking to anybody. I'm sure about that. There wasn't anybody around me. Why did she do it?"

"Maybe she likes you better out of jail than in," Malone said. "Of course, I don't know just how you stand with her."

The young man's cheeks reddened. "There never was anything serious," he said. "Maybe she was just being helpful."

"Or maybe she wanted to establish where she was at the time," Malone said thoughtfully. "The really funny thing about it is that another person also claims to have been talking to you." He told about the visit from Ellen McGowan.

Jerry Luckstone stopped walking for a few seconds. "But why would she do that?"

"I don't know," the little lawyer said amiably. "Unless you'd been running around with her too." As the district attorney laughed, he went on, "It's just that nobody wants to see you in jail." He considered telling about the weeping Arlene Goudge, and thought better of it.

"I don't know what to think," Jerry Luckstone said, "or where to begin. Ordinarily this job of mine is a pretty routine thing. But murder, and especially the murder of an important man like Senator Peveley, and the town full of reporters—"

Helene's car drove up beside them just in time to save Malone from having to give free advice.

"We'll drive you downtown," Helene said. "When's the inquest?"

Jerry Luckstone consulted his watch. "Half an hour."

Later Helene remarked that, even for coincidence, the next few minutes had perfect timing. Malone consulted his wallet and announced that he had to cash a check and had better do it now, in case the bank was closed after the inquest was over. Jake decided he ought to cash a check too. Jerry Luckstone offered to accompany them for identification.

Helene parked the convertible before the two-story stucco building marked FARMERS' BANK OF JACKSON, WIS., announced she didn't want to be left behind, and went in with the men.

The interior of the Farmers' Bank of Jackson, Wis., was small. An el-shaped lobby ran across the front and down one side, around the enclosure which occupied about half the space. Two windows in the painted metal grillwork were marked CASHIER and TELLER, at the end of the lobby a ground glass door announced PRESIDENT.

The bank was crowded even before their arrival. As they entered, Mr. Goudge was going into the enclosure by a small side door. In the enclosure they saw and recognized the gray-haired Miss McGowan and the handsome Phil Smith, who waved to them as they came in. There was a thin, middle-aged, ferret-faced man at the teller's window, and a plump, pretty girl operating an adding machine.

Outside, a high-booted farmer stood at one window, laboriously filling out a slip of paper; at the other, Ed Skindingsrude was just moving up to cash a check, as a housewifely-looking woman moved away and started toward the door.

Malone waited until the farmer and Ed Skindingsrude had finished, made out his check, and stepped up to the window, Jake and Jerry Luckstone just behind him. Whatever might have gone on inside the cage escaped his attention, occupied as he was with his checkbook and fountain pen.

He pushed the check through the slot and said, "Fives and tens please."

Later all that he remembered clearly was Ellen McGowan's warning scream. He had a dim and confused picture of Jake throwing Helene toward the door, and of Helene's ashen face, frozen with horror. In the same instant he felt, rather than heard, a tremendous sound that seemed to come from all around him, the floor beneath his feet suddenly appeared to leap upward, there was a flash of light, and something struck him in the chest with terrific force.

There was another instant in which he realized he was flat against the wall on the other side of the building, pinned there by what had been the teller's window grating. Through the smoke he could dimly see forms, most of them moving. There was blood on the tile floor just in front of him. And the ferret-faced man had completely disappeared.

That was all Malone ever remembered of the explosion that wrecked the Farmers' Bank of Jackson, Wis.

Chapter Thirteen

THE ODOR in the air seemed more settling powder than smoke. Malone opened his eyes gingerly and saw Helene's white face, smudged with dust, bending over him. She was wiping his forehead with a wet cloth.

"You're not dead," Helene said firmly.

Malone shut his eyes again. "I am too dead," he told her.

There was a sharp pain in the back of his head and an odd sensation in his stomach. He decided he was far too uncomfortable to be dead, and opened his eyes again.

"Jake?"

"He's digging somebody out of the wreckage," Helene said. "Ed Skindingsrude, I think. Lie still."

"I am lying still," Malone murmured. The last thing in the world he wanted was to move.

He tried to remember. The flash of blinding light. The noises. The people who had been in the Farmers' Bank of Jackson, Wis. In the distance he could hear somebody say, "Lift that piece of timber over there, its across his stomach," and another voice, partly muffled, said, "Careful there, I think my leg's broke." He wanted to see what was going on, yet he dreaded the sudden impact of daylight that would surely materialize the odd sensation in his stomach into something more tangible and unpleasant.

After a moment he compromised by opening his eyes a narrow crack, protecting himself against the light with his eyelashes. He saw, then, that he was lying on the sidewalk a little to the north of the half-wrecked building, and that an awed circle of spectators was watching Helene bathe his forehead. Beyond them he could see the gray stucco façade of the bank, and through the great gaping hole where a plate-glass window had been, there was a faint movement of men and dust and broken stone and timbers.

"He must have been killed instantly," a woman in the crowd said in an excited, curious voice.

Malone opened his eyes and looked at her. "I was," he said confidentially. The woman screamed and fled.

"Malone," Helene pleaded, "are you all right? No, don't move. Just tell me if you're all right."

"I feel fine," he whispered.

He heard Jake's voice in the distance. "There's nobody else in there." A truck, hastily pressed into service as an ambulance, was driving away. The dust was beginning to settle.

Jake came out from the wrecked building, his red hair whitened by powdered cement, his face black and smudged. There was a small bruise over his left eye. He pushed his way through the crowd to where Malone was lying.

"Excitement's all over now," he reported. He squatted down on one knee beside the lawyer and lit a cigarette. "Of the people who were in there, only—"

A siren screamed. There was a sudden, clamorous

ringing of bells, the crowd on the street scattered in all directions. Malone raised himself up on one elbow. The movement engulfed him in another wave of faintness and nausea, a quick stab of pain shot through his head.

There was one moment of consciousness in which he saw the Jackson Volunteer Hook and Ladder Company come charging down Main Street, a brilliant blaze of red paint and shining brass. He heard yells from the firemen, all still in work clothes.

"By the time that fire department reached the fire," he murmured, "the horse would be out the barn door." As his head fell back on the sidewalk again, he wondered just what he'd meant to say.

Some magic transformed the sidewalk into a bed and a pillow, there was a sheet over him, and a blessed coolness in the air. He might have been in heaven, but he doubted it. He felt that he was alive, in a vague kind of way. It was as comfortable as he'd imagined Heaven to be, but there was some subtle difference. After a moment's reflection he realized the difference was created by the shrill piping of a bird just outside a window, and he knew for sure he was alive. They would never let anything as noisy as that bird into heaven.

Then there was an unfamiliar voice, a masculine one, saying, "He had a nasty bump on the head and another one in the stomach, but he'll be all right if he'll just stay quiet. The chances are he'll be up and around tomorrow, as good as new. But keep him in bed until morning."

A door opened and closed quietly, and there was quiet again, except for the bird.

He wiggled his toes experimentally and found that

they moved according to directions. It was a wonderful sensation just to be alive. No one could ask for anything more, except possibly a quart of gin. Suddenly it seemed very sad to him that people demanded so much of the world, when it was enough to be alive and able to wiggle one's toes, after being snatched from the jaws of death.

From the corner of one eye he could see Jake sitting beside his bed, regarding him anxiously. It was a new and delectable experience. Once he'd imagined how he'd feel if Jake lay before him at the point of death; in fact, he'd imagined it so vividly that he'd wept bitterly on the polished bar of a Blue Island tavern. But he'd never imagined how Jake's face might look if the circumstances were reversed.

It was always fascinating to watch people when they didn't know they were being observed. He suddenly remembered the time he'd pretended to be asleep and managed to watch that gorgeous girl from the Seven-Leven Club going quietly through his pockets. Now, pretending to be still unconscious, he could watch the expression of deep concern on Jake's face. It wasn't the same thing, but it was just as much fun. He'd never imagined Jake, or anybody, would be so disturbed in the same circumstances.

At least, everybody was going to be very, very sorry.

But that doctor, whoever he was, had said there wasn't any danger or serious damage. By tomorrow morning—

He opened his eyes wide, looked up into Jake's face, and said irritably, "I've had banks fold up in my face, but I never had one blow up on me before. What happened, and why, or does anyone know?"

"It was a bomb," Jake said. The look of anxiety

erased itself from his face. "Only a small one, though. The grating off the teller's cage hit you in the belly and knocked you into the wall. That's all."

"Oh," Malone said coldly. "Glad it wasn't anything serious." He paused. "Where's Helene? Is she all right?"

"She's in her room changing her clothes. She had her dress blown off, but she wasn't hurt." Jake located a cigar in Malone's coat pocket, lighted it, and stuck it in the little lawyer's hand. "Listen, Malone. Try to remember. You said something."

"I meant every word of it," Malone said. "Leave me alone."

"Damn it, pay attention to me. We brought you up here and undressed you—"

Malone sat up. "Who do you mean by 'we'?"

"Lie down and keep still. That Miss McGowan and I. She wasn't hurt except for a few scratches, and believe me, Malone, she's handy in a crisis. Never lost her head for a minute.

Malone closed his eyes again. "Even when she helped undress me?"

"Damn you," Jake said, "now listen. Just as I tucked the sheet under your chin you came to for a minute. Remember?"

Malone tried hard to remember. There was something very misty and vague about a pillow under his head, and Jake's ghastly white face, and a momentous discovery that had come to him right out of the blue. But that was all.

"You grabbed at my arm," Jake told him, "and you said, 'This is very important. It was the other story.' Then you were sick for a minute, and then you said again, 'Remember, it was the other story.'"

He leaned over the bed. "What were you talking about? Do you remember?"

Malone was quiet for a moment, his eyes closed. The phrase did mean something, and it was important. Only he couldn't recall what it meant.

"I don't know," he said at last.

Jake sighed. "Well, maybe it will come back to you."

There was a little pause before Malone said, "I suppose it's none of my business, but what about the explosion?"

"I told you it was a bomb," Jake said, wiping his forehead with the back of his arm. "A cute one. We found enough remains to tell it was made in a tobacco tin."

The door opened and Helene came in. She had changed back into the white sharkskin slacks, and her honey-colored hair was loose and damp.

"I washed enough concrete out of my hair to lay a small sidewalk," she complained. Her face was still unnaturally pale. "Malone, what did you mean by 'the other story'? Jake came in and told me about it."

The little lawyer groaned. "I wish I knew." He drew his brows together; the effort sent a pain through his scalp. "There must have been two stories, and one of them was wrong and the other was right. But I don't know which was which, or what either of them was about."

"Maybe another explosion would make him remember," Jake said speculatively.

Helene shuddered. "I'd rather not know. Not even for a small firecracker." She lit a cigarette on the third try.

"Speaking of explosions," Malone said, "go on, Jake. You'd gotten as far as the tobacco tin."

"It went off somewhere right by the teller's cage." Jake scowled. "Might have landed there any number of ways. It might have been dropped there by anybody who was inside the enclosure, or shoved through the cage by somebody outside, or thrown in through a window from the alley outside. No one seems to have any idea. All of a sudden it was there, and it went off."

"I remember," Malone said. The ceiling above him veered sharply to the right, and an invisible hand squeezed his stomach. He dug his fingers into the mattress, shut his eyes, and counted to ten. "The casualty list is what I'm interested in."

"The amazing thing about the explosion," Jake said, "is that the casualty list is so small. One fatality and a small list of injured. I guess everyone ducked. Ed Skindingsrude was buried under the debris, but when we dug him out all that was broken was a watch crystal. Some farmer had his leg broken. Miss McGowan lost her front bridgework, and when I left the scene they were still digging for them in the wreckage. Helene's dress was blown into the next block but she had on a hunk of imported lingerie that made a better showing before the Jackson spectators than the dress ever did, and here you are, slightly battered but practically as good as new."

Malone said very quietly after a moment, "Now tell me what happened to the rest of the people there."

"Jerry Luckstone wasn't touched." Jake crushed out his cigarette and lit another one quick. "Neither was Mr. Goudge. Phil Smith's collarbone was broken, and he was badly bruised." He drew a long breath. "The bank's stenographer had her left arm torn off and most of her jaw. And the teller—his name was Linkermann—was killed."

"You certainly tell everything the hard way," Malone murmured. He closed his eyes and tried to remember how the ferrety little man had looked in those last few seconds.

"His name was Magnus Linkermann," Jake said. Suddenly he was talking in a strange, disjointed rush of words. Malone opened his eyes again and saw that Helene's face had turned an odd shade of gray. "He wasn't just killed. When we started digging, he wasn't there at all, anywhere. He was disintegrated like something in 'Buck Rogers,' literally blown to bits."

Helene said, "Don't!" faintly.

Jake paid no attention to her. "If they try to inter him they'll have to inter all the wreckage of the bank building," he said in a cold, deliberate voice. "There was a little of him hit the wall just behind—"

"Damn you, Jake," Helene said between clenched teeth. She bolted out of the room, kicking the door shut behind her.

Jake was silent, his face white and set. He put his hands in his pocket, walked across the room, stared for a moment at the print of *The Lone Wolf,* sat down again, and said, "She'd have had nightmares about it all the rest of her life. There's nothing like being good and sick to your stomach to clean out the back places in your mind. She'll be all right now."

Malone shut his eyes and said, "Fine. How do you feel?"

"I feel fine," Jake said in an oddly strained voice.

Five minutes later Malone opened his eyes and said, "That makes the second murder in thirty-two years."

Jake blinked at him. "That's right. It was murder. I hadn't gotten around to thinking of that yet."

"Somebody made a bomb and got it into the Farmers' Bank," Malone said. "And it killed this Magnus Linkermann. That's murder in anybody's language. The amazing thing about it is that it wasn't mass murder."

Jake said, "Malone, please lie still and rest. Nobody is going to accuse you or Helene or me of the murder, I hope. Just don't think about it, and let's get out of here as fast as we can." He breathed deeply. "I'd love to get back to the corner of State and Madison for a little peace and quiet."

"Make it two," Malone murmured. "I don't know who Magnus Linkermann was and, frankly, I don't care that he's dead. I would like to know who gave me this bump on the back of my head." He paused. "Damn it, could anybody get a tobacco-tin bomb into that building without its being seen."

"Whoever planted it there," Jake said, "certainly doesn't fool. It may be an effective means of murder, but it's likewise the hard way."

Malone wasn't listening. "The murder of ex-Senator Peveley," he said under his breath, "the blowing up of the bank of which he was president, and the murder of its employee." He paused, wondered if he was going to be sick again, and decided against it. "The hell of it is, Jake, that for a moment I knew who'd murdered the Senator and consequently who must have blown up the bank. Only it was one of those flashes you get when your mind is free, and now it's lost. There's some one little thing that's the key but it's gone from me now and I can't remember. If I could get it back, I'd know who killed the Senator and planted the bomb." He paused, stared at the ceiling, and said, "The other story. No, that doesn't mean a thing to me now. But it must have meant something when I said it. That's a key, but what the hell does it unlock?"

"That's a very nice little riddle," Jake said heartily.

"What about the inquest?"

"Postponed till tomorrow."

The little lawyer was silent for a moment. "Did someone want to murder Magnus Linkermann and do it by blowing up the bank? Or did someone want to blow up the bank and this guy happened to be in the way?" He sat up in bed. "What does it have to do with the murder of Senator Peveley?"

"Lie down and shut up," Jake said.

Malone lay down. His head hurt. "The other story," he murmured. "What other story? Who's been telling us stories, anyway?"

There was a sudden, violent knocking at the door. Before Jake could reach the knob, it had been flung open, and Florence Peveley strode into the room, an anxious-eyed Henry close behind her.

"Don't bother him," Jake said. "He's a very sick man."

She didn't hear him. Henry Peveley closed the door quietly and apologetically.

"I thought you were a friend of mine," she said to the little lawyer. "A hell of a friend you turned out to be, letting somebody blow up my bank."

Malone blinked. "I didn't know it was your bank," he said.

"Well it is. It belonged to Pa, and he must have left it to me." She planted her fists on her hips and stood glaring around the room.

It was obvious that she hadn't taken time to dress before coming over to the General Andrew Jackson House. She was clad, simply, in a pair of khaki-colored shorts, a striped jersey, and an old pair of tennis shoes. There was a grass stain on her right knee.

"What are you going to do about it," she demanded.

Malone closed his eyes. "I'm going to sleep."

"Please, Miss Peveley," Jake began.

She wheeled on him. "Blast you, you know me well enough to call me Florence. Is he going to find out who blew up my bank, or isn't he?"

"It's all the fault of the administration," Henry Peveley said gloomily. "Blowing up banks. They'll be blowing up the Capitol next."

"Don't be absurd," the red-haired girl snapped. "This was something personal."

Malone looked up at her wearily. "You think perhaps someone took a dislike to you?"

"I think someone took a dislike to Pa," she said.

"If you're sore at a guy, the time to blow up a bank is before he's murdered," Malone said. "Why wait until his feelings won't be hurt?"

"But somebody was sore at Pa," she insisted.

"Not necessarily," the little lawyer murmured. "You don't have to have any feeling about a man, like or dislike, to murder him." He closed his eyes. "There are three reasons for murder," he said in a very low voice, "love, money, and fear, and the greatest of these is fear."

The red-haired girl stared at him for a minute. He

didn't move. At last she looked up at Jake. "He isn't dead, or anything, is he?"

"I wouldn't be surprised," came a sleepy whisper from the bed. Then there was a low snore.

Henry Peveley tiptoed to the door. "Come, Florence."

She followed him, momentarily awed. Jake opened the door for her. Henry lingered behind for a moment, drawing Jake out of earshot of the hall, and took a flat, unlabeled bottle from his pocket.

"I thought I'd bring this up to Mr. Malone. It's hard to find a reliable bootlegger in this town if you're a stranger." He slipped out the door and closed it behind him.

Jake stared at the bottle, carried it across the room, and set it down on the bedside table. Malone opened one eye.

"Have they gone?"

"They've gone," Jake said. "Is there anything I can get for you before I go completely nuts?"

"Nothing," Malone breathed, closing the eye again. "Just go away and try to keep out of trouble. Don't get mixed up in anything else."

"No," Jake said slowly. "I think I've got enough to hold me for awhile. A Senator gets shot from under me, a bank explodes in my face, and now I'm handed a bottle of bootleg whisky."

Malone chuckled. "That Henry Peveley. He's living in the past."

Jake shrugged, "Well, anyway, he's enjoying himself."

Chapter Fourteen

FLORENCE PEVELEY and her uncle were waiting for him in the hall.

"He's all right, isn't he?" Florence said in a forceful whisper. "Say, how's your wife? She was blown up too, wasn't she? Is there anything I can do for her? Is there anything I can do for either of you? She's a wonderful person and I like her. Wish I knew where she'd gotten that blue car, I'd like to have one like it. Say, I hope I didn't do Mr. Malone any harm. I know he needed to go to sleep, but I was so all-fired mad." She paused and drew a breath. "It was bad enough, somebody shooting Pa."

One of the nice things about a conversation with Florence Peveley, Jake reflected, was that you didn't have to think of any answers.

"Here comes the sheriff," Henry Peveley said.

Sheriff Kling was coming up the last few stairs, breathing hard. His thick neck was red.

"You're the guy I want to see," he said to Jake.

Jake took out a cigarette. "I suppose I should feel flattered," he said pleasantly. He noticed the sheriff had brought a deputy along, the bigger one.

Sheriff Kling's eyes narrowed. "That's enough, wise guy. We're going down to the courthouse."

Jake thought it over. The last swing he'd taken at a Jackson County officer's jaw had cost him two dollars and costs and six hours in the county jail. He wouldn't get off as easily this time. Twenty-five bucks, Phil Smith had warned him. And maybe they charged more for smacking a sheriff than for a deputy. Anyway there was no point in further antagonizing Sheriff Kling.

"O. K.," Jake said with surprising amiability. "Wait a minute till I tell my wife."

Sheriff Kling turned to the deputy. "Go tell her where he's going."

The hell with the twenty-five-buck fine, Jake decided fast. He grabbed the deputy by the arm. "Now wait a minute."

"At-a-boy, pal," came Florence Peveley's voice right behind him.

Jake waved an indignant finger under Sheriff Kling's nose. "I've had about enough trouble from you. Are you arresting me?" As the sheriff's eyes popped, he went on, "If you are, where the hell's your warrant? All right. You're not arresting me. So you can go climb up a purple rope."

"Listen here," the deputy began.

"Shut your fat mouth," Jake said. "I'm mad now. If you want to arrest me, go ahead and get a warrant, and I'll tell my lawyer to start drawing up a suit for false arrest. If you don't want to arrest me, then get the hell out and quit bothering me. If you just want a cozy little chat with me, write my secretary for an appointment." He turned away.

Sheriff Kling caught his breath on the third try. "Where's your secretary?"

"She's on a vacation in Alaska," Jake hurled back over his shoulder.

"And another thing," Florence Peveley said

quickly. "A swell sheriff you turn out to be, letting some lug come in and blow up my bank. You're supposed to give protection to the taxpayers."

"That's right," Henry Peveley got in. "Have you any idea how much taxes the Peveley estate pays?"

"Why," Florence Peveley finished, "you big, stupid drunken ape—I ought to have the law on you!"

Sheriff Kling decided he was hopelessly outclassed and outnumbered. He retreated, followed by his deputy. On the third step he paused.

"You're not through with me yet," he bellowed. "You'll hear from me."

" Delighted," Jake said. "I'm nuts about fan mail."

The sheriff had just passed the second landing when a door down the corridor opened and Helene stepped out. She was a trifle pale around the lips.

"Is this a private riot, or can I buy a ticket to it?"

"It's all right," Florence Peveley said. "It was just your old man and I, scaring the stuffing out of the sheriff."

"The big dope," Jake muttered under his breath.

"I always miss everything," Helene complained. "Next time you're going to lose your temper, I wish you'd call me first."

Little Henry Peveley was mopping a damp brow. "That was a close call."

They looked at him anxiously. His round face was almost white.

"Suppose," he said tremulously. "Suppose I'd had trouble with the sheriff. And me with a bottle of"— he whispered it—"whisky in my pocket!"

No more than ten minutes after Florence Peveley and her uncle had gone, word came that Jake was wanted downstairs at the telephone.

It was Jerry Luckstone. "Mr. Justus," he said in a worried voice, "I'm sorry you had any misunderstanding, Marv is a little impulsive."

"That's all right," Jake said. "I'm impulsive myself."

"The fact is," the district attorney went on, "I'd appreciate it very much if you'd come down to my office. I think we ought to talk over this business while the details are still fresh in everybody's mind. Would you?"

"I'd be delighted," Jake told him. "Your fat-necked friend should have put it that way in the first place. I'll be there in five minutes."

The crowd on Main Street, considerably increased since morning, was concentrated on two points, the General Andrew Jackson House, and the wreckage of the Farmers' Bank a block down the street. The largest part of the crowd was in front of the bank building, now roped off from the sidewalk, a heap of wood and rubble piled up by its door.

Jerry Luckstone's office was crowded. Ed Skindingsrude was there, and the bald-headed Mr. Goudge, his grim face pale, and Ellen McGowan. Jake was glad to see she had her bridgework back. Even Phil Smith was there, very white and shaken, a huge bandage showing on his neck, and his arm in a sling.

"I guess we're all here," Jerry Luckstone said.

Sheriff Marvin Kling glared indignantly at Jake. "Now," he said, "tell me about this explosion."

Jake sat down on the corner of the flat-topped desk and lit a cigarette. "I don't know what I can add to what you must already know. These people were there too."

"God damn it," the sheriff said, "none of them saw the same thing."

Jerry Luckstone turned around and looked at him, his thin, handsome face wrinkled with anxiety. "Well, after all, nobody—none of us were looking in the same direction or paying attention to what was going on. Nobody there knew there was going to be an explosion."

"Somebody did," Sheriff Kling said doggedly.

"Oh, no," Miss McGowan said suddenly. "That isn't necessarily true. The bomb could have been planted there, or it could have been dropped in from outside. You said that yourself."

"I'm asking him," the sheriff said, indicating Jake.

Jake frowned. "I wasn't paying much attention to what was going on. All I know is that suddenly I heard somebody scream and then everything seemed to go up at once. I shoved Mrs. Justus toward the door and the next thing I knew I was in the middle of a lot of dust and broken glass. Then I sort of caught my breath and began to help digging people out."

"That ain't what I mean," the sheriff said crossly. "I mean, what happened before the explosion?"

"I don't know," Jake said wearily, "except, obviously, that somebody planted a bomb somewhere."

"Where were you standing? Where was everybody else standing?"

"I was somewhere near the door," Jake said. "Mrs. Justus was right behind me, looking out the window. I think Malone was up by the teller's window, but I haven't the faintest idea where anybody else was. I wasn't paying attention."

The sheriff sighed. "Damn it, nobody seems to know what went on. Ed, here, was on his way to the door but he don't remember where anybody else was."

"I was right by Mr. Malone," Jerry Luckstone said. "I'd gone to the bank to identify him so he could cash his check." He paused and added, "and Magnus was right behind the teller's window."

"Hell, I know that already," Sheriff Kling said.

Ed Skindingsrude said, "It seems to me, Marv, that what we need to know is where the different people were inside the enclosure, not out of it. It would've been mighty hard to reach inside and lay down a bomb without somebody seeing you."

"Ed's right," Miss McGowan said. "And I can remember that pretty well. Margaret was sitting at the adding machine. I had just brought in that package of records and put them down." She turned to the county treasurer. "Where'd you go after that?"

"I'd just started into the president's office," Mr. Goudge said. "There was one book that wasn't with those records, and I remembered Gerald had it in his office the day he was killed, so I figured that was where it was."

"That's right," Miss McGowan said. "I remember. And I was over by the safe, talking to Phil." She frowned. "I still think the bomb must have come in through the window."

"Did anybody see it thrown in?" the sheriff asked coldly.

Nobody answered. After a moment Jake said, "For that matter, did anybody see the bomb at all?"

"Nobody saw anything," Sheriff Kling complained. "All anybody knows is that it blew up all of a sudden. 'Cept that it must have been right around where Magnus was standing."

"It certainly pulverized that package of school-fund records," Mr. Goudge said bitterly.

Jerry Luckstone looked up suddenly. "Aren't there any duplicates of those records?"

"Not of that set, there aren't. Probably that one book Gerald had is all right, but it's no use without the others."

"Isn't that just dandy?" the district attorney said gloomily.

"And if you're through with all this," Miss Mc-Gowan declared, "Mr. Goudge and I want to get back to the bank and find out what other records are ruined."

The sheriff nodded. "Harry, you go with 'em." he said to the deputy.

Ed Skindingsrude rose to his feet. "Marv, it seems to me you ain't gettin' very far. Maybe it's none of my business, but that's how it seems to me."

"I'm doing all I can," the sheriff said in an ugly voice. His face had deepened in color.

"Maybe so. Still, I was figuring if I ought to call a special meeting of the county board and sort of discuss the whole business. Maybe there's some better way of handling it than for you and Jerry just to try and worry it out."

"County board can meet until hell freezes over, for all I care," Sheriff Kling muttered, "but I'm the sheriff here, and what I say goes."

The little sandy-haired farmer shrugged his shoulders. "Do the best you can, Marv. Election's coming up in three months now." He put on his hat, said, "Won't call a board meeting for a few days anyway. Good luck, Marv," and left.

The sheriff waited until the sound of footsteps had died away before he said, "Damned old fool."

"Just the same," Jerry Luckstone said miserably, "election *is* coming up in three months." He sat down behind his desk. "Marv, one of those people who was on the second floor of the courthouse yesterday shot Senator Peveley and blew up the bank today."

"I can't arrest 'em all," Sheriff Kling said. "And I couldn't arrest anybody like Phil Smith or Ed Skindingsrude, or Miss McGowan."

"That's a very neighborly spirit and I admire it," Jake said, "but you may have to, if one of them murdered Senator Peveley."

The Sheriff looked sourly at Jake. "I still can't figure just where you fit into this, but by God I'm not going to rest till I find out!"

Before Jake could think of an appropriate answer, a deputy announced that the bomb expert from Milwaukee had arrived, and the sheriff left. Jerry Luckstone sat frowning at the little designs he was making on the desk blotter.

"It's a bad spot to be on," Jake said sympathetically.

"Who was in the bank," the young district attorney began slowly, "who was also on the second floor of the courthouse when the Senator was shot?" He sat thinking for a minute. "Miss McGowan, Phil Smith, Ed Skindingsrude, and myself."

"The bomb might have been planted in the bank by some other person," Jake pointed out. "Or dropped in through the window, though that doesn't seem very feasible. Or the bombing of the bank may not have had anything to do with the Senator's murder."

"Or," Jerry Luckstone said bitterly, "we've all gone insane and none of this really happened. Come on, I'll walk back to the hotel with you." He rose and started for the stairs.

"What's the idea of the big knife the sheriff has out for me?" Jake asked suddenly.

Jerry Luckstone said, "He'd like nothing better than to have you turn out to be the guilty party. Then he wouldn't have the possible political embarrassment of having to arrest somebody like Phil Smith, or Ed Skindingsrude."

"I'm sorry I can't oblige him," Jake said dryly.

"He knows he can't do anything about you," the young man went on, "so he was taking out his cussedness by being as nasty as he could this morning." He pushed open the big door of the courthouse and sniffed the air. "Feels like rain."

"I hope he doesn't do it again," Jake said, "or I'm very likely to forget myself and take out some of my own cussedness on him."

Their progress up Main Street was almost a parade. The crowd still lingered on the sidewalks, and everyone turned to stare after the two men as they walked by.

"I bet I could rent advertising space on my back for a thousand bucks right now," Jake said.

"It's the most excitement Jackson, Wisconsin, has had in a long time," Jerry Luckstone reminded him almost apologetically. "I wish I could understand about Cora Belle. Do you mind my talking to you? It helps me think."

"Go ahead," Jake told him, "what about Cora Belle?"

"Her turning up this morning and claiming she

was talking with me when the shot was fired, when she knew damn well she wasn't, and she knew I knew it. She knows something about that murder. I don't think she did it herself, but I do think she knows something."

"The simple thing would be to ask her," Jake said.

"She'd lie about it," the district attorney said gloomily. "If I could only take her out and get her full of gin, now, she'd tell me everything she knows. She's talkative as all hell when she's drinking."

"Well," Jake said as helpfully as he could, "that one sounds great. Business and pleasure, two birds with one stone, means to an end, and so forth."

"I don't dare, not right now. Everybody knows I'm engaged to Florence, and here her father has just been murdered. If anybody saw me out roadhousing with Cora Belle, it would be just too bad. Especially with the election coming on."

Jake sighed. "You and your damned election." He felt a sudden pang of sympathy for the young man, who looked as completely miserable as it was possible for a man to look.

Helene was waiting on the porch of the General Andrew Jackson House. "Thank God," she called. "I thought you were probably stuck away in jail for the duration." Her face was serene, but very pale.

"Just a few questions," Jake called back. Suddenly all his troubles seemed very small. True, he was detained in the town of Jackson, Wisconsin, but that was unimportant compared to the fix the district attorney was in. To him it wasn't just a matter of a few days inconvenience, it was possibly a whole future. He looked sympathetically at Jerry Luckstone.

"Listen," he said on a sudden impulse, "that little

problem we were just talking about. How about leaving it to me? I have a wonderful way with women."

Jerry Luckstone looked quickly at Helene and back at Jake again.

"She won't mind," Jake said.

Helene said, "Just what are you two whispering about."

"I'll tell you later," Jake told her. "How about it? Do you think she'd go out with me?"

"Oh, sure," Jerry Luckstone said.

"O. K. then," Jake declared. "I'll do it tonight."

Almost immediately a feeling of great gloom settled on his mind. As well as he knew anything, he knew he was going to regret it.

Chapter Fifteen

"THE VICTIM," Jake read aloud, "was a bachelor, with no near relatives. He had been an employee of the Farmers' Baank for twenty-nine years, and for the past eighteen years had been first tenor in the choir of the Evangelical Lutheran Church of Jackson, Wisconsin."

He tossed the newspaper aside. "Hardly a lively career."

Helene sighed. "He doesn't sound like a likely candidate for murder."

"You never can tell," Jake said. "Maybe somebody else wanted to be first tenor."

The steamy warmth of the day had persisted till early evening. The faint haze had lingered, turning a sinister yellow shortly before sunset, then suddenly lifted, leaving the sun to go down behind Heide's Hill like a copper penny dropped into a slot machine.

Jake stepped out onto the tiny balcony outside their room. In the west a pale orange light faded upward into ocherous green. The green ended abruptly at the edge of great black clouds that had suddenly materialized out of nowhere and were slowly settling down toward the western horizon. All at once a quick breeze ruffled the elms on West Third Street, and a mourning dove called sorrowfully from somewhere just behind the Methodist Church.

"It's going to rain like hell and damnation," Jake said, stepping back into their room.

Helene shivered. "As long as the wind doesn't blow. One good healthy puff and the General Andrew Jackson House will be halfway into the next county."

"Well, you wanted to get out of Jackson, Wisconsin," Jake reminded her. He heard a door open and close, said, "There's the doc, I want to find out how Malone is," and went out into the hall, Helene at his heels.

Dr. Spain, a pleasant-faced, bald-headed man in a white suit, said, "Your friend's all right. Just so he stays quiet and in bed until tomorrow. I gave him something to make him sleep for a few hours."

"How does he feel?" Helene asked anxiously.

"He feels like hell," Dr. Spain told her. "But he'll feel better. He ordered a case of beer to be kept on ice in the hotel icebox, and arranged for the clerk to send him up a bottle every fifteen minutes after he wakes up."

"He's normal," Jake said.

Dr. Spain set down his bag and began feeling through his pockets. "Wonderful how a man could get a crack on the head like that and still be able to add. Wish old Doc Goudge wasn't out in the asylum. He used to have a theory about blows on the head making you remember a lot of stuff you'd forgotten except that when you recovered you forgot it again." He located a leather cigarette case in his right-hand coat pocket, and began searching himself for a match. Jake, fascinated, didn't offer him one.

"How about your other patients?" he asked.

"Oh, I guess they're all right. Nasty injuries these bombs leave. Never saw any before myself. Not as bad, though, as the time Emerson Lowell Smith fell into the threshing machine." He found the match and scratched it on his pants.

"Not really Emerson Lowell?" Jake said.

The doctor nodded, lighting his cigarette. "Emerson Lowell Whittier Smith. He was a half-wit. Phil Smith was his uncle. His mother was a Proctor, Hattie Goudge. Always thought she was a little cracked, myself. Lived until she was eighty-two and then went out in the barn and hanged herself." He looked around for a place to throw the match, finally put it in his breast pocket. "She was Doc Goudge's aunt."

"Oh," Helene said. "Today must have seemed pretty dull to you after the life you've lived."

"Not bad at all," Doc Spain told her. "You should have been here the time about five years ago when I had a farmer's wife out on Route Four having triplets, and a woman over in Willow Springs having twins." He puffed at the cigarette and said, "I got three tickets for speeding. You know, I've got a theory about these murders."

"That'll be worth hearing," Jake said.

"I got to looking up statistics in the almanac when I was home for dinner," Doc Spain said, "and I found the per capita homicide rate for the whole country. Well do you know, figuring it out according to the population of Jackson County, we should have four murders every thirty-two years. That leaves us two more coming."

"Interesting," Helene said. "You won't mind if we don't stay to see the fun."

Doc Spain took the cigarette out of his mouth, looked at her, and said, "You know, I bet you've got a vitamin deficiency. Can tell by the color of your skin. Or maybe you just use the wrong shade of face powder. But I'm right about those statistics. Added 'em up twice. So, you can look for two more murders." He picked up his kit.

Jake said, "Maybe you and Buttonholes ought to get together. He calls his premonitions."

"Well, I don't know," Doc Spain said gravely. "I've got a theory about Buttonholes' premonitions. Sort of a combination of extrasensory perception, and electrodynamics. Never forget a telepathic dream I had once back in '22. Remind me to tell you about it sometime." He pulled his Panama hat a little more over one eye, said to Helene, "Better check up on that vitamin deficiency, and darted down the stairs.

Helene counted ten and then wailed, "But, Jake, some people just don't want to look healthy."

"I know," Jake said. "Two vitamin pills, or a change of face powder, and you'd lose all your charm. Just remember I'm the man who even loves you with your face washed." He paused. "Emerson Lowell Whittier Smith. I wonder what they named his uncle. Phil Smith, I mean."

"Philip Smith," Helen said scornfully.

Jake said, "You have no imagination." He took her arm and dragged her down the stairs to the clerk's desk. "Have you a list of the county officers, by any chance?"

The clerk dragged a battered pamphlet, titled *County Directory, 1940,* from somewhere under his desk.

"Thanks," Jake said. He grabbed it and began thumbing through the pages. "Abbott" a few pages slipped through his fingers, "Jones, Jules, Knaimer, Peterkin, Peters, Peterson." He paused, "P-f-e-elwudgin-k-y—the hell with it. Rasmussen, Saintsmith, Satterlee, Saunders, Smith."

"Darling, is this a new game," Helene said wearily, "or have you gone nuts?"

"Curiosity can be a hobby too," he told her. "When the uncle of a guy named Emerson Lowell Whittier is named Phil Smith—" He ran a thumbnail down the directory. "Here. County clerk. Smith." He paused again. "Philomen Ma. Smith."

Helene said, "I don't believe it," and snatched the book from his hands. Thirty seconds later she handed it back and said, "All right. His name is Philomen. Philomen Smith, Ma. The printers made an error."

"No," Jake said, "It's Philomen Ma. Smith. Not Philomen M. A. Smith, but—"

Helene leaned over the desk and turned the full and dazzling candle power of her smile on the weary clerk. "Could you tell us Mr. Smith's middle initial, please?"

The clerk blinked, smiled back, and said, "Which Smith, Stanley, or Livingston?"

Helene raised her eyebrows. "Twins, I presume?"

The clerk looked confused. "How did you guess?"

"It's a small world," Helene said cryptically.

The clerk looked even more confused. "They're Ed Smith's boys. Stanley's in the legislature. **Phil** Smith's their uncle."

"He's the one she means," Jake said. "Phil Smith."

"His middle initial? It's Ma," the Clerk said. "M-a." No, he didn't know what it stood for. Massachusetts, maybe. There was a Massachusetts Wills lived up near Willow Springs.

"Six gets you ten it stands for Madhouse," Helene

muttered as they walked back up the stairs. "And I don't know about you, but I've had all I can stand."

"Sissy," Jake said, "I don't leave Jackson County until I find out Philomen Smith's full name."

"Jake, what were you talking about with Jerry Luckstone? What are you planning to do tonight?"

"Nothing much. A little piece of research I'm doing for him. I can't tell you about it till it's over."

Later he tried to decide what kept him from telling her. It wasn't that he didn't want to, because he did. And there was no earthly reason why he should not. It was just one of those premonitions; they were contagious.

"If it's something dangerous, I'm going along," she said grimly, and added, "it isn't fair for you to have all the fun."

"It isn't going to be dangerous," Jake said, "and it isn't going to be fun, and I can't take you along anyway."

She sighed. "Father always said a wife shouldn't ask questions. Sometime they might get answered. And what I don't know won't hurt you."

"You get dressed for dinner," Jake said, changing the subject fast, "while I get some more cigarettes."

Across the street, in Gollett's drugstore, he bought cigarettes, asked to use the telephone, called Cora Belle, and introduced himself.

"I have a long evening on my hands, and Jerry Luckstone said you might be kind enough to show me some of the county's night life."

Cora Belle declared she would be delighted. "Will you bring your lovely blonde wife with you?"

"She has a bad headache," Jake said glibly.

There was just a shade too long pause before Cora Belle said, "Oh." Then, "Well, drive by around eight or nine, and we'll take in a few roadhouses."

Jake walked back to the hotel room reminding himself that he could always call and break the date, or even just not show up at all. The chances were Cora Belle didn't know anything of importance. If she did, she wouldn't confide it to him, and in any case, it wasn't any of his business. Still, he'd promised Jerry Luckstone, who was in a tough spot.

He found Helene doing a very special job on her right eyebrow before the greenish mirror. Her organdy dress billowed around her like a honey-colored cloud.

"Helene," Jake said, "I love you. You are the most beautiful woman in the world. I never realised how much I love you until right this minute."

She finished with the eyebrow and wheeled around to look at him. "Just what are you up to? Will you promise me it isn't dangerous?"

"Of course it isn't dangerous," he told her, "and it has nothing to do with the subject. I just happened to look at you and think about how much I love you. About how much nicer you are than any other woman in the world, nicer and smarter and more beautiful and much more fun." He had never felt quite as miserable in his life.

A few minutes with Malone after dinner didn't help his frame of mind. He found the little lawyer just wakening from a drugged sleep and preparing to sink into another one. He propped himself up in bed on one elbow and stared sourly at his visitor.

"Don't ask me how I feel, because I feel terrible.

And I'm going to stay right here and stay asleep until we can get out of this town." He lay back on the pillow and looked thoughtfully at the ceiling.

"Jake," he said at last, "there's something deadly and poisonous going on here in Jackson. Far more deadly and far more poisonous than any of us ever even dreamed about. And it isn't finished yet."

"You've been talking to Buttonholes," Jake said crossly. "Shut your eyes and keep still."

Malone ignored him. "It's more than murder. No one goes so far as to blow up a bank full of people without plenty of cause." His voice was thick with sleep. "It's something big and something terrible, and here we are right in the middle of it."

Jake was silent. Suddenly he'd found himself wondering if Cora Belle Fromm had murdered the ex-Senator, and planted a tobacco-tin bomb in the Farmers' Bank, and if she suspected that his date with her tonight was an attempt to pump information. It was perfectly possible. He preferred not to believe it.

"Now pay attention." Malone's voice was very drowsy now. "Keep out of it. Stay close to the ground and keep your head down, and don't stick your neck out."

"Why should I do imitations of a worm?" Jake said. "You won't have to get me out of jail when you wake up in the morning, if that's what you're worrying about."

"Jail," the little lawyer yawned, "would be the easiest place to get out of." His eyes closed, he was asleep.

He was also a brilliant prophet.

Chapter Sixteen

BY TEN O'CLOCK Helene had taken down her hair, brushed it, and put it up again twice, tried to read three different newspapers, and given herself a complete manicure. That was when she put her wrist watch under the pillow and resolved not to look at it again.

Only people with no mental resources, she told herself sternly, were bored and unhappy at spending a lonely evening in a dreary hotel room, with nothing to do.

She gave herself a luxurious facial, tried once more to read the newspapers and gave it up, rinsed out a pair of stockings and hung them to dry on a clothes hanger, and emptied and dusted out all the ash trays. By now it must be well after midnight, and Jake should be coming along any minute. She looked once more at the watch. It was ten-fifteen.

Having exhausted her reportory of the small chores women use to kill time when men keep them waiting, there was nothing to do but begin all over. She took down her hair again for another brushing, tried out several new hair-dos, didn't like any of them, and put it back the way it had been in the first place.

At ten-twenty-five she decided she would rather talk to anybody, even the desk clerk, than to the walls of the room, and strolled down to the bar for a glass of beer. It was crowded, with most of the out-of-town visitors clustered around Buttonholes, buying him drinks while they listened to his description of his premonitions. An impressionable young woman from a Milwaukee paper was writing them down word for word.

There were a few faces Helene recognized. Tom Burrows, talking excitedly with a group of newspapermen. Charlie Hausen, the coroner, playing pinochle at a corner table with the local policeman. Jerry Luckstone sitting alone at the bar, deep in gloom.

Helene sighed. She wished she knew where Jake was and when he would be back. Mostly, she wished that he was here. She was not only bored, she was beginning to be angry.

She climbed up on a bar stool next to Jerry Luckstone. "If Jake doesn't get here pretty soon," she said, "there's going to be murder done."

The first part of her sentence was lost in the hum of conversation. At the word "murder," everyone stopped talking and looked at her.

Jerry Luckstone giggled nervously. He was a little drunk. "What would you do if he were out with another girl?"

"Do?" Helene repeated cheerfully. "I'd wring her neck." She turned to the bartender. "A beer. I'd wring her neck, cut her ears off, and fry them like eggplant, pull her hair out one hair at a time, and finally turn her remains completely inside out."

The girl from the Milwaukee paper was highly amused. "Then what would you do to him?"

"Nothing," Helene called back. "What good would

it do me to make a widow out of myself?" She lit a cigarette. "The only reason I'd wring her neck would be to make sure he never went out with her again."

"A very logical system," Jerry Luckstone said, nodding wisely.

"It works every time," Helene told him.

The gray-haired man from the *Journal* said, "I'll never forget a story out in San Francisco about fifteen years ago—" and in another moment everyone was talking again.

"How's Malone?" the young district attorney asked.

"Asleep," Helene said, staring mournfully into her glass of beer. She wondered if Jerry Luckstone had seduced Arlene Goudge, if he had planned to marry Florence Peveley for her father's money and political position, and if she had blown up the Farmers' Bank. She hoped not.

Five minutes later she left half her beer on the bar and walked out the side door onto Third Street. There was a faint breeze coming up from the river, not much, but it freshened the air. She crossed Main Street and began walking up Third.

From the morning's driving around town, she had learned who lived in most of the houses on what Jackson, Wisconsin, called "The hill." Senator Peveley's had stood on its summit, at the end of Third Street. She noticed that there were lights in all its windows.

Half a block beyond Main, Third Street was dark and quiet and mysterious. Only patches of sky and occasional stars showed through the elm trees overhead, the sidewalk became a narrow pale-gray ribbon running between shadowy squares of lawn. The traffic on Main Street couldn't be heard this far, and in the silence the sound of the crickets was almost deafening.

Most of the little houses that stood four or five to a block, set far back from the sidewalk, had windows lighted. Helene slowed her steps to look in here and there, trying to catch glimpses of their interiors, and the people who lived within. It all seemed so peaceful. Yet here in this house might be a man who hated his wife, next door one who loved his wife and hated her family, here one who was planning to rob his employer, there another who spent his life waiting for a wealthy relative to die, and so on, without end.

Malone was right. The potentiality for murder was like a germ that everybody, including all healthy persons, harbored, but that never developed unless certain conditions arose. It could happen in any one of these little houses.

That was Phil Smith's house on the corner. Helene crossed the street and peeked at it curiously. What kind of house did the man named Philomen Ma. Smith live in? There was a light on upstairs in the front of the house; he himself must be in bed now, nursing his broken collarbone. Downstairs she could see into a long, narrow room lined with bookshelves, only half lighted with the glow that came in through an open door. On the other side of the hall was a brightly lighted room and through its principal window Helene could see four plump, middle-aged women, sitting around a table playing cards. They looked well fed and well cared for and contented, pleased with themselves and their houses and their printed silk dresses. One of them must be Philomen Ma. Smith's wife.

It evidently took more than a murder in town to break up a bridge club, Helene reflected. She remembered what Tom Burrows had said about Jackson County society. The men all went down to the Odd Fellows hall and played pinochle, or went out fishing, and the women met at each other's houses and played bridge. After the initial business of courtship was out of the way, they didn't bother with each other's public company.

She wondered how Philomen Ma. Smith felt about his wife's bridge club meeting on schedule, on the night after he'd almost been blown to bits. Probably it didn't surprise him. Turning back for one last glance, as she went up Third Street, she caught a glimpse of the front upstairs bedroom, one post of a four-poster bed, another bookcase, and a reading lamp. Suddenly she remembered what Tom Burrows had said. "The gentlest man alive . . . everyone in town loves him." Probably everyone in town borrowed his books, too.

At the corner of McClellan Street was a great wooden house, all dark now, and beyond it a smaller, rather shabby one with a screened porch. A little car suddenly came around the corner and parked quietly in the shade of an elm. As Helene walked by it a young male voice was saying, "You don't have to go in yet, do you?"

In the next instant a window opened on the second floor of the shabby house, and a stern female voice called, "Is that you, Geraldine?"

Helene called back, "No it isn't, it's me," in her most lilting accents. The window closed hurriedly and the stern voice was heard no more. Helene strolled on up the street, with a feeling that her good deed for the day was accounted for. The little car started up and drove a block down the street, to park beyond the range of the window.

That would be Henry Peveley's house, on the corner of Third and Maple. It seemed even smaller and more unassuming now in the dark than when it had been pointed out to her by day. Still, it had a far more comfortable air to it than the Senator's mansion, up on the hill, an effect created largely by the fact that it was so pleasantly neglected and run-down. Helene remembered suddenly that Henry Peveley was a widower, and childless. That was fortunate for him. A wife or children might have tried to argue him out of his delightful conviction that it was the year 1929 and would go on being the year 1929. A conviction like that gave a person something to live for.

In one of the windows of Henry Peveley's house hung a poster of a once-famous committee which had demanded the repeal of the Eighteenth Amendment.

Perhaps Jake was back at the hotel now. Surely he must have arrived by this time. Helene paused for a moment, then doggedly resolved to go on to the end of the street. The longer she was away, the better the chances were of his being there when she returned.

Third Street ended at the top of the hill, and for a few minutes Helene stood regarding the late Senator's mansion. She couldn't imagine any ghost wanting to come back to it. Through its windows she could see Florence Peveley moving from one room to another, her flaming red hair bright in the lamplight, apparently doing nothing, just aimlessly moving around the house.

A car parked just around the corner, and Helene drew back into the shadows. A man emerged from the car, crossed the street, and stopped in front of the Peveley mansion. As he passed near a street light, Helene recognized Jerry Luckstone.

He seemed to be deciding whether or not to go up on the porch and ring the bell. He walked halfway up to the steps a few times, pausing each time to look up at the house, and then returned to the curb. At last Helene began moving quietly down High Street, keeping in the shadows. She was halfway down the block when she saw Jerry Luckstone's car go by, and knew he had made up his mind.

The Goudge house was, she knew, just below the corner of High and Second. It was a little too much for a curious person to resist. She walked on slowly to the corner and paused there a moment. Jerry Luckstone's car was parked across the street from the house; as she came to the corner he sounded a peculiar series of long and short notes on its horn. She waited there in the shadows, reluctant to go on past the car in the glare of its headlight, until at last a slim young figure came around the corner of the house, darted across the street and into the car. In the next moment the car was down Second Street and out of sight.

Well, there was the makings of a murder, Helene reflected. The Senator's daughter, and the young district attorney keeping surreptitious dates with another girl. It was a situation that might have had something to do with the sudden death of ex-Senator Peveley. But there wasn't much connection with the blowing up of the Farmers' Bank.

The Goudge house was large and neat and freshly painted, set in a large square of perfectly clipped lawn and restrained beds of petunias. Anyone could tell at a glance it was a house where house-cleaning was done twice yearly, beginning the first day of March and the first Tuesday in September, where the lawn was raked and mowed every Saturday, and the washing was on the line by every Monday noon. It was likewise the house of a man who had done well in all his business transactions and was proud of it.

The blinds were all open, as though to proclaim to the world that the Goudge family had nothing to hide, and through the big front window Helene could see the thin, bald Mr. Goudge rocking by the fumed-oak library table, reading aloud to a pale, plump woman with a lined, unhappy face who sat mending socks on the table's other side. Suddenly Helene remembered, for no particular reason, what Tom Burrows had confided to her about Mr. Goudge, that his particular pride was in the fact that his tomato plants were invariably the first in Jackson to produce tomatoes. Suddenly she felt a pang of pity for the small people who were forced to attend the schools of which he was superintendent. Also she hoped Arlene Goudge had had the foresight to stuff pillows in her bed before she slipped out the back door to meet Jerry Luckstone.

Surely Jake was back at the hotel now! She must have been away for hours.

Helene went on down Second Street, hurrying a little. There was a strange odor of grass and leaves and freshly watered garden flowers that came from all around her, once or twice a toad startled her as it hopped across the sidewalk, and the music of the crickets went on and on, through endless crescendos and diminuendos.

Suddenly she paused. That was Ellen McGowan's house across the street. The blinds were up and the lights were on, and Helen could not resist one peek at its interior.

It was a small house, probably a very old one, but kept in flawless repair. There was a beautiful old mahogany highboy Helene could see through the window, and a pair of well-polished walnut oval picture frames. She crossed the street and walked by slowly.

More oval frames, a precious little cherry table, and a willow ware chocolate set. Wallpaper carefully chosen, and curtains and hangings to correspond. Helene could close her eyes and hear the voices of gushing feminine visitors, praising "your beautiful, beautiful things!"

Helene walked on a few more steps, a burnished copper teapot came into view. Then suddenly she saw Miss McGowan herself, and stood stock-still there on the walk, unashamedly staring into the window.

The tall, gray-haired woman was standing, leaning on a table, her face dead white. There was a visitor in the room—who he was, Helene could not see— but the face of the middle-aged spinster was turned in his direction and, at the same time, toward the window.

Helene felt suddenly frozen to the spot. Whoever that visitor was, whatever the subject of his visit, she had never seen such horror on a human face as on Miss McGowan's. And as she watched, the older woman spoke a few words, quickly and jerkily, waited a moment, then fell to her knees, her thin hands covering her bony face, abject and pleading.

It might have been a moment, or it might have been hours. Helene knew nothing of what was being said within that pleasantly decorated room. Yet suddenly she turned and, with a kind of desperate terror, ran, frantically, stumblingly, toward Main Street.

Chapter Seventeen

HELENE caught herself halfway down the block and paused, leaning against a tree, breathing hard. The chirping of the crickets had become a perfect din in her ears.

She shut her eyes, counted to ten, and opened them again.

"Well, what scared you?" she demanded of herself. "A mouse?"

She looked back up the street to where she could still see the lights of Ellen McGowan's house through the foliage. Someone in that house was frightening Ellen McGowan, frightening her horribly. It might be the murderer.

Helene began walking very slowly back up the street, catching her breath with every step.

It wasn't that she was scared, she told herself firmly. Jake, now, wouldn't be scared at a time like this. It was just that she was being cautious.

Of course, a man desperate enough to blow up a bank full of people wouldn't stop at much.

Still, she had to know who he was.

She passed the last house before Ellen McGowan's and paused for a moment. The man, whoever he was, was still in there.

She left the sidewalk and crossed the lawn between the two houses. There was a cluster of lilac bushes beside the McGowan house; she stepped into the shelter it afforded from the street light and waited a moment.

The crickets seemed fairly deafening now.

Slowly, quietly, she moved up that last step to the window and looked in.

The beautiful little room was empty.

Helene waited a moment, wondering what to do. Then, still in the shelter of the bushes, she went on to the next window.

Through it she could see a corner of the entrance hall. Ellen McGowan stood there, one white-knuckled hand gripping the door jamb. There was no one else in sight.

In the same instant she heard the front door close.

Without thinking, she ran swiftly to the corner of the house, caught herself there just in time, and stood waiting in the shadow the house made. A man was walking down those front steps, only a few feet to her left, taking slow, heavy, deliberate steps. He was only an indistinct shadow in the half-light.

There was an immense syringa bush in the exact center of the lawn. Helene covered the distance to it in one silent bound. A twig broke suddenly beneath her feet and she felt the breath die in her throat.

No, the man on the steps hadn't heard. He was walking down to the sidewalk, his head bowed, his whole posture one of reflection and anxiety. At the juncture of the front walk and the main sidewalk he hesitated for one breathless moment. Then he turned right, toward Main Street, and for that instant the street light shone full on his face.

It was little Henry Peveley.

Helene crouched there in the shadow of the bush, her eyes closed, until the last echo of his footsteps on the harsh concrete had died away.

The only thought she had was that she had to tell somebody, quick. It had to be either Jake or Malone.

There was an alley running the length of the block between the two streets. She recrossed the McGowan lawn into it, and began walking down it. After a few steps the walk broke into a run. It wasn't fright now, it was the urgent need to share the news of her discovery.

The alley was unpaved, thick with pebbles. Several times she stumbled, swearing at the stones, once the cackling of a startled hen in an adjoining back yard gave her a bad moment. Finally, as she reached the next street, she realized that Jake had been perfect in his weather prediction of the late afternoon.

Jake had said it was going to rain like hell and damnation. He'd been right. In fact, he had even understated the case.

Helene reached the doorstep of the General Andrew Jackson House breathless, disheveled, and soaking wet. Her one thought was that Jake must have arrived by now.

The room was empty.

She stared at it for a heart-sinking moment, then went back into the corridor.

She could go and look for him, but she didn't know where. Jerry Luckstone knew where he'd gone, but he was out somewhere in a parked car with Arlene Goudge.

As she stood there, undecided, she saw a local youth, who had suddenly become the hotel's first bellhop in its history, come up the stairs with a bottle of beer in his hand and turn in the direction of Malone's room. She ran after him.

"Is Mr. Malone awake?"

"I guess you'd call it that," the young man said. "At least, he's got his light on and he's speaking. I been bringing his beer up to him every fifteen minutes, just like he told me."

"I'll take this one in to him," she announced, taking the bottle. "And next time, bring up two."

She tapped lightly on Malone's door, heard the lawyer's voice roaring, "Come in."

Malone was still in bed, surrounded by a litter of empty beer bottles, cigar wrappers, and mussed-up newspapers. He stared at her, outraged.

"You can't come in here."

"I am in here," she announced coolly. She set the bottle down on his table. "Malone—"

He was still staring at her. "What the hell has happened to you?"

She glanced down at the ruins of her organdy dress, felt of her disheveled and streaming hair. "It looks like rain outside. Never mind me. Malone, it was Henry Peveley."

He blinked, reached for the beer bottle, and said, "What did he do, turn a garden hose on you?"

"He didn't do anything to me. It's Ellen McGowan. And it wasn't a garden hose, it was the rain." She added in a burst of exasperation, "Malone, pay attention. It's murder."

He looked at her and went on pouring his beer with meticulous care, letting it run slowly down the inside of the glass. "Did she murder him, or did he murder her, and how can you murder anybody with rain?" He added, "There's a dry bath towel on the chair by the dresser, and you'd better pour yourself a drink of that stuff Henry Peveley left me before you get pneumonia."

She took a drink and shuddered. "It's probably poisoned."

"We'll soon know," Malone said cheerfully. "Now go on with what happened to you."

She sat down, began rubbing her hair with the bath towel, and told him the whole story. When she had finished he sat up in bed, staring at her.

"I don't believe it. Not him."

"It was with my own eyes," Helene declared.

He lay back again, his forehead deeply furrowed. "But it doesn't fit. Henry Peveley couldn't have done either of the murders, because he wasn't on the premises. He couldn't have had anything to do with it, because he's such a nice old duck."

Helene sniffed. "That's a hell of a reason. Some of your best friends have been murderers."

"It's probably something entirely personal between them and hasn't anything to do with either of the crimes." He scowled at her. "Shame on you, spying on people's private lives."

"At their age?" Helene said incredulously.

"They may have been engaged for twenty-five years and he just decided to break the engagement."

"If you're right," Helene said, "I hope it was more than a mere engagement. Twenty-five years is a long time."

Malone sighed. "Ah, 'tis better to have loved and lust than never to have loved at all."

The towel she threw at him missed his face by inches.

"Malone, it had something to do with the murder.

She was present when the Senator was murdered, and she's the cashier of the bank he owned, and she was there when it was blown up. And he was the Senator's brother."

Malone was silent for a while. "Go to bed, like a good girl, and don't bother me. I'll dream of the answer and tell you in the morning." Suddenly he raised up on one elbow. "Where the devil is Jake?"

"Out somewhere," Helene said gloomily. "He wouldn't tell me where."

Malone started to bound out of bed, wrapping the sheet around him. "Why didn't you tell me so in the first place?"

"Because you were asleep," Helene said, "and because I didn't know where to look for him anyway, and because he made it very plain this was an excursion of his own."

The little lawyer frowned, finally sank back on the pillows.

"Malone, you don't think anything's going to happen to him?"

"He's probably breaking his way back into jail right now," Malone growled. He stole a quick look at her and added hastily, "Hell no, he probably took advantage of a chance to visit some local dive. He's probably out tripping the light fermented."

She rose, shook out her damp hair, and walked over to the door. "I hope you're right."

"Go to bed," he said again. "Leave me alone. I'm a very sick man."

"You deserve to be," she said, looking at the beer bottles. Suddenly she paused, one hand on the door-knob. "Malone, this whole town. Jake was brought up in a place like this, he knows how it ticks. But it puzzles me."

"I know what you mean," Malone said slowly. "I can't tell you exactly what it is, but there's a difference. The girls wear the same dresses you see on State Street, and every house has a radio, but there's a difference."

"It's like living in a different age," she said.

"That's it," he said in a thoughtful voice. He paused, and added, "Yes, that's exactly it. Here they're still living in the age of innocence." He paused again. "And in Chicago, we're living in the age of consent."

Chapter Eighteen

"I SUPPOSE you find this all very different from what you're used to," Cora Belle Fromm said coyly.

"Somewhat," Jake said, glancing around the Den. It was a large, gloomy, el-shaped room, lined with varnished brown booths, and decorated with posters advertising Drewry's Ale. There was a juke box at the turn of the el, and just beyond it a door led to the minute but crowded bar. "Yes," he told her, "it's quite different. I find it very interesting." Hell, a cheap saloon was a cheap saloon any place, city or country.

She giggled. "It's very quiet tonight."

"I've noticed," Jake said, smothering a yawn. They were the only inhabitants of the big room, save for an occasional couple that drifted out from the bar for a dance.

The bar itself had looked a little more promising. But Cora Belle had suggested that the "lounge" would be more cozy.

Jake sighed faintly, wished he were back at the hotel, sipped his gin rickey, and blinked. "The liquor is a little different here, too."

"Don't you like it?" she asked anxiously, pushing the button beside the table.

"I like it," he assured her, "but it's a little sudden, when you're not expecting it."

The bartender, a big, muscular youth with damp black hair, came out to their table and leaned on it, scowling.

"What did you put in these?" Cora Belle demanded.

"Dollar Gin," the bartender said, as though he were surprised that anyone should ask. He looked at Jake and added, "That's our most popular brand, Dollar Gin. If you don't like it, say so, but—"

"Oh, I like it fine," Jake said. He noticed Cora Belle's glass was empty. "You'd better bring us a couple more."

As the bartender walked away Cora Belle said, "You ought to be here *some* nights. When there's a crowd here."

"I can hardly wait," Jake said.

"Of course," she said, "it must seem pretty dull to you after Chicago night clubs."

Before Jake could answer, a fight broke out in the barroom, resulting in the violent eviction of a couple of lively young farm hands. By the time it had quieted down, Cora Belle had changed the subject.

"It's a terrible place to live. Jackson, I mean. Everybody knows everything everybody else does, and the women just live on nasty gossip. And it's the dullest place in the world. Nothing to do but go to the movies or go roadhousing." She giggled coyly. "Still, I always say the principal entertainments are the same all over the world. Drinking, gambling, and you-know-what-I-mean. So it doesn't matter much if you're in Jackson or Chicago."

"A very fine philosophy," Jake said gallantly.

"But," she added, "Jackson really is a terrible place."

"Then why do you live here?" Jake asked.

She leaned confidingly across the table. "Maybe when I know you better, maybe I'll tell you." She put her head on one side and smiled fetchingly. "But let's talk about you. Tell me all about yourself."

Rule two, Jake thought. Get the man talking about himself. He looked thoughtfully across the table at Cora Belle. From the chin down, she was definitely stocky. Not plump, plumpness had a certain soft curviness to it. Cora Belle was solid. The girdle under her bright print, short-sleeved dress didn't fit any too well, either. But her face was thin, almost too thin. It seemed a little too small for the rest of her, as though it had once been a pretty, piquant little face that belonged on a tiny, appealing girl.

Perhaps it was seeing that small, tilted nose and babyish mouth in her mirror every morning that encouraged Cora Belle to wear her metallic blond hair in ribboned curls. Her voice didn't have a lisp, but her wide eyes did. The total effect would have been good, if it had stopped at the neck.

In Jackson, he decided, she could get away with being the village siren. In any other place she'd have been just another blonde barfly.

Two drinks later she suggested that they move on down to Harvey's. He observed that she nestled a little more closely in the front seat of the convertible than she had on the ride out from town. He fought back an impulse to deliver her back to her door, without pursuing his inquiries, and go back to the hotel for Helene. Helene could have a wonderful time in a roadhouse. Still, a promise was a promise.

Harvey's turned out to be a small shanty between the Jackson-Milwaukee highway and the riverbank, a two-room building housing a bar, a dance floor, and three booths. They paused at the bar for a drink while Cora Belle carried on what passed for gay conversation with the bartender and the two male customers, and while Jake decided that he was developing a preference for Dollar Gin. Either that, or after the first three drinks you stopped tasting it. He wasn't sure.

The booths in Harvey's were smaller and more intimate than in the Den. Jake gave up trying to avoid Cora Belle's knees under the table, and said, "If you dislike Jackson so much, why do you live here?"

"Because," she said, with a devastating mock shyness. "Just because." She assumed a look of extreme self-importance and added, "If you knew the things I know about Jackson, Wisconsin, you'd be amazed. You really would, you'd be amazed."

Jake ordered another drink, lit a cigarette, and sat regarding her. There was a kind of woman he'd come to know well from his newspaper days, a drunken, indiscriminate, and not too good-looking kind of dame, who had read Laurence Hope's poetry and the earlier prose of Ben Hecht, who assumed a look of extreme anguish at hearing either the Tchaikovsky "Fifth" or *My Buddy,* and who always gave the impression of being "in the know" on everything from City Hall staircase politics to the private lives of the upper tenth. Cora Belle seemed to fit into that category.

The hell of it was, though, not infrequently those

babes did know about half of what they pretended to be in on. You never could tell.

"Nonsense," he said coldly. "You can't tell me anything would go on in a place like this."

"That's what you think," she said confidingly. She finished off the gin rickey in a neat gulp. "You've been wondering why I'm here. All right, I'm going to tell you." She leaned so far across the table that she was breathing on his necktie. "It was because nobody asked me to the Junior Prom."

"A good reason," Jake said gravely.

"You think I'm kidding, don't you? All right, you just listen. In a place like this, everybody's all mixed up together. There's no sorting out in fancy private schools and plain public schools and slum schools. It's all one. Flo Peveley and Cora Belle Langhoff, the saloonkeeper's daughter, right in the same high-school class."

Jake said, "That's democracy."

"Democracy hell," Cora Belle said indignantly. "Do you think those babes like Flo Peveley—well, I take that back, she wasn't so bad—but Nellie Proctor, and Kathleen Hansen, and Maybelle Smith—can you imagine them inviting me to come over for supper, or stay all night after a date? Oh sure, all the boys wanted to make up to me." She paused to light a cigarette, a little unsteadily.

"I can't imagine any boy not wanting to," Jake said. He knew this was not the occasion for subtlety.

"But not in public, you understand," Cora Belle said. "Sure, their fathers hung out in my old man's speakeasy. But you wouldn't catch one of them taking me to a movie. It was all right to date me up to go out for a ride, but if we got a drink or a hamburger on the way home, we got it somewhere out of town. My old man bought me the swellest clothes of any girl in Jackson, but you wouldn't catch anybody walking home from school with me."

"I think I can stand one more," Jake said, pushing the bell to call the bartender. "How about you?"

"Oh sure," she said. "I can stand a lot more. Well, anyway, along comes the Junior Prom. I knew I wasn't going to be dated for it, but you know how a kid that age is, I kept right on hoping something would happen, right up to the last minute. Well, a few days before I heard a couple of girls talking down in the high-school toilet, about some guy who hadn't been able to get a date for the Prom, some awful jerk. One of the girls finally says, 'Oh well, he can always take Cora Belle,' and they both haw-hawed about it. That was the finish for me. I stole some money from my old man's pants, and took all the stuff he'd ever given me that I could hock, left a note for him, and beat it to Milwaukee."

"I don't blame you," Jake said. "But why did you come back?"

"I always intended to come back," Cora Belle said. "I had a couple of jobs in Milwaukee, but I always kept my eyes open for a good chance. Well, along came Danny Fromm and we got married. He was a racketeer, but he was a swell guy, and when we finally split up he settled a big hunk of money on me. So I just moved back to Jackson—my old man was dead by that time—and bought that cute little house, and I've been here ever since. And do these dames here hate me!"

"Maybe it's this gin," Jake said. "But I don't get it."

Cora Belle laughed nastily. "Because they have to be polite to me. They don't know what I might do if they weren't. Sure they don't invite me to join the Music Study Club and they don't drop over for visits, but they sure are polite when they meet me on the street. Because they know their husbands and boy friends are taking me out, every chance they can get. And just to make it worse, they see me going around in swell clothes they can't afford, and driving a nifty new Chrysler roadster. They hate me like poison, and they have to stand it, and that's just how I intended it would be." She emptied another glass of Dollar Gin and soda water. "And that, pal, is why I stay in Jackson, Wisconsin."

"I see," Jake said. He felt a little vague about things.

"And I know plenty about all of 'em," Cora Belle said. "Like that old biddy, Ellen McGowan. She'd like to see me ridden out of town on a rail, just because her nasty little brother hangs around me. She's just so damn refined I can't stand it. But you just ask her sometime. Her father was supposed to go to California for his health, wasn't he? Well, you just ask her sometime if she ever got a letter from him. Just one letter, all the time he was away. And ask her if she can produce anybody who saw him out there. Just ask her." She pounded on the table and called, "Harvey!"

Jake's brain whirled a little, but he thought it was more the Dollar Gin than anything Cora Belle had said. Perhaps one more would clear his head a little.

After that outburst, Cora Belle did not seem disposed to discuss Jackson, Wisconsin, and Jake couldn't think up any of the right questions. They moved on to a slightly more ornate roadhouse called Lakeside Inn where Jake managed to ignore the pointed advertisements for tourist cabins, "by day, week, or hour," and to a tiny crossroads tavern called The Owls' Nest where Cora Belle fed a dollar's worth of nickels into a slot machine.

It might not be the gin, Jake decided. It might be the weather. The one-room interior of The Owl's Nest was like a small steam bath, heavily scented with stale beer and Dollar Gin. The line of stuffed brids and animals over the bar seemed to feel the heat too, their fur or feathers hung limply, and their glass eyes were dull. The bartender himself was lethargic and half asleep.

Jake yawned heavily, and suggested to Cora Belle that the outside air might be cooler. She dropped one more nickel into the slot machine, and agreed.

Night life in Jackson County, Jake thought.

There was an agonizing quality about the drive back to town that he knew he would never be able to forget. Dollar Gin appeared to have an entirely deadening effect. It was hard to keep his hands on the wheel. Cora Belle nestled close to him, her damp, sweaty hair spread over his shirt front. The edges of the road were faintly blurred, he drove slowly and with painstaking care, slowing almost to a stop whenever the headlights of an approaching car appeared. It wasn't that he was afraid of being killed, but it was Helene's car he was driving.

Besides, it had suddenly begun to rain. Hard.

Poor little Cora Belle, he thought. What a miserable life for such a nice girl. He slowed the car down to the barest minimum of speed and glanced at her. Her pretty little face looked drooping and sad.

It was a dirty trick to take a nice girl like this out just to pump information from her.

That reminded him that he'd been singularly unsuccessful in his attempt. He blinked and shook his head once or twice, in the vain hope that it would clear a little.

Dollar Gin was hardly the stuff with which to ease into drinking again after a long stretch on the wagon.

The idea of pouring Dollar Gin into a sweet kid like Cora Belle, just to learn something from her. The poor, pathetic little creature. He wished he could do something nice for Cora Belle. Maybe she'd like another drink.

She said that she would, and indicated a tavern just on the edge of Jackson. Jake never did learn what its name was, or remember much of what it looked like.

The drink did settle his head a little. He resolved to be very stern. Mustn't let good old Jerry Luckstone down. A little coaxing might help.

He slipped an arm around Cora Belle and managed a few rather tentative pats on her neck. She giggled. It was all in a good cause, he told himself, but couldn't quite remember what the cause was. They went back to the car. His resolve slipped away from him momentarily, and he began driving down the road again.

The exigencies of driving down the wet, blurred highway drove her temporarily out of his mind. He gripped the wheel with a desperate determination, his teeth clenched.

The drive across the bridge was a thousand miles long.

He turned off at Milton Street, turned one more

corner with meticulous care, and stopped approximately in front of Cora Belle's house.

The streetlight shone on her face through the rain, hiding the wrinkles and the loosened skin and the make-up. Just a poor little high-school girl, Jake murmured, and everybody picking on her. Including him. A very nasty thing to do.

Nothing personal about this, he reminded himself, as he patted her again. All in a very important cause.

She nestled down against his shoulder.

"Cora Belle," he said thickly, "who murdered 'at man in the courthouse?"

She giggled again. "Bet you wish y'knew."

"Bet you don't know," he said, picking up the cue.

"Bet I do too. Know who wanted to, an' why. Know who blowed up the bank, too, an' why. Know that much, anyway." She hiccuped.

"Bet you don't," Jake said monotonously. "Bet you can't tell me."

She hiccuped again, faintly, and was silent. Jake waited awhile before he looked at her closely and realized she was going to be silent for a long time, probably hours.

Well, at least she did know. He'd learned that much.

She looked very comfortable there. Jake gave up trying to hold his eyes open, and settled back on the seat for a good, long nap.

Chapter Nineteen

H E DIDN'T know what he'd done, Jake decided, but whatever it was, he would never do it again.

The back of his head materialized first. It ached. Then suddenly it vanished, and his forehead came to life. For a little while nothing existed save his forehead. At last his stomach entered the picture, behaving in the most unpleasant way possible.

He was, he realized, in bed. Just what bed, and how he had gotten there, was a mystery that would have to be taken up later. He opened one eye just enough to discover that it was daylight, and closed it again hastily.

For a while he was content to lie there and suffer. Then little by little he began trying to think things over. It was a painful effort and singularly unsuccessful.

Something vague about carrying someone—he couldn't recall who—up a short flight of steps, and banging his knee in the process. Something equally vague, and faintly terrible, about trying to find his way home through a maze of streets that kept twisting and wheeling to confound him. Then a definite gap in memory.

Someone laid a cold cloth, scented with menthol, on his face. It felt wonderful. Kind hands bathed his face with cool water. It was even more wonderful. He opened his eyes and saw that a blonde angel was holding a cup of coffee to his lips.

The coffee was strong and reassuring. It was no more than safely down when a voice on leave from some angelic choir said, "Take this, darling."

He obediently swallowed a couple of small tablets and a few drops of water and lay back on the pillow to await improvement. The blonde angel went on bathing his face and reapplying the cold cloth on his forehead. The throbbing ache began to fade.

He had never seen anyone so beautiful, so gentle, or so kind. That long golden hair that fell over her shoulders, the filmy white gown that clung to her—he couldn't quite decide if it was an angel's vestment or a nightgown—the cool, exquisite, heavenly touch of her hand.

Suddenly she threw her arms around him, kissed him, and clung to him for a moment. His head spun. This might be an angel, but definitely not a celestial one. He tried desperately to remember where he was, how he had gotten here, and above all, what accounted for the presence of the angel. It was no use. Everything was terribly vague, and his thoughts went round and round. Maybe he had amnesia. Or was amnesia a medicine? Milk of amnesia. No, amnesia was a confused state, like California. California had the tallest trees. He opened his eyes suddenly and looked at the angel.

"Trees a crowd," he said happily.

Her answer was to stroke his forehead.

"Darling," he said, gazing at her, "you're wonderful. You're beautiful. You're an angel. Darling, will you marry me?"

Her answer was to kiss him lightly on the forehead and say, "Yes, dear."

He fell back on the pillow and closed his eyes, reflecting on his good fortune. Sixty seconds later he sat bolt upright in bed, his eyes wide. He'd just remembered who the angel was. Helene.

He groaned.

Helene poured out another cup of coffee from the thermos bottle on the dresser and handed it to him. Then she lit a cigarette and slipped it between his shaking fingers.

"It's all right," she said soothingly. "I don't know what you've done, but I forgive you."

He drank the coffee, complained that the cigarette had been made of old mattresses, and said, "Well, I didn't. I guess she expected me to, but I didn't."

Helene asked, "Who?"

"Cora Belle. Cora Belle Fromm."

Helene said, "Oh."

There was a longish pause before Helene announced furiously, "If you think I'd suspect you of any kind of hanky-pank with that faded blonde floozy, you're an insane man. Did you find out anything from her, and what gave you the idea in the first place?"

Jake swung his feet to the floor, sat up a minute, then hurriedly lay down again. "If I weren't already in love with you," he declared, "I'd fall in love with you now. Or maybe you have second sight, like Buttonholes."

"It isn't second sight," Helene said. "It's first sight. One look at Cora Belle. Did she tell you who murdered the Senator, or didn't she know?"

"It's like this," Jake said. "It was Jerry Luckstone's

idea." He went on to resurrect the past evening as best he could, including the story of Cora Belle's return to Jackson. His account ended at the point where he'd begun worrying about how to get Cora Belle from his car to her house.

"Then everything gets very confused," he told her.

Helene frowned. "I hope you didn't just leave Cora Belle on the sidewalk."

"I don't think I did. In fact, I'm sure I didn't." He paused. There was a badly mixed-up memory of hauling her up the front steps, fishing through her pocketbook for the key, dropping a curious miscellany of pocketbook contents on the porch and crawling around to pick them up, of shoving Cora through the door and dumping her on a sofa. "No, I know I got her in the house. Then I guess I left."

"Darling, don't you know?"

"I must have left," Jake said. "Or why am I here? And how did I get here?"

"You came roaring up to the door at six o'clock," Helene said. "I let you in, you apologized for breaking into the wrong room, and collapsed. I put you to bed."

"Six o'clock?" Jake said. "But it wasn't more than one or two when I delivered Cora Belle. It couldn't have taken all that time to get here."

She shrugged her shoulders. "All I know is that the sun was up."

Jake blinked. "Helene, the car."

"It's all right, darling," she said soothingly. "I can get another one if I have to."

"No, that isn't what I mean. I mean—hell, I was very careful of the car. But—wait a minute. I sort of remember getting in the car and curling up for a nice nap. Then I woke up and got terribly lonesome for you, and started out to find my way here. It was very hard, because the streets kept getting all mixed up. Anyway, I got here."

"That's the one thing I'm sure of," Helene said. "You did get here."

"Only the car." He wrinkled his brow. "I know I came back here. So I must have left it there. Parked right by Cora Belle's house. It must be there now."

Helene said, "And the good people of Jackson can just assume that you were there too."

He scowled at her. "You mean you don't care?"

"Why should I care?" Helene asked pleasantly. "It's your reputation, not mine."

Jake moaned, and lay back on the pillow again. It was very comfortable to be there, to lie quietly on a bed and not have to move, not have to fight his way through twisting streets to a place that was secure.

"Helene, what do you think about what she told me?"

"You mean about her life? I think it's very beautiful and very, very sad. Go to sleep."

"I don't want to go to sleep. I mean, do you think she knows who murdered Senator Peveley and blew up the bank, and all that?"

"If she does," Helene said firmly, "let a better man try to find out."

Jake was silent for a moment. "What do you think about what she said about Miss McGowan?"

"I think she has a nasty mind."

"Helene, please be serious. What do you really think about what she said?"

"I think," Helene told him, "that Miss McGowan probably murdered her father, for reasons I would prefer not to discuss, and faked the story of his being in California to hide her crime. Furthermore, I think that Senator Peveley found out about it and so she killed him. Then she blew up the bank because she'd never really liked the place. Now shut up, and go to sleep."

Jake obediently closed his eyes.

Later he claimed that he had not slept a wink. Helene declared that he'd slept like a baby for three hours. But to Jake, the period was one of confused thoughts and confusing dreams, of half waking and half sleeping, trying to reach either one state or the other.

He'd curled up the pillow under his head and tried to settle down. Bits of Cora Belle's story came up to haunt him. At sixteen or seventeen she must have been an attractive young thing in a helpless sort of way. She'd stolen her old man's dough and gone off to Milwaukee. Jake dozed a bit there. Florence Peveley came up and invited him to go to a Junior Prom. She was dressed as an Indian, and explained to him that it was going to be a costume party. He was wide-awake, turned over, punched the pillow again, and resolved *firmly* to go to sleep. He would never drink Dollar Gin again, in fact he would probably never drink anything again.

Who had murdered Senator Peveley? Did Cora Belle really know? The bartender at the Owl's Nest was setting a glass down in front of him, and someone said, "Look out, it's a bomb." The bomb exploded, and someone with a pickax began working on the wreckage, pounding and cracking and pounding and cracking, with a sound that grew steadily louder and louder.

With a groan he sat up, wide-awake now. The pick-ax had turned into someone knocking on the door.

Helene called, "Who's there?" cautiously, one hand on the doorknob.

"It's me," Malone roared, out in the hall. She let him in.

Jake lay down again and pretended to be asleep. But the little lawyer paid no attention to him. Instead, he addressed himself to Helene.

"You would have to say a thing like that," he told her crossly, shutting and locking the door behind him.

Helene raised her eyebrows. "What did I say?"

"Down here in the bar last night, where everybody in the world could hear you, you said that if Jake went out with another woman you'd wring her neck." He mopped his streaming brow. "Even if you didn't know Jake was out with another woman right at that minute, it was damned tactless of you."

"She didn't know it," Jake murmured from the bed.

"You shut up," the lawyer told him. "I'm talking to her."

Jake felt he shouldn't let anyone bully an angel, but was unable to cope with it. He kept still.

"Well?" Malone demanded.

Helene shrugged her shoulders. "What does public opinion expect me to do about it, go out and murder Cora Belle?"

"Public opinion seems to be that you already have," Malone said. "Early this morning the milkman found Cora Belle murdered. Somebody, it seems, had wrung her neck."

Chapter Twenty

"AS A MATTER of cold, hard fact," Malone said, peeling a cigar, "Jake is the one who gets some of the credit for this."

The little lawyer looked at Jake thoughtfully for a minute. "What were you drinking last night?"

"Dollar Gin," Jake said, "and so help me, if I ever touch another eyedropperful—" But Malone was out the door and halfway down the stairs.

He returned five minutes later with a bottle and a glass. "This will fix you up."

Jake shuddered. "Go away," he said faintly.

"Never look a Greek in the mouth when he comes bearing a gift horse," Malone said cheerfully. He paused in the act of opening the bottle. "I mean beware of the Greek when he comes bearing a horse in his mouth."

"Never mind," Jake said in a feeble voice. "Let's get this over with."

Dollar Gin proved to be every bit as bad as he had remembered it.

"Now," Malone said. "What time did you leave Cora Belle?"

"I wish to heaven I knew," Jake said miserably. He looked up at the lawyer's face, it was white and drawn. It made him feel a little happier to realize that someone else was suffering. "How did you know I was out with her?"

Malone lit his cigar, tossing the match toward the washstand. "Everybody in town knows you were out with her, and knows where you went. The convertible is still parked by her house, and three bartenders report seeing you with her."

"I think they missed a couple of bartenders," Jake said, thinking back. He gave Malone a brief sketch of the evening. "The hell of it is, I didn't learn anything from her, and I'd counted on it."

"You should have had a practice session with Dollar Gin first," Malone said, chewing savagely on the cigar. "What time did you roll in?"

"Helene says it was sunup, and roll is not the word."

"Then where in God's name were you in the meantime?"

"Probably crawling up the sidewalk on my hands and knees," Jake said bitterly. He lit a cigarette, puffed at it experimentally, and put it out fast. "All right, let's have the gory details."

Cora Belle Fromm, Malone told them, or rather, Cora Belle's body, had been found about six-thirty that morning by the milkman, a personable young fellow named Harold Krause. Harold, questioned by the sheriff and fourteen reporters, had declared that Cora Belle was one of his best customers for Jersey cream, and so when he'd seen her front door open, he'd taken the liberty to go up and close it, thinking that maybe she'd come home a bit high, and knowing what the flies were like this time of year. He was just reaching for the doorknob when he saw Cora Belle's body, sprawled half on the davenport and half on the rug.

It hadn't been so great a shock to the young milkman. "I just thought she was plastered," he told the reporters. But when he came a little closer, with an idea of moving her into a more comfortable position, he'd gotten a good look at her and immediately rushed to the telephone to call Doc Spain.

Why Doc Spain instead of the sheriff? He hadn't known she was dead, and besides, people always sent for Doc Spain when there was unidentifiable trouble.

Dr. Spain had discovered that Cora Belle had been strangled to death with a bath towel, probably not more than a few minutes before the milkman had found her. Her body had still been warm. Her clothes had been ripped to pieces and her face and body badly bruised.

The milkman's wife was reputed to have entered a suit for divorce, within two hours of the discovery of the body.

Everybody in town was talking about the fact that the robin's-egg-blue convertible had been parked by the house.

"And there you are," the little lawyer finished angrily. "You've got yourself into a fine mess, and the Lord only knows if I can get you out of it." He relit his cigar. "All right, you've made your pipe, so put that in your bed and smoke it."

Jake said indignantly, "I didn't murder her and nobody can pin it on me, especially a small-town sheriff in a purple suit."

"Shut up," Malone said. "I want to think." For a full five minutes he stood staring out the window, puffing furiously at his cigar. Then he turned around to glare at the man on the bed. "All I need to do is take a night off to get some sleep, and you go right out and race into trouble. Now I don't know when I'll get back to Chicago."

"Who asked you to stay?" Jake said stiffly. "You can go right back to Chicago on the next bus."

"All right, I will," the lawyer roared. He dived out the door, slamming it behind him. Thirty seconds later he was back in the room.

"Up to this morning," he said, ignoring the previous conversation, "my interest in who had murdered ex-Senator Peveley was purely academic. Now I've got to find out who it was, and why, because the same person undoubtedly strangled this blonde wench. If I don't do it, nobody else will. All that sheriff has done for the past two days is sit on his hands and scratch his head."

"Neatest trick of the week," Jake murmured.

Malone ignored him. "The bomb expert from Milwaukee states that the bomb at the Farmers' Bank—a homemade affair—could not have been planted in advance. It had to be set off a few seconds before it did its work. No one but myself in Jackson seems to be paying any attention to that bit of information, which is considerably more important than the strangling of Cora Belle Fromm."

"Why?" Helene wanted to know.

He looked at her disgustedly. "Because it proves that the planter of the bomb was one of the group in the bank when it went off. Assuming the same person murdered Senator Peveley, it narrows the field considerably."

He found a scrap of paper in his pocket and began

writing. "Not counting ourselves and the man who was killed, the following people were in the bank at the time. Jerry Luckstone, a farmer named Krause-meyer, Ed Skindingsrude, and inside the cage, Miss McGowan, Phil Smith, Mr. Goudge, and the girl at the adding machine." He scowled at the list. "What members of that group were on hand when the Senator was shot?"

"Miss McGowan," Jake said, "Jerry Luckstone, Ed Skindingsrude, and Phil Smith. Four promising names." He looked up, first at Helene, then at Malone. "Yes, I know what you're thinking. Jerry Luckstone could have asked me to take out Cora Belle last night, so that suspicion would fall on me when she was found strangled. But I hope it wasn't that way."

"So do I," Malone said, "and that reminds me of a bit of local gossip. The Goudge girl—Arlene—slipped out for a date last night, and her old man found out about it and wouldn't let her in when she came back. She spent the night with Jerry Luckstone's mother. It's as interesting to the townspeople as Cora Belle's murder." He relit his cigar. "I don't know where that fits in to the murder of Senator Peveley and the bank teller and Cora Belle, but you never can tell."

Helene lit a cigarette and sat cross-legged on the end of the bed. "How about motives, Malone? Jerry Luckstone was engaged to the Senator's daughter and was running around with another girl, and possibly seeing Cora Belle on the side. The Senator didn't like him."

"Wrong set of murders," Malone said. "If he was marrying the Senator's daughter for her old man's political pull, he'd hardly murder the old man, and blow up the bank that held the money."

"That's for you to figure out," Helene said. "Or how about Philomen Ma. Smith? Nobody seems to pay much attention to him."

"He got his collarbone broken in the explosion," Jake objected. "He'd hardly break his own collarbone."

"He might," Helene said, "if he couldn't duck as fast as he'd expected. After all, whoever blew up the bank took some risk himself."

"But why would Phil Smith blow up the bank?" Jake demanded.

"Why would anybody?" Malone asked crossly. "That's a question that hasn't occurred to anybody yet. Magnus Linkermann appears to have been the mildest, most inoffensive guy who ever sang in a choir. He'd never had any trouble with any of the people involved in this, nor any particularly close friendships with them—or with anybody else."

"It's still possible nobody intended to murder him," Helene pointed out. "He just happened to be there."

Malone nodded slowly. "In which case the only possible conclusion is that the bomb wasn't intended to destroy any person in the bank, but to destroy a thing. What thing?" He paused again. "You wouldn't ordinarily expect a man to throw a bomb into a building full of people, no matter how desperate he was, if the same effect could be accomplished without mayhem." He was fast assuming his best courtroom manner. "Therefore, the object to be destroyed must have been one which was not in the bank previous to its opening in the morning. Then why not wait until after the bank was closed? I believe it was in order to prevent that object from being seen by persons in the bank."

Jake yawned. "Why not say it was that package of records Ellen McGowan brought over from the courthouse, and be done with it," he said crossly. "I figured that out all by myself, simply because the bomb was planted as close to the package as possible."

"I might as well go back to Chicago," Malone said stiffly.

Jake sighed heavily. "That's where you came back in again. We're not progressing."

"Don't worry," Malone said reassuringly. "Even a Jackson County jury wouldn't convict you with me for your lawyer."

Helene stood up. "All this talk is very fine," she declared, "but I'm beginning to crave action. Malone, what do you propose to do first, or are you just going to wait for a premonition?"

"I'm going to talk with Jerry Luckstone," Malone said. "I'm going to suggest to him that everything points to some kind of monkey business at the bank and that an investigation might be in order. Then—" He paused. "I don't know yet. I'll just make it up as I go along."

Helene began pulling stockings out of the open suitcase on the table. "Wait for me down in the lobby. I'm going with you."

Malone turned to Jake. "As for you—you stay here and keep quiet. Understand?"

Jake nodded. "There's nothing in the world I want more to do than just keep quiet. For a long time."

"Then do it. Go to sleep. Don't answer any questions. And if before we get back that fathead sheriff comes around to arrest you"—he paused—"send for me and I'll come and knock his block off."

He had waited less than five minutes in the lobby when Helene came down the stairs, looking as though it had taken her five hours to dress.

"Breakfast?" Malone asked.

"I've had some," she told him. He saw that her face was very pale. "Malone, suppose they should arrest Jake."

"They'd never convict him," he said. "And if they should, don't worry, he's been in jail before, and worse ones than this."

At any other time in his life, he would have enjoyed the walk up Main Street with Helene, conscious of the admiring glances she attracted. Today he was worried. He knew the glances were not solely admiration. There was considerable curiosity about the wife of the man who had probably committed a hideous crime the night before.

Malone mopped his brow with a crumpled handkerchief. It was not a pleasant situation. The three crimes seemed to be unrelated in their methods. An ex-Senator had been shot in the back. A rabbity little bank clerk had been pulverized by a bomb. A hard-drinking town woman had been strangled. Yet he sensed that they were all part of one deadly pattern. He knew, too, that the desperate hand behind them had too big a stake to stop now, whatever stood in its way. There was still a sense of impending doom in the air.

"If you see Buttonholes," he muttered to Helene as they went up the courthouse steps, "ask him how he feels."

She sniffed. "Are you a lawyer, or a fortuneteller?"

"I wish I could be both," he said unhappily.

The interior of the courthouse seemed slightly more normal than it had on his previous visit. Typewriters and adding machines were clicking in various offices. As they came in, Buttonholes, a mop and pail in his hand, vanished through a door that led to the basement. Mr. Goudge was bent over his desk; in the next office Phil Smith, a plaster cast reaching to his chin, was propped stiffly in an office chair, dictating to one of his deputies.

Through one of the long windows they could see the jail building and the door of the sheriff's office. That was where the newspapermen had gathered.

As they started up the big staircase, they met Jerry Luckstone racing down, a batch of papers in his hand. He stopped suddenly, stared at them, and said, "Thank God! Come up to my office, I want to talk to you alone."

Upstairs in his office he sent his secretary out and shut the door.

"I can't tell you how sorry I am I got him into this mess. I'll get him out of it, though, somehow. Poor Cora Belle. Isn't it the most horrible thing! And to think that only a week or so ago, I—" He paused, lighted a cigarette, and drew on it deeply. The smoke seemed to calm him.

Malone started to speak, the young district attorney shook his head at him. "Before you say anything, look at this. I just got it."

Helene and Malone bent their heads over a hastily mimeographed sheet of paper.

CITIZENS' ANTICRIME COMMITTEE

*Meet for organization
purposes at 12 noon today
at Gollett's Hall.
Everybody come.*

*If our law enforcement offices won't
take care of criminals, we citizens will.*

Malone looked at it for a long time. "Well, you know the country better than I do," he said quietly. "Where will we hide him?"

Chapter Twenty-One

IT WAS no time to quibble over legal technicalities, Malone declared. He agreed that a district attorney could not—or at least should not—have any part in evading the law. On the other hand, he pointed out, Jake was not a fugitive from justice. Jerry Luckstone had no official information that the sheriff, or anyone else, wanted him.

Nor, Malone went on, not giving the unhappy young man a chance to get in a word, would he be aiding a criminal to escape. Jake was no criminal, he was simply a victim of circumstances, most of which Jerry Luckstone himself was responsible for. The least Jerry Luckstone could do now was provide him with a hideout.

Helene came in with a good second chorus by looking reproachful and saying, "You couldn't let him down *now!*"

Plans were made quickly. There was, it seemed, a fishing shack belonging to the Luckstone family about eight miles out of town. No one would think of looking there.

Jerry Luckstone would park his car by the Third Street bridge, leaving his keys in it. Helene and Malone would waken Jake, and she would lead him down the back staircase of the General Andrew Jackson House and down the alley that ran back of Wilk's

Garage to Third and Water Streets, where the car would be waiting. The rest was up to her.

She noted down careful directions about how to find the fishing shack. "With Jake out of harm's way," she said, "Malone and I can pitch in and help you find who did murder all these people."

"The bank," Malone said suddenly. He told the district attorney what he had reasoned out that morning.

"But," Jerry Luckstone said in a puzzled voice, "but there isn't anybody in the Farmers' Bank who would steal any money."

"You never can tell who would steal money," Malone told him. "Ask any deacon who passes a collection plate."

Jerry Luckstone frowned. "It'll have to be investigated, of course." He caught his breath. "And if you're right, it'll have to be done right away. Before any other records are destroyed."

"Or anyone else is murdered," Malone said. He looked at his watch. "This isn't any time to stand around chatting. Let's get Jake out of town first, and think afterwards."

They parted from Jerry Luckstone at the courthouse steps, he to get his car, they to go back to the hotel. There seemed to be even more activity than usual on Main Street; the crowd was no larger but it was moving around more and forming into small discussion groups on every corner. The curious glances directed at Helene and Malone were definitely unfriendly.

Malone bought the newly arrived Madison newspaper and glanced at it as they went up the street.

JACKSON VILLAGE BELLE
ASSAULTED AND SLAIN

STRANGLED ON
THIRD DAY OF
CRIME WAVE

In the center of the front page was a feature story by "Lily Lake," headlined "Just Like a Butterfly Caught in the Rain."

Malone snorted, and tossed the paper into the nearest dustbin.

"Just a lost child, coming home," he muttered. "A fragile little butterfly, beating her lovely wings against . . ."

"For the love of Mike, Malone," Helene said.

"I should have been a reporter," the lawyer growled. "Just give me a catalogue of popular song titles and I'll be a second Lily Lake." He looked at Helene out of the corner of his eye. Her face was very white, her eyes wide and shadowy. "Just think of the life stories you can give the papers while Jake is being tried."

"I'll give them the secrets in the life of a shyster lawyer," she said grimly. "And is the entrance of the General Andrew Jackson House an unusually popular spot, or is it my imagination?"

"Whichever it is," Malone hissed in her ear, "just keep—"

He was interrupted by the noisy arrival of the sheriff's car in front of the little hotel and took a firmer hold on Helene's arm. The crowd parted as Sheriff Marvin Kling and his deputy climbed out of the car, crossed the sidewalk, and stopped before Helene and the lawyer.

"Where's your husband?" the sheriff demanded, as though Helene had him hidden in her handbag.

Malone felt the muscles in her arm tighten. "I don't know. Are you looking for him?" Her voice was as serene as a summer breeze.

"You're damned right I'm looking for him," Sheriff Kling growled.

A reporter pushed his way through the crowd and all but climbed up the sheriff's red necktie. "Sheriff, can you tell me if you're—"

Sheriff Kling straight-armed the reporter and a couple of spectators. "I'll tell you everything you want to know later. Right now—"

A photographer popped up from nowhere, caught a quick shot of Helene, Malone, and the sheriff, and disappeared again. Sheriff Kling pushed on into the building with his deputy, sweeping Helene and Malone before him.

As they reached the lobby, Helene kicked the little lawyer in the ankle and said, "Mr. Kling, I think he's gone to get the car."

The sheriff paused. "What car? You mean your car?"

Helene nodded. Malone sauntered through the crowd and up the staircase of the hotel. "He said he was going to get it, when I last saw him—"

"The car's in the police garage," Sheriff Kling said. "It's evidence." He scowled at her. "Maybe he's gone to get it and maybe he hasn't, but we'll take a look in his room first." He spotted Malone halfway up the staircase and bellowed, "Hey, you. Where were you going?"

"I was going up to my room to change my shirt," the lawyer said in a hurt and surprised voice.

The sheriff charged up the stairs, his deputy and Helene right behind him. Malone waited until Helene reached his side, then took her arm and went up with her, letting the sheriff and a few courageous spectators go ahead.

"It's all right," he murmured to her, under his breath. "Jake will be as safe in the Jackson County jail as any other place. Just as long as the Citizens' Committee doesn't get hold of him, don't worry."

Ahead of them they could hear Sheriff Kling pounding furiously on the door.

Helene paused a moment. Her slender fingers on Malone's arm suddenly turned ice cold, but there wasn't so much as a tremor on her face. Rather there was a look almost of boredom, plus a faint annoyance as at some trifling inconvenience.

The sheriff turned to her with badly suppressed fury in his eyes. Helene's impervious calm froze any angry words that might have risen to his lips; for a moment he glared at her silently. When he did speak, his voice was almost gentle.

"Do you have your key with you, Mrs. Justus?"

"Sure," Helene said cheerfully. "You mean you're going to open the door the easy way?"

Sheriff Kling nodded, speechless.

Helene found the keyhole on the second try, hesitated no more than an instant with her hand on the key, then deliberately turned it in the lock, reached for the doorknob, and opened the door, stepping aside to let the sheriff and his deputy enter first. Malone's hand on her shoulder steadied her, and she followed them in.

The room was empty.

The bed, a disheveled mass of wrinkled sheets

when she had seen it last, was neatly and freshly made up. The cigarette ashes on the carpet had disappeared. So had Jake's clothes that had been thrown across the rocking chair. So had Jake.

"He's in the clothes closet," Deputy Harry Kline said helpfully.

Jake was not in the clothes closet. Nor was he under the bed. Nor was he hanging out the window on the fire rope.

The sheriff had a single-track mind. "Where is he?" he demanded loudly.

Helene shrugged her shoulders. "He probably went to get the car, and get some breakfast, just as I told you. He didn't know you'd want to see him."

"Oh yes he did," Sheriff Kling said nastily.

Malone said, "Now look here, if you're arresting Mr. Justus, go ahead and arrest him and get it over with, or else stop annoying him. He didn't know you'd be looking for him, or else he'd have been here waiting for you. He hasn't any reason for hiding from the law. If you go out and walk the length of Main Street, you'll probably find him. Try the restaurants and the barbershops." He drew a quick breath. "The way you go on, anyone would think he was accused of a crime."

The sheriff roared, "He left his car last night at Milton and First Streets."

"Well," Malone said, "this is a hell of a lot of fuss to make about a parking violation."

He ducked just as the sheriff swung at him, slid on the corner of the rug, and sat down heavily on the floor. By the time he had caught his breath, the sheriff and his deputy were standing in the doorway.

"I'll find him, all right," the sheriff raged. "I'll

find him, and when I do, no Chicago lawyer is going to get him out of jail, either." He slammed the door and was gone.

There was a little murmur of noise from the stairway, and then silence.

Malone waited a moment, got up off the floor, straightened his tie, and for a good three minutes talked about the sheriff of Jackson County, his origin and his personal habits, bringing in improvised facts which would have dumfounded any congress of anthropologists, and touching on his family connections, his friends, and his lack of ordinary cleanliness.

Helene let him finish. "It's probably all the truth," she said calmly, "and the same thing goes for his great-grandmother, too. But how did Jake know enough to get out of here before he came pounding on the door?"

Malone looked at her. "Jerry Luckstone found out what the sheriff had in mind, and instead of waiting for us to walk over here, he beat it up the back stairs and got Jake out to his car."

"I hope you're right," Helene said grimly.

They waited a few more minutes until the last excitement outside the General Andrew Jackson House had died away, and then went cautiously down the back stairs, behind the barroom, past the kitchen, and into the alley. The space between the alley door and Water Street was completely empty of people, a dusty expanse of sunlight and weeds.

"If he came down here," Malone said, "nobody stopped him."

At the corner of Water Street they turned and looked around. Near the bridge was Jerry Luckstone's car, empty. Helene ran up to it and looked inside. The keys were in the dashboard, just as Jerry had agreed to leave them. There was no sign of Jake anywhere.

Helene caught at Malone's arm. "Malone, he didn't know anybody was looking for him, and he just wandered off somewhere by himself. Maybe he went out to get a shave, or a cup of coffee."

"Maybe," the little lawyer said.

"We've got to find him before anyone else does."

She began sprinting up the weed-grown walk that ran from Water Street up to the General Andrew Jackson House. Malone reached out and grabbed her wrist.

"Don't look so damned hurried. Wait a minute and powder your nose and fix your hair. Somebody might see you and think you were worried about something."

She glared at him furiously, then paused to take out her compact and do as he had suggested.

"There's plenty of need for hurry," Malone added, "but for the love of Mike, don't show it."

They strolled into the lobby of the hotel as though they hadn't a care in the world.

Had the clerk happened to see Mr. Justus go out that morning?

No, the clerk had not. In fact, nobody in the lobby had seen anything of Mr. Justus that morning. Anyone there would have remembered seeing him, because several reporters were waiting for him.

Mr. Justus was not in the restaurant. He had not been in the restaurant since the night before.

Mr. Justus was not in the barbershop, nor in the drugstore, nor in any of the barrooms. He was not in the offices of the *Jackson County Enterprise,* nor in the courthouse.

Mr. Justus had not made any attempt to retrieve the Buick convertible from where it had been left the night before, nor had he called at any garage to inquire after it.

The sheriff appeared to be covering the same ground as Helene and the little lawyer, but in a far less casual and unconcerned manner.

It was near noon, the hour set for the meeting of the Citizens' Anticrime Committee in Gollett's Hall, when Helene and Malone faced each other in a room of the General Andrew Jackson House and came to the same unavoidable conclusion.

Whether or not of his own volition, Jake had simply disappeared from the face of Jackson, Wisconsin.

Chapter Twenty-Two

THE Citizens' Anticrime Committee was swiftly renamed, under the direction of Alvin Goudge, the Citizens' Law Enforcement Committee. Citizen Goudge restrained himself to a plea for restoring law and order to Jackson, Wisconsin, and a recommendation that a reward be offered for the apprehension of the criminal, but Danny Gollett (brother of the Golletts of Gollett's drugstore) rose up to declare he was all for finding the dirty so-and-so and hanging him. (Muffled applause.)

Beyond that point the meeting confined itself to organization work and plans for a second meeting to be held at five in the afternoon. "At which time," Citizen Goudge said ominously, "we may be forced to take the law into our own hands."

The meeting adjourned at twelve-forty-five. By one o'clock a hastily lettered poster appeared on a telephone pole at the corner of Third and Main Streets, offering a reward of $1000 for finding the murderer of Senator Peveley, Magnus Linkermann, and Cora Belle Fromm. A local wit declared that $500 had been subscribed by Florence Peveley, and $500 by old sweethearts of Cora Belle, at a dollar a head.

Helene and Malone spent the rest of the morning and the noon hour in the back shed of the *Jackson*

County Enterprise, a refuge from both the heat of the day and the curious stares of the Main Street crowds, repeating to each other at intervals, "Jake's all right." "Jake can take care of himself anywhere." "Someone must have tipped him off, and he had sense enough to beat it." "Jake will get in touch with us as soon as he can, there's no need to worry." Tom Burrows returned from covering the meeting of the Citizens' Committee to report on its deliberations and conclusions.

"I might be able to carry off that thousand bucks," Malone said wistfully. "It's not very much, though, for the trouble I'd be put to."

Tom Burrows unloaded a paper bagful of beer cans. "Do you know our local murderer?"

"I feel as if I ought to," Malone said. "I feel as if some one little fact that would point to him is right at my finger tips, something that I already know. Only I can't seem to think what it is."

"Don't mind him," Helene said. "It's the way his mind always works."

"Is there anything one can do about it?" the young newspaperman asked. "I mean, could we jar him, or something?"

"Nothing does any good," Helene said. "Nothing but time." She paused. "I don't suppose it's important, but had you heard about the fair Arlene being bounced out of her bed and board?"

Malone said, "A very crude, unladylike way of putting it," and popped open a can of beer.

"Of course I've heard about it," Tom Burrows said. "Do you think anybody could keep anything like that a secret in Jackson, Wisconsin, for more than an hour?" He added, "I'm not the man she was out with, if that's what you were trying to find out."

Partly because he was curious, and partly to take Helene's mind off Jake's disappearance, Malone asked, "Are you in love with this Arlene girl?"

Tom Burrows threw a beer-can top into the river and watched it floating down toward Beloit. "No, I'm not. She's unbelievably appealing, in a limp, lost-kitten kind of way, but it's a different thing from love. She doesn't love me, either, which simplifies everything."

"My first impression," Helene said, "was that she did."

Tom Burrows shook his head. "I've asked her to marry me three times since that night, and she turned me down every time. She's even confided to me that I'm not required to marry her, if you know what I mean. Of course those two facts, even taken together, don't prove anything. But the truth is, that sad look on her little mug when you saw her calling me up from the courthouse just meant that she thought she'd lost her last boy friend."

Malone said, "Either love life in Jackson, Wisconsin, is incredibly complicated or I'm still suffering from that blow on the head."

"It's like this," the newspaperman said. He scowled at a reflection in the river. "Arlene was so full of gratitude to any man who'd pay any attention to her that he could have his own way about anything. She wasn't especially amorous, but she sure was grateful as hell. In a town like this it's a terrible thing for an unmarried but marriageable girl of Arlene's age not to have a boy friend and not to have dates."

"Well, damn it all," Malone said, "she ought to

be attractive enough to suit any guy. What d'ya want here in Jackson anyway, little Venuses?"

"Arlene's attractive enough," Tom Burrows told him. "But it raises the devil with a girl's popularity to have an old man who won't let her go to school parties when she's in high school, and won't let her go to the movies, or go to dances, or have dates. Especially when there are so many other equally attractive girls who are a lot more accessible."

Malone thought for a minute, and then said, "How about leaving home?"

"There's no place to run to," Tom Burrows said. "Not in Jackson, Wisconsin." He tossed another beercan top into the water. "But she did find out that she could make it down the back stairs after she was supposed to be in bed." He scowled again. "I had an idea Jerry was crazy about her, from seeing them together. Then suddenly he turned up engaged to Florence Peveley. I took Arlene out about four or five times, first out of curiosity, then because there wasn't anything better to do, and finally because I was so doggoned sorry for her. But then she began to act as though she was afraid I might get away from her, and I decided to call a halt."

"And now?" Helene asked.

"Now," Tom Burrows said, "she won't marry me. She won't even borrow any money from me." He added, "I suppose I've acted like a son of a bitch, but I don't see what else I could have done at the time."

He threw one more beer-can top into the river with a sudden violence, rose, and was halfway up the wooden steps before he paused.

"The whole thing is just her imagination," he said

in an oddly cracked voice, and went on up to the *Enterprise* office.

Helene listened for his last footsteps to die away and then counted ten before she said, "A very pretty story, and how much of it do you suppose is true?"

"I'm a gentleman," Malone snorted. "I'll suppose it's all true."

"I'll testify for part of it," she said thoughtfully. "Old man Goudge wouldn't let his little girl go out with the boys, or she wouldn't have been sneaking out the back way when I saw her last night. I'll also testify that a spot like that is a terrible handicap for a lively girl. But our young friend Mr. Burrows seems entirely too anxious to prove his innocence."

"I'd do the same thing in the same situation," Malone lied. He threw his cigar into the river. "What did he mean was just her imagination? Was she imagining he and she had a gr-r-r-eat bond between them, or was she imagining she was going to have a baby, or both?" He sighed, and said, "Frankly, I don't give a hoot."

Five minutes later Helene said, "You don't think anyone could have murdered him, do you?"

"If you mean Jake," Malone said, "no."

Ten minutes later she said, "If he's just gone out on a bender, I'll massacre him when he gets back."

"You can't massacre just one person," Malone told her. "One is a murder, two is a sex slaying, three is a massacre."

"All right," Helene said gloomily. "If he's out on a bender, I'll massacre all three of him."

The afternoon dragged along. Helene slowly grew more colorless and silent, faint lavender shadows began to appear below her eyes. Malone tossed an endless succession of badly frayed cigar stubs into the placid and disinterested river. Tom Burrows came downstairs at intervals with what little news there was.

Jackson County had been thoroughly searched, according to Sheriff Marvin Kling. The county's four highway policemen were out scouring the countryside for the missing man. The interstate-police radio was sending out descriptions at fifteen-minute intervals. And the Chicago police had rounded up eleven red-haired, freckle-faced men and asked Sheriff Kling to come down and take his pick of the lot.

Malone had met the last item with a hasty long-distance call to Chicago, and eleven innocent red-heads had gone back to their favorite bars.

The Jackson, Wisconsin, police force (two men and one motorcycle) had quelled an incipient riot around an enterprising young man selling hastily made picture postcards of Cora Belle Fromm's house.

Madison had offered to send over a ballistics expert. No one was sure why, inasmuch as Cora Belle Fromm had been strangled. By this time the murder of Senator Peveley and the bombing of the bank had paled into insignificance in the public eye.

Once, during the longest hour of the afternoon, Helene said sharply, "We'll hear from him. Sooner or later we'll get a postcard saying, 'Wish you were here.'"

"With an 'x' marking the jail," Malone said.

For the most part, Malone sat staring out over the river, lost in thought, going over and over the circumstances of the three crimes. Someone had murdered Senator Peveley, blown up the bank, and strangled Cora Belle Fromm. Phil Smith, the gentlest man in Jackson, had lost his position as a teacher of the classics, through Senator Peveley's influence with the school board. That was a number of years ago. Ed Skindingsrude had quarreled with the senator over a stock deal. That too had been several years ago. He had also been a director of the Farmers' Bank, but had resigned in a huff. As far as anyone knew, Ellen McGowan had never had any trouble with the Senator. She had worked for the Farmers' Bank for many years. Jerry Luckstone—the matter of the Senator's daughter and Arlene Goudge. Malone sighed.

There was some all-important fact that he was overlooking, he knew. It was the one thing he needed, and he couldn't find it.

Meantime, Jake might be anywhere, anything might have happened to him.

The murder of the Senator and the bombing of the bank had to be related. They simply couldn't be two separate crimes. The Senator owned the bank, the same people were present at both crimes, everything fitted together. As for the murder of Cora Belle Fromm, she had known something that fitted her into the same set.

It was about four o'clock when high-heeled footsteps sounded on the wooden stairs. Helene and Malone looked around to see Florence Peveley descending the steps. It was the first time either of them had seen her in a skirt, and that alone called for a second look. She was wearing a chiffon afternoon dress, of what Helene later described as a violent violet, and carrying a wide-brimmed violet horsehair hat in one hand. Her blazing hair was blown to every point of the compass, and there was an ice-cream stain down the front of the dress.

"This is a screeching mess, isn't it?" she said as she reached the last step. "I hope nothing's happened to your husband, Helene. You don't mind if I call you Helene, do you? I didn't think so. He didn't really rape Cora Belle, did he?"

"I don't know," Helene said pleasantly. "He never gives me their names. Have a bottle of beer?" Only Malone noticed that she was white around the lips.

"Thanks," Florence Peveley said, sitting down on a packing box. She cracked open the beer bottle on a protruding nail, tore her skirt on another nail, exploded one surprising verb, and said, "Well, I hope he's alive. How do you feel? I did this damn burg from end to end, looking for you."

"He's probably alive," Helene said. "I feel wonderful. And you just looked in the wrong places first."

Florence Peveley leaned her elbows on her outspread knees and grinned at Malone. "She's wonderful, isn't she? Is it any wonder I like her?" She tilted up the beer bottle and drank from it with a pleasantly gurgling noise. "I'd be something like her if I weren't so damned homely and neurotic. It's very bad to be both, you know. There was a doctor up at Rochester—" she interrupted herself with the beer bottle, lit a cigarette, and then said, "Can you imagine that dirty little bastard running out on me like that last night?"

"No," Malone said, gasping for breath. "Who?"

"Jerry. He took out another girl. I can imagine why, too." She finished with the beer bottle and tossed it into the river with a loud splash. "Will you get the hell out of here, *Mister* Malone? There are times when we women want to talk in private."

Helen took a quick look at the girl's face, and said,

"I need cigarettes anyway, and you want a nice walk."

Malone got up off the grass with difficulty, retied his tie, grunted, and started toward the stairs. Halfway up he paused and said, "You could have asked me anything you want to know and gotten detailed information on it," and was out through the *Enterprise* office before either of them could say a word.

The damp hotness of the street struck him like a blow. He stood for a moment in the doorway, blinking at the sun. It was a big, round sun, blazing down on a big round world, and somewhere in that world was Jake.

A doorway marked DENTIST OFFICE ONE FLIGHT UP offered the only shelter he could see on the street. Malone moved into it, discovered the shade was, if anything, hotter than the sun, but decided to stay there anyway.

A lot of people went by, almost all strangers. Among them was the tall, thin Alvin Goudge, his bald head turned faintly pink in the sun. He saw Malone standing there, shuddered, and drew away as though someone had left a dead horse in the street. More people went by. Ten minutes later an old-model Buick leaped ten inches over the curb, bounded back into the street, rubbed the paint off an adjoining fender, and stood still. Ed Skindingsrude got out, and bellowed something indignant about the fatheaded town commissioners and the condition of the streets. He didn't notice Malone, but went on down the street. Still later plump little Henry Peveley walked by briskly, casting occasional anxious glances to right and left as though he expected the revenue officers to be following him.

A nerve stirred in Malone at the sight of him; Helene's report of her night wanderings came into his mind. The little lawyer stepped out into the thick stream of pedestrians and followed him. Henry Peveley was the murdered man's brother. Henry Peveley was executor of the estate which included the blown-up bank. Henry Peveley had been threatening Ellen McGowan with heaven-knew-what. Malone had a sudden feeling that Henry Peveley might lead the way to a key to the murder.

At worst, he would lead the way to a place to buy a drink.

Malone followed him down Main Street to Milton Street, down Milton Street to Frederick Street, and half a block to a small, white, almost Colonial house with bright-blue blinds. The lawyer blinked at it for several minutes before he recognized it from its newspaper pictures. It was Cora Belle's house, the house where she had been murdered.

There was a line of cars driving slowly past the house, their occupants peering out curiously. A traffic cop (borrowed from Delville) stood in the street to keep them moving. The pedestrian sight-seers were kept at their distance by a rope stretched between the elm trees. A deputy sheriff was smoking a pipe and dozing on the top step.

Henry Peveley turned up the alley. Malone followed him. There was a little garage a short way down the alley, behind it a path led to a neglected backyard and to the back steps of Cora Belle Fromm's house (already named "the murder cottage" in the Milwaukee press).

Malone hesitated one moment in the shadow of the

garage. Henry Peveley opened the back door of the cottage, which appeared to be unlocked, and went right on in.

The least that could happen, Malone told himself, was that he'd either be murdered or thrown in jail. He crossed the back lawn as though he owned it, slipped through the door, and began walking through a tiny entryway as silently as a nervous mouse.

Cora Belle's house appeared to have been left deserted save for the front-steps guardian. Malone paused at a doorway and stood peering around its corner.

He could see a brightly decorated room, crammed with a collection of highly modernistic furniture and a few pieces of badly imitated early American. There were end tables and ash trays everywhere, and a cunning little glass-and-chromium bar in one corner. The rug in front of the davenport was mussed up a little.

Malone took all that in at a glance. Then he settled back in the shadow of the doorway and watched Henry Peveley go through a thorough search of the room. At the same time, the little lawyer searched it with his eyes.

There was the open secretary desk, with the topless ink bottle. It looked as though Cora Belle might have been writing a letter. Henry Peveley was going through the desk drawers methodically. There was a tiny spot of ink on the rug near the desk. She might have been interrupted at her writing. He saw a fountain pen under the chromium bar. There was another spot of ink on the davenport. But the letter she had been writing appeared to be gone.

Anyone in Jackson, Wisconsin, might have murdered Cora Belle Fromm, shortly before six that morning, he told himself. The little house was sufficiently secluded that no one, who was not deliberately watching, would notice that anyone entered or left.

No one questioned so far had offered any alibi. Everyone claimed to have been home in bed, but Malone knew from long experience, not only with the law, that that was no alibi.

Then there was always the possibility that the strangling of Cora Belle was a totally unrelated crime, and had nothing to do with the other two. A woman like Cora Belle usually had any number of people, male and female, who wanted to murder her. One murder in a community could set off other murders that had been smoldering for a long time. Malone had known such things to happen.

Yet Cora Belle did fit into the other picture. She had been in the courthouse at the time of the Senator's death. She had claimed to Jake that she knew who had murdered the Senator and who had blown up the bank, and why. Jerry Luckstone, already pretty well involved with two other women, had had dates with her. Ellen McGowan had been afraid she would marry the former's brother. And now, the late Senator's brother was searching her house.

No, Malone decided, the three crimes were all part of a pattern. Though, he told himself, the murderer certainly showed a catholic taste in weapons. A gun, a bomb, and a bath towel.

Henry Peveley had completed a thorough, but amateurish search of the house, and now stood, puzzled and unhappy, in the middle of the living-room rug. Malone completely forgot he hadn't been invited and stepped out into the room.

"From past experience," he said, "I'd suggest trying behind the pictures and under the sofa pillows."

Henry Peveley automatically looked behind the pictures and began picking up the cushions. From under the center one of the davenport he drew out a long white envelope. A happy light came into his mild blue eyes, then faded in a flash, replaced by a look of alarm.

"How did you get here?" he asked Malone. His voice was a little squeak.

"I came down the chimney, rehearsing for Christmas Eve," Malone said wearily. "Don't let me bother you. I'm just trying to help."

Little Henry Peveley leaned against a chair for a moment. Slowly the terror faded from his face. "I have a feeling you're someone I can trust. I hope I'm right, because I guess I have to anyway."

"I'm trustworthy as the day is wide," Malone told him in his most reassuring voice.

"This is it," he announced. There were two papers in the envelope. He looked first at one and then at the other. "She wrote a letter last night after she came home. The date is at the top of it. This is it."

Malone frowned. "Then she heard someone coming, and stuffed it under the sofa cushion. The someone turned out to be the murderer."

Henry Peveley handed over the two papers. "You can see why I was anxious to find them," he said.

The first was a letter, written in a round, childlike, and definitely staggering hand, addressed to Florence Peveley:

Dᴇᴀʀ Fʟᴏ:

When we were kids in school you were the only one who treated me like a human and I never forgot it. I made your old man give me this because I was sore, but I've got all over being sore now. It isn't what you think, I did him a favor and made him pay for it. But I don't want the damn money, I got enough of my own. So the hell with it."

Cᴏʀʀɪᴇ

The other paper was a badly typed document, dated a week before. It was a will, signed by Senator Gerald Peveley and witnessed by Henry Peveley and Arlene Goudge.

Malone read it slowly and carefully. It directed that the Senator's estate be divided equally between his daughter, Florence, and Cora Belle Fromm.

"You see?" Henry Peveley said brightly. "Now, do you see why I was so anxious to find it?"

Chapter Twenty-Three

MALONE took a cigar out of his pocket, put it back again unlighted, and finally said, "She wasn't murdered because of the will. Or it would have been found and destroyed. It wasn't really hidden, it was just slipped out of sight until her visitor left."

"So it couldn't have been Florence or myself," Henry Peveley said. He looked searchingly at Malone. "You weren't thinking it was either Florence or myself."

"I wasn't thinking anything of the kind," Malone assured him. He started to sit down on the sofa, caught himself, and chose a gaspipe-and-pink-leather chair instead. "But you did know about this."

"I knew about it, and I disapproved of it. Gerald brought it up to my office about a week ago. He said he wanted to sign a paper with Arlene—she's my stenographer—and me for witnesses, without either of us looking to see what it was. Arlene put her name down all right, she never asks questions. But I insisted on seeing it and finally Gerald showed it to me."

Malone was trying to accustom himself to hearing the late Senator referred to as Gerald. "Did he give you any reasons?"

"He said Cora Belle had done him a very important service. He didn't tell me what it was. But I can tell you this, he was very angry. He was angry all week, and he was angry right up to the time of his death."

Malone sighed. "If we knew what he was angry about, we might know who murdered him," he said thoughtfully.

The white-haired man looked at the papers in his hand. "Mr. Malone, you are in my confidence. About this will. Cora Belle is dead. She has no heirs, that I know of, who would benefit from this. It would not affect me, in any case, as I am not named in Gerald's previous will, which left everything to his daughter. Filing this would not only mean a considerable loss to Florence, with no worthy person to benefit, but a very definite personal embarrassment. I don't want to do anything illegal, but—" he paused. "Well, she herself wanted it out of the way."

Malone reached out a hand. "I have a stake in this affair too. My friend's missing, possibly hiding from the police, possibly kidnaped, possibly dead. I'd be very happy to keep that will for you until I can verify the fact that you don't benefit under the old will."

He'd expected to see opposition in Henry Peveley's eyes. Instead there was a friendly gleam. "Why, of course." He handed over the document as though it had been a calling card. "I sent the old will up to Florence; you can go up there and see or even just telephone her. Then you can meet me, and we'll tear this up."

Malone shoved it into his inside pocket and said, "I'll meet you in the Hermitage speak"—he'd almost said "tavern"—"at nine tonight."

"Fine," Henry Peveley said. He moved toward the door. "But whatever you do, don't let anybody see that will in the meantime." He opened the door and said, "We'd better not leave together. And when you go to the Hermitage tonight, give three slow raps on the door and say you're a friend of Henry's."

Malone waited five minutes, then slipped out the back door and down the alley. It was a wonderful county, he reflected, where there weren't enough police guards to handle both entrances of a house. He picked a reasonably quiet street and went back to the *Enterprise* office, where he found Tom Burrows proofreading a long column of "personals." There was no news of Jake yet. The Citizens' Committee was considering demanding that Sheriff Kling resign from office. The half-ruined Farmers' Bank was locked to the public and Jerry Luckstone and a state bank examiner had been inside there since noon. Helene was still downstairs.

The little lawyer went slowly down to the riverside shed, wishing he could tell Helene that there was news of Jake, and that it was good. At least he didn't have to tell her any news that was bad. Not yet, anyway.

Florence Peveley was evidently just preparing to leave.

"An awful lot depends on the man, of course," Helene was saying in an advice-to-the-young voice.

Florence Peveley said, "Yes, but if—" saw Malone, blushed, and said, "Well, I've got to be running along."

"Don't hurry on my account," Malone said. He started unwrapping a cigar. "Say, Miss Peveley—all right then, Florence—I wish you'd tell me one thing, just to satisfy my curiosity. What kind of will did your father leave?"

She stared at him. "He left every cockeyed cent to me, of course. What would you have expected Pa to do?"

"What about his brother—your Uncle Henry?"

"He didn't leave him anything. Henry had his own dough."

"That's fine," Malone said, lighting the cigar.

She stared at him an instant, then turned to Helene and said, "Thanks," and went up the stairs, three steps at a time.

There was a short silence. Then, "Where did you go?" and "What did she want?" were asked simultaneously.

"Never mind what she wanted," Helene said. "It had nothing to do with murder or with Jackson County or with anything of the sort, and none of your damn business, and I wouldn't tell you anyway."

Malone puffed at his cigar and said, "I hope you told her that helpless stuff was no good any more. And does she have anyone in particular in mind?"

A faint pink came into Helene's cheeks. "No one. Just general information in case she spots someone. Now answer my question."

Malone hesitated. "I'm breaking a confidence when I tell you this," he said, looking at his cigar end, "but you and Jake and I are the only people in the world who ever will know." He told her of the curious last will and testament of Gerald Peveley, ex-Senator.

Helene scowled becomingly. "What was the idea? It couldn't have been one of those things. Or maybe it was, but this was something else. Do you know what I mean?"

"Not quite," Malone said. "Try it again."

"I mean, even if he was quietly keeping company

with Cora Belle, it wouldn't quite account for his making this will. There had to be some other reason."

"I gathered that already," Malone said. "But what was it?"

"Well," Helene said, "it seems like a pretty gaudy gesture to make out of pure friendship. She couldn't have been blackmailing him, could she?"

"She could," Malone told her, "and she probably would have if the opportunity presented itself. But it seems like a silly way to blackmail anybody. Remember me in your will, or I'll tell the world you did such-and-such. There's a kind of sweet unreasonableness about it that doesn't appeal to me." He paused and added thoughtfully, "Besides, it wouldn't work. You could make a will and give it to the blackmailer, and then quietly go away and make another, later one, and leave it in a good safe place and then go ahead and die. Blackmail isn't very effective on a ghost."

Helene shrugged her shoulders. "All right. You tell me what it was."

"At a time when he was already pretty sore at his daughter," Malone said, "as we already know—Cora Belle, according to her letter, did him an important service. My hunch is that she gave him some information that was highly valuable to him."

"What kind of information?"

"I think I know that too," Malone said. "And if I'm right—"

He was interrupted by the sound of clattering footsteps down the rickety stairs. For a moment he held his breath. No, those weren't Jake's footsteps. A sudden cold perspiration broke out on his forehead.

It was Jerry Luckstone, pale, tired, and harassed, but with a new light in his eyes.

"Malone, will you come over to the bank with me? I think we know pretty much what's what there, but I'd feel better if I had you along."

The lawyer rose stiffly to his feet. "This isn't really my party, you know," he pointed out. "I'm just a visiting spectator. But if you want me to come along—" He'd have nursed a broken heart for days if the district attorney hadn't come for him.

"I guess I can have an unofficial expert lend a hand," Jerry Luckstone said.

Helene had risen too. "You're not invited," Malone told her.

"I didn't expect to be. I'm going back to the hotel and take what passes for a bath in the General Andrew Jackson house, and get dressed up." She pushed back a strand of hair. "I want to look my best when Jake comes back."

Malone and the district attorney exchanged a quick glance and said nothing.

"And stop looking so anxious and protective," she said firmly. "There's nothing to worry about."

As they passed through the *Enterprise* office, they found Dr. Spain giving the young editor a news item about a pair of twins just born at Jay Creek. He looked at the trio curiously.

"Is this an arrest, Jerry, or are you just going out to lunch?"

"He's the worst old gossip in the county," Tom Burrows said. "Never tell him a thing."

"Just curious," Dr. Spain said.

"Well, it's not an arrest," the district attorney told

him. "I'm just taking advantage of Mr. Malone's kindness to get some expert assistance.

"Good idea," said the doctor. "No amateur ought to monkey with anything important. Like the time Luke McGowan tried to lay a new concrete floor in his sister's basement."

"What happened to it?" Malone asked, fascinated.

The doctor was feeling through all his pockets. "Oh, the floor turned out fine," he said. He finally produced a tobacco tin. "But it took nine hours to get the concrete off Luke." He started hunting for his pipe as he added, "He was damn near petrified."

They parted from Helene at the entrance to the Farmers' Bank, she going on to the hotel. Malone looked around the little building curiously. The debris had been carefully swept away, and a hastily constructed wooden affair, resembling a picket fence, was serving as a teller's cage. There were a number of broken spots on the plastered wall. Malone looked at them with an uncomfortable interest, wondering which one his head had made.

Jerry Luckstone led the way back into the office, a room untouched by the explosion save for a cracked pane in the glass door. It was a small, very plain room, with two windows overlooking the river twelve feet below, furnished with an imitation-mahogany desk, a bookcase, and an assortment of uncomfortable chairs.

At the moment the room seemed fairly crowded. Ellen McGowan was there, and Phil Smith, Mr. Goudge, Ed Skindingsrude, and a man who was introduced to Malone as "Mr. Pepper from Madison, the bank examiner," a razor-faced, unhealthy-looking citizen with gold-rimmed glasses.

Phil Smith said, "Ed dropped into the office just as

I was leaving and I thought I'd better bring him along. He was a bank director when most of this was going on."

Malone sat on the window sill and stared down into the shiny green water of the river. He didn't want to watch any of the faces in the little room, and he was going to be glad when this was over. There was a cold, uncomfortable feeling in the pit of his stomach.

Mr. Pepper cleared his throat. "The situation still requires considerable study," he began stiffly. "I should estimate it will take a week of careful checking to make the entire picture clear."

"Never mind that," Ed Skindingsrude said. "Is there any money missing, and how much, and who got it?"

"There appears," Mr. Pepper said, "to be a shortage of approximately $76,000, evidently embezzled over a period of some years. I am of the tentative opinion—"

No one paid any attention to his last words. Jerry Luckstone walked over to the desk and began fingering a handful of papers. "These notes—"

"Undoubtedly forgeries," the examiner said in a cold voice. "As I said, it will take about a week—"

"No it won't," Ellen McGowan said suddenly. "I can give you all the details in half an hour."

Malone couldn't avoid a quick glance at the spinster's face. It had suddenly grown very old. He rose and stood looking out the window, his back to the room. This was the part he hadn't wanted to see.

Ellen McGowan's voice was clear and perfectly calm. She might have been giving a treasurer's report to the Federated Women's Club as she told the story of her embezzlement of $76,000 over a period of six years. She gave facts and figures and dates, referred to forged notes made to cover up shortages, and to duplicate ledger statements of scores of accounts. Malone paid little attention to the details. Any discussion of financial matters, beyond a simple business of debts versus cash on hand, bored him. The important point was the missing money, and the identity of the embezzler. No, there was one still more important point.

When the woman had finished talking, Malone turned around. Everyone in the room was completely silent, every face as expressionless as a board.

"You've left out something," Malone said wearily. "What did you do with the money?"

She looked at him, her gray eyes blank. "That doesn't matter. It's gone."

"It does matter," Malone said. "You didn't spend $76,000 in seven years."

The faces in the room were all looking at him now. He lit a cigar with slow deliberation and tossed the match into the river.

"How much money was your father short in his accounts when he died?" Malone asked.

Ellen McGowan's face was white as chalk. "He had debts, but he hadn't stolen any money. He expected to pay every penny of it back."

Malone made a quick examination of his memory. "It was from the school funds, wasn't it?"

"Yes." Her voice was a shade lower now. "But it wasn't an embezzlement. In those days the treasurer took the district's money and kept it in his own account, simply being obligated to the county for the amount. There's a different arrangement now. But," she caught her breath, "he was perfectly honest. It was just that when he died, he owed the county about twenty thousand dollars."

"How did you guess it?" Jerry Luckstone asked, looking at Malone with a kind of wonder.

"I didn't guess," Malone said. "I'd heard that her father was something of a gambler, and that she adored him. When she admitted to this embezzlement, it looked like covering up for him." He was looking at the end of his cigar, not at any of the faces in the room. "I knew it must be the school funds, because those records that were destroyed were the school-fund records." He added, "The important thing is where the rest of the money—some fifty thousand dollars—went to. Or rather—who it went to."

"The important thing," Ed Skindingsrude said, "is who murdered Senator Peveley," he breathed heavily, "and planted a bomb in the bank and strangled poor Cora Belle."

"I don't know!" Ellen McGowan's voice suddenly had a high, shrill tone. "I don't know anything about it. That hasn't anything to do with it."

"Oh yes you do," Malone said. He spoke coldly and deliberately. "You know, and you're the only person alive who does know." He paused. "Except one. The murderer."

She stared at him, her eyes wild. He could see the last color draining from her face.

"I know you do," he went on in that same, clipped tone. "Because I remember a little of the explosion. I remember two things, your scream and the explosion itself. And you screamed before the bomb went off. Because you saw it and you knew what it was."

Everyone in the room seemed to be moving a little closer to the gray-haired spinster. She was swaying a little.

But Malone never finished what he was going to add. This time the scream that he heard came from outside the bank. He wheeled around to the window. As he moved he saw Ellen McGowan fall across the imitation-mahogany desk, in a strange, distorted posture.

It was all too quick for him to realize what was happening. There were a couple of people running frantically on the Third Street bridge. The scream had come from one of them. As he looked, something struck the water with a splash. There was a faint struggling in the water as the something was caught in the current and swept downstream toward him.

He moved instinctively, scarcely realizing he had thrown off his coat and dived from the window of the Farmers' Bank until he felt the cool water of the river on his body.

Chapter Twenty-Four

A DISTINGUISHED alumnus of the old swimmin'
hole, Chicago River Chapter, South Branch,
which in his childhood had been the bathtub of the
city's lower West Side shanty town, Malone still
dived like a bullfrog, but he swam like a wharf rat.

The current favored him. Swimming with it, he
worked his way out to midstream just as the struggling girl was carried down. He managed to reach and
grasp her, and for a moment paddled frantically, keeping them both afloat. Her long, wet hair swept across
his face, blinding him, until he managed to shove it
aside.

Fighting there in the water, he was surprised that
his mind was so clear. From the shore he could hear
shouts and voices. Damn-fool thing to do, he was telling himself. Go to work and get drowned in a river,
with the best years of your life ahead of you, just
because you wanted to make a hero out of yourself.

The girl had become limp as a wet potato sack. He
held her with one arm, trying to work toward shore.
A voice near him yelled something about a rope. He
hoped they wouldn't send for the fire department to
bring a rope.

Ahead of him was the curve in the river, just
beyond the *Enterprise* building. He headed for it,
using the current to his best advantage, hampered by

the dead weight of the girl, as well as by his clothing. Those on shore had seen the direction he had taken and were moving that way. Through a film of spray he saw Helene going down the edge of the river, running like a deer.

Someone had found a rope. As the current swept by the curve Malone worked close to the shore just as Jerry Luckstone grabbed the rope and threw it. His aim was faultless. Malone caught it with his free arm, clung to it, and was half propelled, half dragged across a mudbank and up onto the grass.

For a moment he lay there on the grass, panting, his eyes closed. Then he sat up and wiped the mud from his face.

"Did—any one of you God-damned so-and-sos—pick up my cigar—" he gasped indignantly.

Helene shoved him back on the grass. "Wasn't anybody in this crowd ever a Boy Scout?" she was demanding. "You're supposed to kneel on his stomach."

"If anybody kneels on my stomach," Malone managed to get out, "I'll kill the bastard."

"Oh thank heaven," Helene said. "You're all right!"

He lay there on the grass, gazing up at the treetops and the hot, blazing sky beyond. The sky had never looked quite so beautiful before. There were voices all around him, but he paid no attention to them. It was a wonderful world, a perfect world, and here he was in it, alive, and able to enjoy it. Nothing else mattered very much.

Somebody said, "Here, this'll revive him," and held an old-fashioned flask to his lips. Malone automatically swallowed, strangled, gasped, exploded, "What are you trying to do, murder me?" and looked up into the apologetic face of Henry Peveley, who was hastily reconcealing the flask in his hip pocket.

Malone struggled to his feet, pushing aside the hands reached out to help him. The combination of wet clothes and accumulated mud seemed to weigh a ton.

"Who was she?" he demanded. He looked around. "And where is she?"

"Arlene Goudge," Helene said. "And Dr. Spain just took her down to the shed back of the *Enterprise*."

Malone shook himself a little, like a collie just out of a bathtub, took Helene's arm, and started up the path toward the shed. The rapidly fading voices back of him were discussing the rescue in excited tones. At the entrance to the shed a little crowd had gathered at a respectful distance. Malone pushed their way through and went on into the shed with Helene.

Arlene Goudge was lying on the ground, looking beautiful, pale, and completely alive. Dr. Spain, on one side of her, was searching anxiously through his pockets for something. Tom Burrows was standing on the bottom step of the stairs, watching everything. And Jerry Luckstone was kneeling on the ground, holding both of her hands.

"Darling," Jerry Luckstone was saying incoherently. "Darling, I love you. Darling, why did you ever do such a crazy thing? Darling, aren't we going to be married?"

Arlene opened a pair of reproachful brown eyes. "Are we?"

"Of course we are," Jerry Luckstone babbled.

She sniffed faintly. "But you'd never asked me."

Dr. Spain had found what he was looking for. It

was his cigarette case. He took one out, put it in his mouth, and began hunting for matches.

"She'll be all right," he pronounced. "A good healthy girl like that can stand a lot more than a ducking in the river even in her condition."

Jerry Luckstone looked up. Malone wouldn't have believed his face could have turned paler than it already was, but it did. He said hoarsely, "Condition? What are you talking about?"

Dr. Spain, having just found the matches, dropped them. "Do you mean to say she hasn't told you?"

Malone glanced down at the girl. In spite of the fact that she had been half drowned, a definite blush was beginning to grow on her colorless face. The little lawyer grabbed Helene's arm.

"This is no place for an audience."

They pushed on up the stairs into the *Enterprise* office. At the same moment Ed Skindingsrude opened the street door and came in. Malone stopped dead in his tracks.

"Here's your coat," Ed Skindingsrude said, holding it out.

"Thanks," Malone said. He felt in the pocket to make sure his cigars were all right. They were. His lips were suddenly stiff as he formed the words, "How's Miss McGowan?"

Ed Skindingsrude stared at him with stunned eyes for a moment. He didn't say anything.

Malone strode to the head of the stairs and bellowed, "Dr. Spain! You're needed!"

Dr. Spain came puffing up the stairs, muttering, "If the darn-fool girls would only— Well, what's the matter up here?"

Malone explained quickly about Miss McGowan,

how she had fallen on the desk, how her face had looked.

"Stroke," Doctor Spain said, taking a firm grip on his little satchel. "Always thought she'd have one. Wouldn't think as thin a woman as that would have high-blood pressure, would you?" He kicked open the door. "Where'd you say she was, the bank?"

Malone caught up with him in a bound. Helene and the county board chairman were two steps behind.

"But I remember a farm woman near Delville," Dr. Spain was saying.

"Doctor," Malone said, trying to use his breath for talking and racing at the same time, "if it's a stroke, will she be able to talk?"

Just about this time Phil Smith joined them.

"Talk?" Dr. Spain had broken off in the middle of a word to repeat it. "Maybe. Maybe not. You never can tell about these cases. Take old man Waterman, here in town. Had a stroke when he was seventy-one. Lived to be ninety-two. Never spoke a word in all that time. Three days before he died, he started talking clear as a bell. Fact is, though, I always suspected he could talk all the time, and was just too mean to do it. But with a stroke—"

Alvin Goudge caught up with them at this point. "Stroke? Who's had a stroke?"

Malone wanted to say, "You will have, when you hear about your new son-in-law." He didn't have the wind left for it. Instead he pointed dumbly to the bank.

Main Street was nearly deserted, everyone having gone down to the riverbank. Halfway down the block Dr. Spain made the turn into the Farmers' Bank on one rubber heel, without slowing down. No spectators noticed what was happening.

They followed him into the private office, Malone, Helene, Ed Skindingsrude, Phil Smith, Mr. Goudge, and the bank examiner who had somehow been picked up on the way.

Ellen McGowan still lay across the flat-topped desk, exactly as she had fallen. Yet there seemed to be a difference in the way she lay there, some indefinable thing that had to do with nerves and muscle.

Dr. Spain put down his satchel and began a quick examination, while the silent little group watched from the doorway.

"Now this woman near Delville," he began. Suddenly he straightened up. "Well, I'll be dumfounded!" His voice showed only a faint surprise. "That's funny. Her throat's been cut."

Chapter Twenty-Five

MALONE was the first to recover his speech. "Well, doctor, your statistics were right. This makes four."

There was just a shadow of a pause before Doc Spain said, "I hope the statistics were right."

"If you added them up wrong," the little lawyer said savagely, "either Ellen McGowan isn't dead, or else there's one more murder coming." He felt that he had never been as angry in his life. "Maybe you'd better check up, to make sure." He strode across the room and grabbed the telephone from the desk. The movement of its wire flipped the dead woman's hand to one side. Someone in the group still by the door gasped, he didn't know who it was but he was sure it wasn't Helene. "Get me the sheriff's office," he growled into the mouthpiece.

In the brief pause that followed he looked indignantly at the shocked faces. "A few more murders and somebody in this town will know what to do when one happens. If there isn't a doctor in the house, call the police. If there is, call the police anyway. If the— Hello?" he roared at the telephone. "The sheriff? Deputy hell, I want to talk to Sheriff Kling." Another moment passed, in it his anger began to fade. By the time a voice snarled over the wire, he was able to say, very cheerfully, "Hello, sweetheart. You'd better drop

over to the bank. We have another murder for you."
A pause, and, "No, you bastard, I'm not kidding."
He slammed down the receiver.

In the interval before the sheriff and his henchmen
came roaring in, he looked over the spectators. There
had been that little lapse between the time he'd im-
petuously dived into the river and when he'd remembered Ellen McGowan. During that time, no one in
Jackson, Wisconsin, had noticed where anyone else
was at any one moment. Practically the only person
in the town who couldn't have murdered Ellen Mc-
Gowan was Arlene Goudge.

"I had nothing to do with it," he answered the
glare Sheriff Kling directed at him from the doorway.
"And the fact that I'm as wet as the St. Lawrence
Waterways right now is my only alibi."

He explained what had transpired, with a little
help from the spectators.

"Obviously," Sheriff Kling said coldly, remembering his high-school English and the fact that a reporter might creep in at any moment, "when the dead
woman was alone in the room somebody murdered
her."

"Obviously," Malone said, "you're full of small
pieces of flypaper." He pushed his way out of the
room, grabbing Helene's arm on the way. Her flesh
was like ice.

He paused in the lobby of the half-wrecked bank
and looked at her. From inside the private office he
could hear Sheriff Kling calling Charlie Hausen, the
coroner. The little lawyer looked at Helene; the color
had all drained out of her cheeks.

"Malone, at least they can't pin this on Jake. He
wasn't here. They—" Her breath caught sharply in

her thoat. "Well, when we find him we can tell him there was one murder he didn't do. When we find him."

"Aw gw'an," Malone said, weighing every word. "He could have sneaked in through the window."

"He couldn't have if he's—" She broke off, reached for a cigarette, and managed to light it with the fourth match. "Malone, Arlene Goudge."

"She picked the damnedest time to jump," Malone said. "One minute more—"

"That's not what I mean. Did she jump?"

Sheriff Kling hurried through the lobby, ignoring both of them, followed by one deputy.

Malone waited till he had gone and then said, "This sounds like an old song or something. Did she fall, or was she pushed?"

"There were other people on that bridge," Helene said through tight lips. "And one of them was Tom Burrows. Why didn't he jump in and save her?"

Before Malone had a chance to speak, Jerry Luckstone came into the lobby.

"Ellen McGowan's been murdered," Malone told him.

"That's too bad," the young district attorney said. "Say, is Phil Smith—" He stopped suddenly and said, "What did you say?"

The little lawyer repeated it, with details.

"But that's terrible," Jerry Luckstone said. His voice didn't seem shocked or even surprised. Obviously there was something on his mind. "I can't believe it. Ellen McGowan. Is Phil Smith in there?"

Malone nodded. He called, "Mr. Smith." The white-haired, handsome man came out, looked wonderingly at him and at Jerry Luckstone.

"Listen, Phil," the young district attorney said in a voice that had a lapel-grasping quality to it, "do you have to wait five days for a marriage license?"

Phil Smith blinked. "You know the law as well as I do, Jerry."

"Damn it. I don't want to wait five days."

Malone decided to be helpful. "I know a little about Wisconsin marriage laws," he suggested. "There's such a thing as a special dispensation—"

The county clerk looked at Jerry Luckstone. "How about it, Jerry? If Doc Spain will say the word—"

Dr. Spain was called into the conference. He said, "Hell yes, enough for half a dozen dispensations," and went out on the street to watch for Charlie Hausen's ambulance.

"In that case," Phil Smith said, clearing his throat. He paused. "How about Florence?"

"That's all right," Jerry Luckstone said. "I called her up and she drove right down here. She's taken Arlene up to her house to spend the night, and we'd like to get married in the morning."

Malone counted to ten and decided he could trust himself to speak. "Well, I certainly wish you all the happiness you deserve."

"Thanks," the young district attorney said. For the first time in their knowledge of him, there was a relaxed, almost happy look on his face.

There was a howl of brakes in the street outside, and Charlie Hausen's assistants began preparing to move Ellen McGowan's body into the ambulance.

"Wait a minute," Malone said suddenly. He drew Jerry Luckstone into a corner of the lobby. "What authority do you have to get here in the county to exhume a body?"

Jerry Luckstone turned pale. "Why?"

"I'm just asking."

"Well, Charlie Hausen can give an order. Here in Jackson County the coroner has the authority to give permission to open a grave."

"Then get it from him while he's here," Malone said quickly, "before he drives off with Ellen Mc-Gowan's body. Or better yet, get him to send an assistant to drive the ambulance, and have him stay here."

"All right," Jerry Luckstone said, frowning. "But why?"

"You ask too God-damned many questions," the little lawyer said. "Just get Charlie Hausen to stick around, and get the necessary order to open Ellen McGowan's father's grave."

This time the young man turned completely white. He opened his mouth, shut it again, finally managed a completely unintelligible sound.

"I said not to ask so many questions," Malone snapped. He relit his cigar. "Her father presumably died out in California and his body was shipped back here for burial. Am I right?"

Jerry Luckstone nodded, without saying a word.

"I thought so," Malone said, looking fixedly at the match that had burned out in his hand. "You get that order through in a hurry and make arrangements to open the grave tonight and investigate that coffin that was shipped back from California." He snapped the match in two and dropped it on the floor. "Because I'm pretty damned sure you're going to find it's empty."

Chapter Twenty-Six

HALF a dozen reporters had cornered Mr. Goudge, of the Citizens' Law Enforcement Committee, and were asking him (a) did he know that his daughter had just been pulled out of the river, (b) could he suggest why his daughter had jumped into the river, and (c) did he have any statement to make regarding his daughter's act and any possible connection with the series of crimes that had taken place in Jackson.

Mr. Goudge upheld a fine old tradition, and utterly delighted the reporters, by setting his jaw hard and announcing grimly, "Gentlemen, I no longer have a daughter."

As far as the Committee's plans were concerned, he had nothing to say, save that it was hardly fair of the *Journal* to refer to it as a "vigilantes mob."

At that point the reporters caught sight of Helene and Malone, on their way to the hotel, and set after them in full cry.

Malone yelped, "No you don't!" grabbed Helene by the elbow, and ran, calling back over his shoulder, "You can't talk to me till I get my clothes changed." He had dragged her into Wilk's Garage, behind two parked trucks, through the back door, up the alley and into the rear entrance of the hotel before the astonished press had time to catch its collective breath.

"A lot of nerve," he growled, "wanting to interview a man when he's covered with mud."

"Usually the procedure is reversed," Helene said acidly, wiping her forehead with the back of her hand.

"For that matter," the little lawyer said, starting slowly up the stairs, "why did the double-damned idiot jump in the river? Especially," he added, "right at that particular moment."

"Didn't you ever go to the movies when you were a boy? The girl always jumped in the river after her old man had turned her out. You couldn't expect much originality from a girl like Arlene."

Malone sniffed. "Well, I wish she'd waited five minutes longer," he complained. "Though even so, I doubt if— What the hell's the matter?"

Helene had stopped suddenly, one hand flung against her white cheek, staring at a step just ahead of them. "Malone!"

"Well, *what?*"

"That's Jake's necktie!"

Malone stared at it for a moment, then picked it up from the corner of the stair.

"It's one of those silly-looking hand-woven ones. I'd know it anywhere. Malone, how did it get here?"

The little lawyer turned the necktie over and over in his hand as though he expected to find a code message written on it.

"Why didn't we see it when we came downstairs this noon?" he wanted to know.

"Because it was way over in the corner. You wouldn't see it going downstairs, you'd have to be going up." She drew a quick breath. "I don't care why we didn't see it, I want to know what it was doing there. Malone, *where's Jake?*"

"Shut up," he said. His voice was like the crack of a whip.

It worked. After a moment she took out a cigarette and lit it with fingers that trembled only a little.

"Malone, he wasn't dressed when we left him. And we weren't gone such a long time. Something happened that made him get up and dress in a hurry, and go out by the back stairs." She took a deep drag on the cigarette. "He was in such a hurry that he left with his necktie in his hand, intending to put it on on the way. His shoelaces must have been untied, too, I've seen Jake dress to go to a fire when the hook-and-ladder company went by the window." She dropped the cigarette and stepped on it with her high heel. "Then in his hurry he dropped it here."

"Damned good reasoning," Malone said absent-mindedly. He scratched the back of his neck. "Then he left the hotel down these back stairs. I thought so all along. Otherwise someone in the lobby would have seen him." He paused, scowled. "That means he didn't leave the hotel alone."

"What do you mean? How do you know?"

"Because," the little lawyer said patiently, handing the necktie to Helene, who held it as though it might turn and bite her, "he wouldn't have known about the back staircase. We wouldn't have known about it if Jerry Luckstone hadn't told us where to find it, and where it led. Even if he'd stumbled on it by accident—which is unlikely since you have to open a door to get to it—he wouldn't have known where it led. So someone must have come up here, routed him out, and gone with him down these stairs."

"But who? Why?"

Malone shook his head.

She looked at him blankly. He realized how very pale, how very weary she was. He suspected that she had slept little, if any, the night before. Her cheeks were almost marblelike, her eyes two great pools of blue shadows. She turned and started up the stairs again.

"I always knew Jake would lose that necktie sometime," she said coldly.

At the door of her room she paused a moment, one hand on the doorknob. "Let's meet for dinner in half an hour. Do you think you can get all that mud off in half an hour?"

"If I can't," Malone said gallantly, "I'll be here anyway."

He closed the door of his room behind him, caught hold of the corner of the bed, and leaned on it for a minute, breathing deeply. A curious monster, evidently originally dressed in white, now covered with half-dried mud, weeds, and green slime, looked at him from the mirror above the dresser.

"I never felt better in my life," Malone assured himself.

He clung there for a moment, then threw himself on the bed, face down, his arms above his head. For five minutes he sprawled there, his eyes closed, not thinking of anything at all, not thinking of Jake, nor of Ellen McGowan's face as she lay across the desk, nor of the wet hair blinding him as he struggled in the river, nor of the empty coffin they would dig out of a Jackson, Wisconsin, grave that night.

At last he rose and regarded the monster in the mirror with loathing.

"A good thing you didn't run into a photographer," he told it. He could imagine the caption. "Malone the Merman."

He stripped to the skin and commenced an involved bathing process in the tiny washbowl. The clean water on his skin improved his spirits. By the time he began hunting for clean shirts and socks, he felt almost normal.

By the time he finished tying his shoelaces he was singing a highly improvised version of "Oh, what a time I had with Minnie the mermaid—down at the bottom of the sea—"

Helene had decided to show the world how she felt by wearing a dress that was almost flame-colored, a light, bright color of an unnamable shade. If there was such a thing as "pale red," Malone decided, that would be it. He stood in the lobby admiring it as she came down the stairs. It was a filmy little thing, without enough decoration to put in your right eye, not a dinner dress and not a daytime dress, but something in between and indefinable, exactly the right dress to wear in Jackson, Wisconsin, on a summer evening. Her hair was sleek and smooth on her head, and coiled on the back of her neck like freshly pulled taffy. Her lips were painted a red just the barest shade darker than the dress.

He hoped that they were being noticed as he led her into the dining room of the General Andrew Jackson House.

"Malone, it's funny he didn't leave a note," she said as she sat down at one of the tables.

"Who?" He was looking at the menu.

"Jake. Of course."

Malone said, "Maybe he'd forgotten you knew how to read. Pay attention to your dinner."

The General Andrew Jackson House offered a choice of roast beef, roast pork, pork chops, and liver and bacon. Malone muttered something about people who came to the country in hopes of finding good food, and worried through the meal with the help of beer brought at ten-minute intervals from the bar.

Jerry Luckstone was waiting for them in the lobby by the time they had finished.

"I got the order to open up the grave," he said in a low voice. "But you've got to come along." He looked anxious. "I don't know what's going to happen if you're wrong."

"I'm never wrong," Malone said matter-of-factly. He glanced at Helene, pictured her left alone in the hotel to think about Jake. "You don't mind if she joins us, do you?"

Jerry Luckstone glanced at him, understood what Malone meant, and said, "No, of course not. Come along, my car's outside."

Helene ran upstairs to get a wrap. While she was gone Jerry Luckstone fidgeted for a minute, looking at Malone out of the corner of one eye.

"I'm not going to ask any questions," he said at last, "I'm just assuming that you know what you're doing."

Malone sighed. "I do. I'm going to find your murderer for you. And not," he added, "for the sake of justice. I just want to make sure Jake doesn't have a murder rap hanging over him when we find him." He emphasized the "when."

Jerry Luckstone frowned. "There hasn't been any word about him, not from anywhere."

"I know it," Malone said. He heard Helene's heels on the stairs. "We'll talk about that later."

The sun had gone down, and the twilight had begun to create strange little purple caves under the elm trees by the time they reached the Jackson Riverside Cemetery, an overlandscaped patch of ground on the outskirts of town. Jerry Luckstone parked his sedan halfway up one of the drives, and they walked on up a short rise. It was very shadowy and very still.

There was a small group waiting for them: Charlie Hausen and several of his assistants, Sheriff Kling and his deputy, Joe Ryan, and the cemetery's caretaker, a cheerful, toothless individual who turned out to be Buttonholes' brother.

Sheriff Kling scowled by way of greeting. "Have you any idea what you expect to find?"

"I think so," Jerry Luckstone said confidently. His brow was deeply furrowed.

The sheriff shrugged his shoulders. "Well, it's your funeral." He grinned broadly. "Or vice versa."

Charlie Hausen blew his nose loudly, and tucked a large blue handkerchief into his back pants pocket. "All right, boys," he said briskly. "Dig."

Malone yawned and looked away, to inspect a small, neat granite headstone just above the field of operations:

HAROLD McGOWAN

b 1869　　　d 1937

Jerry Luckstone was looking at it too. He touched the little lawyer on the arm.

"Malone, there's something wrong. 1937 was only four years ago. Presumably Ellen McGowan started her embezzlement on her father's death. But"—he paused, figured a minute—"if she started appropriating money six years ago—"

"That discrepancy in dates," Malone said shortly, "is what convinced me I was right." He refused to say anything more, but stood looking critically at the polished granite stone. It was refined, all right, but entirely too small and too plain for his taste. He preferred something really nice, with angels and sheltering wings and doves.

The old marble stone near it was more to his liking, showing a decorative pair of clasped hands and a drooping rose, the latter beginning to disappear under the wear and tear of the elements. He stooped down to examine the inscription.

LUCIUS MCGOWAN
b Jackson Wis 1840
d Jackson Wis 1887
R.I.P.

Next to it was another, similar one. This one did have a dove carved just under its arch. Malone admired it for a moment.

WATCHFUL MCGOWAN
b Elmira N Y 1841
d Jackson Wis 1870
Fond wife of Lucius, loving
mother of Harold M

Harold was evidently a motherless child, Malone reflected. Not even a stepmother, as far as he could see. There was no stone indicating that Lucius McGowan had taken a second wife. In fact—he counted rapidly on his fingers—Ellen McGowan's father had been left an orphan at the age of eighteen.

Helene had found another, older stone, and was

trying to make out its well-worn inscription in the gathering dusk. Malone knelt beside her and lighted a match.

AILANTHUS McGOWAN
b Burlington Vt 1817
d Antietam 1862

There were some words, almost entirely obliterated, having to do with honor and glory.

A change in the sounds just back of him made him wheel around. A great pile of sod had been accumulated by the driveway, and Charlie Hausen's assistants were beginning to hoist the coffin out of its grave.

"Lift 'er out, boys," Charlie Hausen said. A moment later he added, "I told you those plated coffins wouldn't ever rust," with professional pride.

"There's something in there, though, all right," one of the assistants said, puffing. "It's not so heavy, but I can tell."

Jerry Luckstone frowned and looked anxiously at Malone.

"Open it up," the little lawyer said hoarsely.

There was a hideous, wrenching sound as the lid of the coffin was pried open. Helene put her hands over her ears and looked away.

For just a moment, Malone didn't dare look. He heard Charlie Hausen's assistant say triumphantly, "There, I told you so. Told you it wasn't empty."

He opened his eyes. There was a skeleton inside the coffin.

Charlie Hausen and Sheriff Kling had turned accusingly to the young district attorney. "Well, Jerry," the sheriff began in an ominously quiet tone.

"Just a minute," Malone said. He tried to keep the

excitement out of his voice, but it bubbled up in spite of himself. "Just a minute." He looked thoughtfully into the opened coffin. "In the first place, that body was never embalmed."

"That's right," Charlie Hausen said slowly. After a moment he said, "Well, it isn't my fault. He was shipped here from California and we never opened it up. Held the services in Ellie McGowan's house, with the coffin closed." He blew his nose again. "Just the same though, he's there."

"Oh no he isn't," Malone said very quietly. "That isn't Ellen McGowan's father. Because, whoever it is, that's the skeleton of a woman!"

Chapter Twenty-Seven

D R. SPAIN confirmed Malone's pronouncement. "Darned funny business," he said, "but I remember a case up near Two Rivers where a man and his wife were—"

Malone never heard the rest of the story. He'd had another thought. There was something Henry Peveley had said to him that night in the Hermitage Tavern—!

He announced his theory to Jerry Luckstone, who promptly sent for the high-school physiology teacher to come to Hausen's Undertaking Parlor.

The physiology teacher identified the skeleton as the one that had been stolen from the high school four years before. He knew it by the initials Arthur Wilks had carved on the right clavicle, back in '28.

Jerry Luckstone sat down heavily on one of Charlie Hausen's folding chairs, waited till Dr. Spain and the high-school teacher had gone, and said helplessly to Malone, "But why? Why would anyone steal a skeleton from the high school, and bury it in Harold Mc-Gowan's grave?"

Malone wondered if it was etiquette to light a cigar in a small-town undertaking parlor. He decided that it was. "Why?" he repeated. "Because Ellen McGowan was afraid some question might arise sometime in the future, and there might be a disinterment. She didn't know that anyone could tell the body had never been embalmed, and she didn't remember that a female skeleton looked any different from a male one. All she knew was that there was a skeleton in the high-school building."

"You mean," Sheriff Kling said stupidly, "you mean she put it there?"

Malone looked at the sheriff and then at Jerry Luckstone. "He isn't very bright, is he?"

"Well God damn it," the sheriff said, his neck reddening, "why didn't she put her own pa's body in his grave, since he was dead?"

Everyone looked expectantly at Malone.

"Because," the little lawyer said, looking at his cigar, "she couldn't get it out from under the concrete floor in her basement." He added wearily, "I suspect we'd better get Ellen McGowan's brother in and talk to him."

He refused to make any more explanations in the meantime. However, he did agree with Jerry Luckstone that the basement floor in the McGowan house had better be investigated, and at once.

For a long hour he sat with Helene, Jerry Luckstone, the sheriff, and Charlie Hausen in the old New England parlor of the house where Ellen McGowan had lived since her birth, forty-six years before. The sound of pickaxes rang from the cellar below, and occasional voices of workmen.

No one said very much. The deputy sheriff had driven out to Luke McGowan's farm to get him. By some miracle the reporters had not discovered yet that anything was going on. For this little while, there was peace.

However, it was an uneasy peace. Helene sat turning

over the pages of a woman's magazine, without looking at them, her dress like a spot of flame in the
shadowy room. Sheriff Kling and Charlie Hausen sat
talking in low tones about the proper procedure to
follow in case Malone was right about what lay under
the concrete floor of Ellen McGowan's basement.
Jerry Luckstone was silent, looking at Malone out of
the corner of one eye, with almost a kind of super-
stitious awe. And Malone just sat and worried.

Once the lawyer rose, went to the telephone, and
called Dr. Spain. He wanted to know the exact state
of Harold McGowan's health before he presumably
went to California.

"Bad heart," the doctor said. "Very bad heart.
Might have gone like—that, anytime." Malone could
visualize him snapping his fingers. "Or he might have
lived for twenty years." He went on to cite two cases
he knew of that had lived for twenty years, before
Malone could stop him.

Shortly before the deputy arrived with Luke Mc-
Gowan, the young district attorney could hold back
his questions no longer.

"She didn't murder him, did she?"

"No," Malone said. "No, she didn't murder him."
That was all he would say.

A few minutes later Joe Ryan came back with the
awkward, gangling, sunburned man Malone recognized as Luke McGowan.

Evidently the deputy had told him nothing. The
big farmer stood still for a moment in the middle of
the floor, listening to the unmistakable sounds from
the basement below, turning white under his tan.

"You aren't—" he began, and stopped. "You can't

—" He shut his lips firmly, as though he'd resolved not to say another word.

"Now look here, Luke," Sheriff Kling began in an officious tone.

Malone held up his hand. "Just a minute, Mr. Kling." He paused and looked around the room. "If we go through a procedure of questioning Mr. Mc-Gowan here, it's going to take us all night. There aren't any questions we need answered anyway. At least there aren't any I don't know the answers to. So I'm just going to tell you what did happen, and Mr. McGowan can tell you if I make any mistakes."

"He's right, Marv," Jerry Luckstone said.

Charlie Hausen nodded briefly.

Malone paused to mop his brow and look around him uncomfortably. This was the first room he'd been in where he was sure he shouldn't light a cigar.

"Ellen McGowan's father had a bad heart," he began slowly. "He knew it because he'd seen Doc Spain. The chances are his daughter knew it too; they were pretty close."

He paused again, glancing quickly at Luke Mc-Gowan. The farmer's face was impassive.

"Maybe he planned to go to California for his health. Maybe he didn't. I don't know. I just know these two things. He was short about twenty thousand dollars in his accounts. Before anything could be done about it, he dropped dead."

There was an uneasy little stir in the room.

"You're guessing," Sheriff Kling said.

"Sure I'm guessing," the lawyer told him. "If you can make a better guess, go to it." There seemed to be a different tone to the sound of the pickaxes from the floor below. "I was guessing when I told Jerry here to have that grave opened up, too."

He looked to see what effect this pronouncement would have on Luke McGowan. The big man was frowning in a dazed way, looking from one to another in the room.

"He dropped dead," Malone repeated tersely. "Doc Spain just told me it might have happened at any time. If the news of his death had been made public, his accounts would have had to be balanced. The shortage would have appeared, and everybody in the world would have said he'd embezzled county funds to play the market. Everybody except Ellen McGowan."

Malone turned slightly so that he couldn't see Luke McGowan's face any more.

"She was a proud woman," he said. He took a cigar out of his pocket, looked at it lovingly, and put it back again. "And she worshiped her father. There must have been some pretty terrible hours while she decided what to do. Finally she went for her brother Luke, and they buried their father's body in the basement, and a few days later Luke laid a concrete floor over it."

The sound of pickaxes had ceased now and there was another sound, a strange, rasping one.

"Ellen McGowan got away with the fiction of his having gone out to California," Malone said. "And in the time he was supposed to be there, she appropriated—let's not say embezzled—enough money from the Farmers' Bank to wipe out the shortage in his accounts. Then—knowing she couldn't keep up the fiction indefinitely—she announced his death, out in California. Still, there was the danger that even if she arranged to have an empty coffin sent from California, and saw to its burial here, someone sometime might begin asking questions and investigating. She remembered the skeleton in the high-school anatomy class—" Malone wheeled around like a top to face Luke McGowan. "Did she steal it from the high school or did you?"

"I did," Luke McGowan said almost automatically.

There was a moment of absolutely dead silence in the room.

"There you are," the little lawyer said, mopping his brow. He looked accusingly at Luke. "And if you hadn't blabbed the whole story to Cora Belle Fromm one night when you were full of gin, she'd be alive today."

Luke McGowan dropped his eyes. "I didn't know anything would happen to her if I told her. I didn't mean her no harm."

"If," Malone began, and stopped suddenly. It was as though a blinding flash had suddenly gone off in his brain. Cora Belle had learned the story. The Farmers' Bank belonged to Senator Peveley. Cora Belle had done the Senator a "great service" for which he'd made a will leaving her half his estate. The Senator had gone around being angry for a week. He'd had a book of the school-fund records in his office the day of his death. He'd come over to the courthouse in a rage, and he'd been killed *by someone who knew he was going to be there.*

"What is it?" Jerry Luckstone asked anxiously.

"Nothing," Malone lied. Someone knew he was going to be there, and hid in the broom closet at the top of the little staircase, waiting for him.

But there was more to it than that. There was something else. And he didn't know what it was.

There were heavy footsteps on the cellar stairs. A voice said, "I guess you better come down here."

Malone turned to Helene. "Don't you dare go down those stairs. You wait right here."

He led Jerry Luckstone, Sheriff Kling, and Charlie Hausen through the door to the stairs. Luke McGowan looked toward the door and shook his head, the deputy sheriff stayed behind, watching him.

A few minutes later Malone returned, wiping great beads of perspiration from his brow. His face was very white.

"Well, I was right," he said.

The other three men came into the room close behind him.

"I don't know how you do it," Charlie Hausen said, shaking his head admiringly.

Sheriff Kling scratched behind one ear. "Then I guess the Senator found out about it and she killed him, and she must of blew up the bank to get rid of those records, and then Cora Belle—"

Malone was silent. It would be so easy, now. All he had to do was say now, "Yes, she did. Yes, that's the way it was," and the worry and terror would be over. The words formed on his lips.

But there was that air of quiet pride in the little old parlor, there were those names he'd read only that evening, Ailanthus McGowan, b. Vermont, 1817, who was killed at Antietam; Watchful McGowan, and Lucius McGowan. Ellen McGowan had lived six years with her father's body buried beneath the cellar floor and had embezzled thousands of dollars to save his name and her pride. His fingers tightened on the

smooth walnut back of an old chair that must have
been brought out from Vermont long before the Civil
War.

"No," he said in a curiously flat voice. "No, she
didn't murder anybody."

"But," the sheriff said stupidly. "Then who did?"

"I don't know," Malone said. "I almost know, but I
don't quite."

There was a Bacchanalian howl from the street as a
car screamed around the corner on two wheels. Malone
lifted the window curtain and looked out.

"Citizens' Committee stuff," Deputy Ryan said.
"All the hard-drinking young punks in town have
joined up and they're searching houses, and burning
down back fences, and raising hell generally."

He paused and looked anxiously at the sheriff.
"Also they're putting up posters demanding you resign."

"Well, damn it," Marvin Kling said testily, "I'm
doing all I can."

"They're saying Cora Belle was raped," the deputy
said. "They say they're going to—" He remembered
a lady's presence in the room and stopped with a sudden gulp.

"She wasn't raped," the sheriff said. "Doc Spain
would of said so. She was just murdered. And I'm
doing everything I can to find the murderer. His voice
was wild. "You go put up posters telling 'em I'm doing
everything I can. Election's coming in three months."
He looked at Malone with desperate red-rimmed eyes.
"For the love of God, mister, if you know who it is—"

"I don't," Malone said. "But maybe if you'll just
stop heckling me for a while, I will."

Helene's voice broke in suddenly. It had a strange,

high-pitched note, though her face was rigidly calm.

"It doesn't matter," she said. "Who the hell cares who murdered all these people? Where's Jake? Forget all this stuff and think about that for a while. *Where's Jake?*"

Chapter Twenty-Eight

"I AM NOT overwrought," Helene said firmly, "and stop treating me like a mentally deficient child."

Malone sighed. "Helene, everything that can be done is being done. You've just got to be calm."

"I'm perfectly calm," she said.

That was the trouble, Malone thought, she was. A little hysteria would almost be a relief.

She had been all right during the early evening, when there were things to distract her. "I'm on the verge of finding out who murdered Senator Peveley and—" he began.

"I don't give a damn who murdered Senator Peveley. He was probably a nasty old man who went around pinching girls in streetcars and elevators. Why the hell do you care who murdered him?"

"Because the Citizens' Committee offered a reward of a thousand bucks," Malone said in a nasty voice.

If he could find out who murdered Senator Peveley, he could find Jake, or find out what happened to him. That was the link. Or maybe it worked the other way.

He looked around the desolate hotel room. It was hardly a place to spend a long night of waiting. But there was nothing else for her to do. There was nothing else for him to do but go back to his even more desolate room and try to find a cool place on the pillow, and try to remember the one thing that would tell him the name he wanted to know.

But Helene—

He looked at her thoughtfully. "If I promise to go out and find Jake, will you do something for me?"

"Something? Anything!"

"Then make yourself all comfortable and tuck yourself in bed, and I'll go down to the bar and bring you up a nice nightcap, and you go to sleep like a good girl. And when you wake up in the morning—" He paused.

"I suppose Santa Claus will be coming down the chimney," she said bitterly.

"Shut your mouth," he said. "Jake will be here, and I'll have lost another night's sleep."

A wan smile formed on her face. "I don't know why I should trust you like this, but I do. Go get my night-cap, and make it a good one."

"A good one," Malone thought, as he pattered down the stairs, was going to be an inadequate name for this nightcap.

For the first time since his arrival in Jackson, the bar of the General Andrew Jackson House was almost empty. All the newspapermen were out, trying to keep up with the Citizens' Committee. The few lucky ones who had stayed behind were now over at the jail, getting Sheriff Kling's statement about the discoveries of the evening.

Malone stepped up to the bar and spoke confidentially to the bartender. "I want you to mix me a very special drink." As the bartender reached for a glass, he began naming ingredients.

Halfway through, the bartender stopped him. "You're not going to drink this yourself, are you?"

"No," Malone said crossly, "I'm taking it to a friend. Go on now, a jigger of Carioca Rum, and a —"

The bartender was a visibly shaken man when Malone marched away from the bar, carrying a tall glass in his hand. He wished he'd written down the recipe. Not that he had any enemies in the world, but he'd have liked one sip, to find out how it tasted.

The little lawyer paused at the door, his face knitted into a terrific scowl. This concoction, for all he knew, might lay Helene out for a couple of days. He hoped it wouldn't take that long to find Jake, but it might.

He knocked timidly on the door.

"Just a minute," Helene called. A moment later he heard the key turn. "One more minute." A pause, with a very faint, indistinct rustling. "All right, come in."

He opened the door slowly, balancing the glass in his hand. Helene was already tucked in bed, her favorite pale-blue personal coverlet—he'd seen her pack and unpack it half a dozen times—drawn up to her chin. There were two wisps of gray chiffon outside it; he looked at them again and saw that her slender, white arms were inside them. Her hair shone on the pillow like a reflected light.

Malone stood there a moment, then walked across the room and handed the glass to her. He had never realized that her face was so childlike, so exquisite before. Angelic, that was the word.

She tasted the drink, and gasped. "What the hell did you put in this, Malone?"

"Don't you like it?" he asked anxiously.

"Like it? It's wonderful." She took a long, deep swallow.

"I thought it up myself," he said proudly.

He lit a cigarette for her, and while she finished the drink he wandered restlessly around the room, deep in thought. For a few minutes he gazed out the window, over the town. Somewhere out there he would find Jake. He had to find Jake now. He couldn't come to Helene in the morning, when she woke up, and say that Jake was still missing.

"Drink's all gone," the clear voice behind him said.

He turned around. Helene looked like a sleepy, wistful child, her head propped up on the pillows.

"How do you feel now?"

"Fine." She smiled faintly.

Her eyelids were drooping a little. He stood looking at her for a while, until he could see that she was half asleep.

"Don't worry about anything," he whispered. "Just go to sleep and don't worry. I'll find him."

He tiptoed to the door, paused for one more look at her, turned out the light, and slipped quietly out into the hall. He paused there outside the door, leaning against the wall, breathing hard. Helene was going to sleep, expecting that Jake would be there when she woke up. He *had* to be, that was all.

Did the Citizens' Committee know yet about the evening's discoveries? Not that it would make any difference to them now. They were out to find Jake, and to hang him to a tree for the murder of Cora Belle Fromm. Then the sheriff would save his face, and the election, by announcing that Jake had committed the other two crimes. That was the planned routine. Now all he had to do was find Jake before the inflamed members of the Citizens' Committee did. That was all.

Had Jake left the hotel of his own volition, was he hiding out somewhere, unable to send a message? Or had he been carried away, and if so, by whom, and why?

The little lawyer decided that he could think better down in the bar. It was now entirely empty save for the bartender. He climbed up on one of the stools and buried his face in his hands.

"Same thing for you?" the bartender asked hopefully, wiping a glass.

"Lord, no!" Malone said.

He ordered a double gin and was sipping it disconsolately when the street door opened and Buttonholes came in. The gnomelike janitor joined him at the bar and began speaking in confidential tones.

"I've been looking all over for you." He glanced around as though to make sure no one was listening. "Look. I've got a bloodhound."

"Who cares," Malone said crossly. "I knew a fellow once who had a Saint Bernard. It was a lot more use when he needed a drink. What will you have?"

"Thanks," Buttonholes said. "Dollar Gin," he told the bartender. After a moment he tugged at Malone's sleeve. "Listen. This is serious. You want to find your friend, don't you?"

Malone turned and glared at him silently.

"So," Buttonholes said, "I've been looking for you to tell you you could have my dog, for nothing. The Citizens' Committee wanted to take him, but I said nothing doing. You can have him, though. He's half great Dane, but he's a damned good bloodhound, Hercules is."

"Hercules?" Malone repeated in a fascinated tone.

"That's his name," Buttonholes said. "And he can find Mr. Justus if anyone can."

"I haven't any doubt of it," Malone said. He wished Buttonholes would go away and leave him to suffer in solitude. With a little effort he managed to adopt an expression of great interest and went on thinking his own thoughts. Buttonholes' voice broke in at intervals.

Jake must have had a terrible hangover. He could have wandered away without knowing what he was doing. Perhaps he'd only gone down the hall to the bathroom, opened the door leading to the back staircase by mistake, and just kept right on going.

"Never forget the time Herb Flannery's little girl was lost over in Duncan's Woods," Buttonholes was saying. "Hercules led us right to the—"

Or perhaps someone had lured Jake away. But with what? Jake was a hard man to lure. Who could have done it, and who would have wanted to, and for what motive?

"—got a feeling Hercules could lead you right to the place where he is—"

Could the murderer of Cora Belle have believed Jake had been lurking about in the bushes, or possibly under the bed, or in any other imaginable place where the witness to a murder might lurk?

"—can't help remembering what my grandmother always used to say—"

Or could there possibly be a homicidal maniac loose in Jackson, Wisconsin? It hadn't seemed altogether unlikely on a few occasions.

"—keep having this same funny feeling about what's going to happen next—"

Buttonholes' premonitions had an uncanny accuracy about them. Could his belief that Hercules could find Jake be correct? How did one operate a blood-hound, anyway?

A car went around the corner of Main and Third Streets on two wheels, its horn going full blast. The Citizens' Committee again.

Malone wheeled around on his bar stool. "Where is this Hercules?"

Buttonholes grinned widely. "I got him tied up outside in my car."

"Bring him in," Malone said. It was a forlorn hope, but it was the only hope he had.

"Hercules is a good dog," the bartender volunteered, pouring a drink; the first one anybody had seen him buy since the newspapers had invaded Jackson, Wisconsin.

The door opened again to the accompaniment of heavy footfalls. Malone turned around.

Hercules was not only a good dog, he was a large dog. In build and coloring he appeared to be all bloodhound, otherwise he might easily have been mistaken for a small pony. The lawyer stared at him.

"He's big, isn't he?" he said at last.

Buttonhole beamed. "That's the great Dane in him."

Hercules padded across the floor gingerly, as though it was red hot, sat down near the bar, and pounded his tail on the floor with a noise like a bass drum.

"His feet hurt," Buttonholes said, half apologetically. "But that don't keep him from being a good bloodhound." His voice became suddenly affectionate. "Make friends with the gentleman, Hercules."

Hercules licked Malone's hand with a rough, wet tongue and looked up at him with great eyes that appeared to be full of tears. Malone patted his head very hesitantly and murmured something that sounded like "Nice doggie."

"Now all you got to do," Buttonholes went on, "is give him something to smell that smells like Mr. Justus, and start him out at the last place you know Mr. Justus was at. Just leave the rest to Hercules."

The big dog corroborated this with a high-pitched whine.

"That—" Malone stopped suddenly. He'd started to say, "That ought to be easy." But all Jake's personal belongings were in that room upstairs, and Helene had just settled down to a badly needed night's sleep. "I don't know what I can give him to smell." He explained the situation to Buttonholes.

For a few anxious moments the lawyer, Buttonholes, and the bartender discussed what to do. At last it was Malone who had the idea.

"Jake had been drinking some particular brand of gin last night," he suggested. "He must have reeked of it when he left the hotel. Do you think that would appeal to Hercules?"

"It's the very thing," Buttonholes declared, his face lighting up. "What brand was it?"

"Dollar Gin," Malone said.

The bartender reached for the bottle, unscrewed the cap, and handed it to Malone, who held it under the big bloodhound's nose.

Hercules sniffed, accomplished a backward leap of about six feet, sat down again, and gave a reproachful howl.

"Well," the bartender said, looking at him, "even a bloodhound has to draw the line somewhere."

"That's all right," Buttonholes said cheerfully. "He may not like it, but he'll remember it. Just the same," he added to Malone, "you'd better carry a bottle of it with you, to let him sniff now and then."

Malone nodded unhappily. "Give me a bottle of it," he told the bartender. After a moment's reflection he added, "You'd better make it a quart. Hercules and I may have a long way to go." He turned to Buttonholes. "You're coming along, of course."

Buttonholes shook his head. "I can't. I'm supposed to be up at the courthouse right now, cleaning it up. I don't want to lose my job."

"You mean," Malone said, "you mean I'm going to go out alone with that—" he started to say "monster," finally said "dog." He had an uncomfortable feeling that his voice had squeaked. He had an even more uncomfortable feeling when the bartender said, "Do you mean a big man like you is afraid of a little dog like that?"

"Of course not," Malone said in a voice approaching falsetto. He and Hercules looked at each other for a while. "No, of course not," he repeated.

He felt in his pocket for his wallet to pay for the gin, ran into a folded document, and suddenly remembered the appointment he'd had.

"On your way back to the courthouse, could you run an errand for me?"

"Sure," Buttonholes said agreeably.

"Wait a minute," Malone said. He disappeared into the men's room. Five minutes later he returned, an envelope in his hand. "Will you give this to Henry Peveley, at the Hermitage Tavern, and tell him it's from me?"

Buttonholes grinned. "Knock three times on the door and say you're a friend of Henry's."

He reached for the envelope and put it in his

pocket without discovering it contained nothing but ashes.

"And now," Malone said, looking hopefully at Hercules.

Buttonholes said, "Just lead him to near where your friend disappeared at, and leave the rest to Hercules." He added as though by way of encouragement, "Don't worry. He knows what to do."

Malone hoped so. He tucked the quart of gin under his arm, bought another drink for Buttonholes, and promised to return Hercules unharmed ("Just turn him loose and he'll come home," Buttonholes had said. "He's just like a pigeon that way."), picked up the leash, and led his new companion around the corner to where the back stairs of the General Andrew Jackson House opened into the alley.

Hercules sat down, looked up at him, and wagged his tail hopefully.

"Well," Malone said after a moment. "Well, commence."

Chapter Twenty-Nine

"IT'S A lovely night," Malone agreed, "it's a beautiful moon."

Hercules moaned again. The little lawyer had found it was possible to carry on a highly intelligent conversation with the big bloodhound. Whatever he said, Hercules answered.

After a moment or so of anxiety back in the alley, the expedition had gotten underway. At first Hercules had just sat there looking at him, with what Malone considered a silly grin on his face. Malone had finally decided to fortify himself with a taste—no more than a taste, mind you, he told himself—of Dollar Gin. He'd held the bottle out to Hercules in the same manner he'd have offered a drink to a compatriot. The big dog had coughed, uttered another protest, suddenly begun sniffing excitedly at the air and the ground, and at last trotted off down the alley, pulling Malone after him.

They were now halfway across the Third Street bridge.

"Good old bloodhound," Malone said. "Good old Hercules."

He felt an upstirring of renewed hope, and a sudden charging of excitement through his nerves. Everybody knew that bloodhounds could track down missing persons in ways that were positively uncanny.

Look at the stories about the Georgia chain gangs. And Eliza crossing the ice.

"Good old Hercules," he repeated.

Hercules paused unexpectedly on the bridge, nearly upsetting the little lawyer, and sat down, looking up at the moon. Malone caught his breath, looked in the same direction, and leaned on the rail of the bridge. He knew just how Hercules felt.

Hercules cried something appropriate about the moon.

"Silvery," Malone agreed again. "Very beautiful." He looked reproachfully at the dog. "Fine thing. We're not out to look at the moon, we're out to find Jake. Jake, do you understand, *Jake*. Here." He opened the bottle of Dollar Gin, held it under the bloodhound's nose, then held it under his own nose for a man-sized drink.

Hercules didn't protest this time, he just sneezed. Then he gave a few more sniffs and started off once more, Malone holding desperately to the leash.

Behind the Third Street bridge the town of Jackson was left behind, and they were out in the open country. Malone looked around anxiously for a sidewalk, found none, and contented himself with trotting down the macadam pavement. There were immense, shadowy trees on both sides of the road now, and wide stretches of fields on beyond them, no houses, no buildings, only the fields and the trees, all strange shades of blue and black and silver under the moon.

It reminded Malone of Lincoln Park, except that there were no street lights. He missed them.

They went up the road for about a mile, pausing once or twice to open the bottle of Dollar Gin and renew the scent. Hercules seemed to be overcoming his aversion to Dollar Gin little by little; at the last stop he not only sniffed, but licked the top of the bottle.

Once during the mile the headlights of a car showed in the distance, and Malone hastily hauled Hercules off the road and into the shadow of a ditch. It wouldn't do to have some carload of Citizens' Committee find him now, going down the road with a bloodhound. He patted Hercules on the head and murmured, "Nice doggie, don't make any noise." Hercules muttered something in his throat and licked Malone's left ear.

The headlights proved to belong to a farm truck with a single passenger, chugging toward home. The little lawyer waited until it was out of sight, then they were on their way again.

The shadows on the road were almost purple, the surface of the road itself was like polished aluminum. Somewhere at the end of it, Malone told himself, they would find Jake. They would find him alive and unhurt, and Malone would lead him back to the General Andrew Jackson House and hide him from the Citizens' Committee, then he would find out who had murdered Senator Peveley and Magnus Linkermann and Cora Belle Fromm, and in the morning he would deliver Jake to Helene safe and sound, just as he had promised. There was something about the moonlight on the macadam pavement that made him think beautiful thoughts.

Suddenly, at a bend in the road, Hercules paused. For a moment he stood still, his nose against the pavement. Then he began running in small circles, almost overturning Malone. Then he sat down, his tail lying limply on the ground, and looked up unhappily at the little lawyer.

"Come, come now," Malone said. "We can't have this." He opened the bottle again, taking a somewhat longer drink this time to reassure himself. Hercules sniffed at it, and began stalking about the pavement in circles again. At last he sat down once more, looked up at his friend, and howled miserably.

"Oh dear," Malone said. He wondered what to do next.

Apparently, so did Hercules.

For a few minutes they stood there, looking help-lessly at each other.

"Look here," Malone said. "You've gotten this far, you can't give up now."

Hercules answered with a mournful whine. He looked very tired. Maybe, Malone thought, his feet hurt again. He encouraged the big bloodhound to get up again and led him off to the side of the road, where there was grass underfoot.

"We've got to find Jake," Malone reminded him.

Hercules gave a few tentative sniffs at the ground and suddenly bounded off the roadside and into the field beyond, nearly dragging Malone off his feet. Once in the field he gave a couple of encouraging yelps and began trotting over the grassy ground.

"Hey," Malone said, "you're off the road." He thought about it a moment, and finally decided per-haps Hercules knew what he was doing. "Just so you don't get lost now," he admonished.

Besides, he liked it in the field. Apparently Her-cules liked it too, his steady trot threatened to break into a scamper at intervals. Here it was all silver underfoot, a moon-white world below and a star-dazzled sky overhead. Malone repressed an impulse to halt Hercules while he lay on his back in the meadow and gazed up at the sky. The field they were in seemed to be completely ringed with dark, mysterious trees; in some strange manner the sky appeared to be ringed with the same trees. It was a wonderful phenomenen, and one that interested Malone very much. He couldn't quite understand it, but it interested him. If some curious explosion of the universe should occur right now, and the whole thing were suddenly reversed, he would be walking on the sky, being careful not to step on the stars, and the meadow, with its tender grass, would be over his head.

It was, he thought, like being in a little box. But the mere business of being alive and on earth was one of being in a little box. People tried to break out of their little boxes, and all kinds of calamities resulted. Things like the murder of Cora Belle. Suddenly he felt inexpressibly sad over the murder of Cora Belle. She could have been out in this same meadow under the stars and the moon, she could have been drinking from a bottle of Dollar Gin, and here someone had gone and murdered her. Malone paused in his thoughts to reopen his own bottle of Dollar Gin.

If a prospective murderer ever stopped to think, Malone reflected, about the wonderful things of the world he was taking from his prospective victim, there would surely be no more murders. It was one thing to shoot a man down in cold blood, or to strangle him or to poison him. But it was quite another to rob him of smooth meadows pale under the moon, of this wonderful sensation of being hung somewhere between the earth and the stars, of Dollar Gin, of the remembrance of plump giggling girls with pretty dimples in their knees and elbows, and of the companionship of a dog like Hercules. Malone almost sobbed aloud.

It was some time before he realized that the bloodhound had been transcribing a circle around the meadow and getting absolutely nowhere. Indeed, Hercules seemed to discover it first, he stopped in his tracks, sniffed at the ground, came back to Malone to lick his hand, and howled miserably.

"Lost?" Malone asked sympathetically. " 'At's all right. Le's go right back to where we started from and try it again."

He led an abashed Hercules back to the road. There they paused a moment, deciding what to do next. One more drink of Dollar Gin, Malone concluded, might help him think of something. Hercules consented to lap a little of it out of Malone's cupped hand.

Thus fortified, the pair stood for a while in the center of the road. Hercules sniffed intermittently and sadly at the pavement, and Malone stood wondering which direction led back to town. At last Hercules went on a few steps, picking his feet up uncomfortably. They probably did hurt, Malone decided. A little rest wouldn't do either of them any harm.

He looked around for a park bench for several minutes. While he was looking, a bird suddenly rose from the deep grass of the ditch beside the road, startling both of them. Hercules gave a joyous yelp and started in the direction the bird had taken, dragging Malone after him, entangling them both in the leash, and finally landing them in a confused heap in the bottom of a ditch.

Malone pushed Hercules' front quarters off his chest and lay still. It was very cool and quiet there, and very pleasant. He didn't care if he never moved again. The soft grass stirred gently against his face, the trees beyond were whispering sympathetic and loving words. He opened his eyes and saw a vast panorama of stars, almost as clear and almost as beautiful as the Adler Planetarium, among them the moon, round and shiny as a silver dollar, appeared to be moving in an intricate and graceful design.

Malone shut his eyes for a moment and opened them again. The moon stood still now; he decided he liked it better that way. It was so marvelous and so far away, so shimmery and cold, and yet so friendly. It reminded him, somehow, of Helene.

Hercules had been looking at the moon too. Suddenly he sat up, Malone sat up with him, putting one arm affectionately around his neck. They looked at each other, then up at the moon again, and then, simultaneously, burst into song: Malone caroling joyously *My Wild Irish Rose,* and Hercules improvising a melancholy but effective little number of his own.

The moon slid coyly behind a tree, and the serenading stopped abruptly.

"Look here," Malone said severely. "This is all very fine, and a lot of good clean fun, but we came out here on a mission. We're out here to find Jake." He stood up, and gave Hercules a gentle shove with the tip of his shoe. "Get a move on, you sentimental son of a bitch."

They climbed out of the ditch and up on the road again. All at once Hercules gave a sniff, an excited yelp, and started galloping up the road, pulling Ma-

lone after him. The little lawyer caught his breath
after the first two bounds, took a firm hold on the
leash, and ran.

Good old Hercules. He might stop along the way
for a little fun, but he went on tending to the important business at hand just the same. Bloodhounds,
Malone decided, were his favorite dogs. If Buttonholes wouldn't part with this one for a reasonable, or
perhaps even unreasonable, consideration, he meant
to purchase one the minute he got back to Chicago.
Surely the Loop hotel in which he lived wouldn't
object to his keeping just one bloodhound in his room.

There could be no doubt about it, Hercules had
picked up the scent again. He was running now exactly like the bloodhound Malone had seen years before in a production of *Uncle Tom's Cabin,* with a
combination of excitement, self-assurance, and grim
determination.

Somewhere up this road he would find Jake. Malone
was sure of it now. Hercules had finally made up his
mind.

They raced down a stretch of pavement, around a
curve in the road, across a small culvert, and past a
crossroads where Hercules didn't even pause to look
around. He knew where he was going.

Malone hoped it wasn't going to be far. He was
getting out of breath.

He remembered suddenly that they had left the remains of the bottle of Dollar Gin back in the ditch.
For a moment he considered going back after it. No,
it wouldn't do to interrupt Hercules right now. Obviously the big dog didn't need another sniff to remind him what scent he was following. And they

could always stop and pick up the bottle on the way back. Malone made a mental note of its location, he wasn't sure what the landmarks were like, but he was sure of the sky. The spot where the bottle had been mislaid was directly underneath the Big Dipper.

Ahead of them Malone could see a small, yellowish light burning beside the road. As they drew nearer his eyes made out a building, too small to be a house and too large to be a shanty; the light came from one of its windows.

Hercules slowed down a little, but kept on in the direction of the light at a steady, even trot.

There was a painted wooden sign hanging over the front door of the building. It read:

CHARLIE'S CASINO

GIN AND BEER
GAS AND OIL

A slow fury began to rise in Malone's brain. Jake hadn't been kidnaped. He hadn't been lured away to a horrible doom. He'd just wandered off to a saloon, and obviously, he was still there.

Hercules led the way right up to the battered screen door, sat down, looked up at Malone, and whined hopefully for appreciation. Malone patted his head, opened the door, and led him in.

It was a small, unadorned room, with a battered wood bar running its full length. There were no cus-tomers, and a thin, black-haired man in a white shirt stood reading a newspaper back of the bar.

"Where's Jake?" Malone asked hoarsely.

The bartender looked up at him and grinned. "You got the wrong place, pal. My name's Charlie."

The hideous chill of reason was beginning to creep through Malone's veins. "I'm looking for a friend of mine," he said stiffly. "A friend named Jake."

Charlie shook his head. "Ain't nobody named Jake been in here, far's I know. What does your friend look like?" He added, "I only been open since six o'clock. Close up all day now that harvestin's on."

"He's tall," Malone said. His voice seemed very far away. "Tall, and he has red hair and freckles." He drew a quick breath. "You must have seen him."

"Sorry," Charlie said. "Nobody like that's been in tonight. Fact is, nobody's been in here that I don't know, and none of 'em is named Jake."

Malone sank down on one of the bar stools. His eyes found the row of bottles that stood between the cash register and the wall. A long line of them were labeled Dollar Gin. An opened bottle on the bar was labeled Dollar Gin.

He looked indignantly down at the anxious Hercules and muttered something, of which the only intelligible word was "Judas."

Chapter Thirty

"**M**IGHTY fine dog you've got there," the bartender said.

Malone looked down at Hercules, who was asleep on the floor.

"I'd sell him to you right now for a nickel," he said bitterly, "if he belonged to me."

He'd been sitting for the past half-hour at the far end of the bar, his chin resting on his palms, deep in gloom. There was only one thing to do, he'd decided, that was to abandon Hercules, go back to Jackson, and start all over again.

By this time, it might be too late. The Citizens' Committee might have found Jake first.

"Another beer," he told the bartender. He would not only never trust a bloodhound again, he would never trust Dollar Gin.

He took a gulp of the beer, looked at the sleeping Hercules, and suddenly gave him a sharp kick on the rump. The big bloodhound lifted his head and stared up at Malone with hurt, reproachful eyes.

"Helene trusted us," Malone told Hercules, "and look what you did."

Hercules sighed, and buried his nose in his paws. Malone took another gulp of beer and buried himself in his thoughts. He failed to notice when a car drove up in front of Charlie's Casino and a trio of young men entered the room, sitting down at the far end of the bar.

Jake is somewhere, Malone was thinking. He's got to be somewhere. If there was only one clue, one faint thread leading in the direction of where he might be! He considered leading Hercules back to the alley behind the General Andrew Jackson House and starting all over again. No, his faith in Hercules had been shaken. Besides, his own feet hurt by this time. But he couldn't face Helene in the morning unless he'd found Jake.

"How do you know he's there?" one of the young men at the end of the bar said loudly. Malone caught the phrase and suddenly felt the skin stiffen along his spine.

"We were tipped off, weren't we?" another one said. "Give us another drink, Charlie."

"Make it a double one," the third man said.

Malone shifted so that he could look at the trio. One was a heavy-set, blond boy with a broad, impassive face reddened by the sun. The one who was stripped to undershirt and dungarees was tall and thin, with bulging muscles under his freckled shoulders; he had a narrow, almost chinless face, and a beetle brow under thick, black, heavily oiled hair. The third, in a denim work suit and cap, had a sunburned face that seemed older, harder; his eyes were small and shifty.

"Don't worry, we'll get him," the man in denims said. He licked his lips as he spoke.

There was a long, low, whispering rumble in Hercules' throat. No one seemed to notice it except Malone.

"Just so that thousand-buck reward don't have to be

split up among no nine hundred guys," the blond boy said. His companions laughed noisily.

Suddenly Malone found himself very sober, very purposeful, and very calm. A pure blue flame was beginning to flicker in his brain. He slid a coin across the counter to the bartender, nudged Hercules in the stomach with his toe, and walked inconspicuously toward the door. The big bloodhound rose and followed him, moving silently.

The three young men didn't seem to notice them.

Their car, a slightly battered Ford sedan, was parked near the road, at the end of the driveway. For a mad moment the little lawyer considered climbing into its back seat and concealing himself under a rug. On second thought, he gave it up. There probably wasn't a rug in the car. Besides, there wouldn't be room for Hercules.

He examined the tracks made by the wheels of the car, and discovered that it had come from the same direction he and Hercules had followed. In that case, the chances were that it was going on up the road. If the three young men were really out on a man hunt, they wouldn't drive out of their way to go to Charlie's Casino, they'd be stopping on their way.

With that in mind, he went on up the road a short distance, the big dog padding silently behind him. He hadn't the remotest notion how he meant to keep up with the car, when it got started again, he just had a serene hope that he would be able to follow it.

As much as he'd wished for anything in his life, he wished that Helene were here, at the wheel of the robin's-egg-blue convertible that could catch up with anything on the road or on the rails, not excluding the Burlington Zephyr.

He had gone about a hundred yards up the road when his ears caught the sound of a car starting behind him. Hercules growled softly. Malone looked over his shoulder; a pair of headlights were moving slowly in the driveway outside of Charlie's Casino, headed toward the road. The little lawyer pulled Hercules into the ditch and stood there a moment, waiting to see which direction the car would take. It swung around the curve and came toward them, creeping up the road at a pace that would have disgraced any respectable snail.

The car came near and slowed down to the very minimum of movement. Malone grabbed Hercules around the neck, pulled him down into the shadows of the ditch, and hissed a forceful, "Keep quiet!" in his ear. Someone in the car turned on a flashlight and began moving it back and forth, spraying its light on the field just beyond Malone's head.

"I tell ya, I saw sumpin' move," a voice said.

Malone held his breath, his face half buried in the ditch. He recalled, for the first time in years, a similar moment when he'd lain face down in a ditch in the Argonne forest, while a light played back and forth across him, missed him, and finally moved away.

"Wait a minute," another voice said. An instant later a horrible clatter broke out as a tin can full of pebbles was thrown across the ditch to land in the field beyond. Malone cupped a hand over Hercules' nose and waited. There was something reminiscent about that, too. Except that on that other occasion the things that were thrown over his head had exploded somewhere just beyond him.

"What're we doing here?" a voice muttered. "He ain't anywhere around here, we know where he is."

"We was told to watch the roads on the way," the first voice said.

There was still another detail in which this occasion differed from that other one of years ago, Malone lamented. That other time he'd been hugging a quart of cognac stolen the day before from the captain's orderly. He'd gotten away with most of it, too, before he collapsed in a mudhole, to wake hours later in another mudhole hugging two machine guns and sitting on a recumbent prisoner. He hadn't figured out how he, the machine guns, or the prisoner got there, or what he'd done with the rest of the bottle of cognac, but he had silently accepted the young lieutenant's recommendation for a citation. It had given him a memorable five days' leave.

He pinched himself as a sharp reminder of where he was. The car had started moving slowly again. He waited until it had gone a hundred feet or so, and then began slowly creeping along the edge of the ditch, Hercules at his heels.

The occupants of the car knew where they were going. Someone knew where Jake was, and had tipped them off. It wasn't Hercules who was going to lead him to Jake, it was the carful of drunken young ruffians inspired by the Citizens' Committee. Just the same, he was glad to have Hercules with him. It was a comforting kind of moral support.

The road curved sharply, went down a steep little hill, and curved again. Suddenly, ahead of him, Malone could see a cluster of buildings, most of them large. A high-arched wooden gate stood at one side of the road. The car he had been following suddenly turned off its lights, slid past the gate, and stopped. Malone again put a hand over Hercules' nose and waited in the shadows, while the three men piled out of the car and slipped inconspicuously through the gate. Through the darkness he could see other cars parked along the road.

He stood there until all was quiet again, then went slowly and cautiously up the side of the road until he stood directly below the arch. Through it the buildings seemed vast and mysterious; only a few lights showed here and there. He looked up at the lettering on the wooden arch: JACKSON COUNTY FARM AND INSANE ASYLUM

Malone sank down on the grass by the side of the road, pulling Hercules after him. The county asylum. That was where old Doc somebody-or-other was, the one who had some theory about blows on the head. Maybe a good quick blow on the head was what he needed right now.

Another car drove up the road, its lights turned off, and parked near the arch. Two men walked within striking distance of Malone. As they passed, one of them said, "He's here all right. We'll get him out if we have to tear the place down."

Malone looked desperately up and down the road. Inside the gates everything was very quiet and peaceful, yet a group of angry, drunken men, their minds intent on that thousand-dollar reward, were gathered somewhere in the shadows. And, for some reasons he could not understand, Jake was somewhere in that enclosure, too.

On the other side of the road, nestled in its next curve, was a farmhouse. Malone spotted it, grabbed Hercules by the leash, and raced for it. The farmer might be one of the Citizens' Committee, or he might not. It was a chance that had to be taken. The little lawyer dived up the two, rickety front steps and pounded noisily on the door. Hercules howled.

There was an agonizingly long pause before footsteps sounded and the door opened. A plump, gray-haired woman in curlpapers looked out.

"—use your phone—" Malone panted.

The woman didn't ask any questions. She lighted the hall lamp and pointed. "There it is." As Malone stared at it dumbly she added, "One ring for Jackson central."

Malone turned the crank, picked up the receiver, and said, "The sheriff and Jerry Luckstone. Well, dammit, can't you give me both at once? All right then, Jerry Luckstone."

Central found the district attorney in his office at the courthouse.

"There's a mob," Malone said, without explanation. "They're tearing down the county farm. Jake's here." He caught his breath and said, "For Pete's sake bring the police." He almost said "the marines."

He found his hostess in the act of giving Hercules a hambone, offered to pay for the call, thanked her, and started back toward the wooden gate. Hercules followed him, carrying the bone.

The group of buildings inside the arch clustered around a central brick structure with a high, decorative tower. Two low houses stood on each side of it; to the left was a collection of barns and shed, and to the right, a long, two-story wooden building. Malone paused in the shadow of a hedge and considered the situation. Only two lights showed anywhere; one was in the entrance hall of the main structure, and the other was in the wooden building. He thought it over for a minute. If Jake were, indeed, in one of those houses, he probably was not quietly sleeping in some dark room. Therefore, the light in that wooden building was the best chance.

He went on cautiously toward its entrance. Suddenly Hercules, close behind him, let loose a low-pitched, warning growl. Malone froze in his tracks and stood in the shadow of a bush, looking around him.

Just inside the high wall that ended at the arched gate, a group of men had gathered, almost hidden by the shadows. Malone looked closely; it seemed to him that a few of the heads were turned toward the wooden building.

If Jake was in there, it would be Jake, himself, and Hercules against the Citizens' Committee, until Jerry Luckstone and the sheriff arrived. That is, unless there was another way of getting out of the enclosure besides passing through the gate.

He took a long breath and began working his way up to the door, staying close to the bushes. There was a small patch of moonlit lawn between the last bush and the steps; he paused an instant, then covered it in a single leap, Hercules landing on the step beside him.

The door was open. Inside, he found himself in a long hall, from which innumerable doors seemed to open. If he once got lost in here, he warned himself, he would never find his way out again.

But Hercules suddenly showed a renewed and frantic excitement. Malone caught a faint, almost inaudible whine, looked down, and saw the big bloodhound sniffing at the floor.

"Come on, Hercules," he whispered, "good old Hercules. Find Jake."

Hercules was already padding silently up the long hall. He went around a corner, paused for a moment of anxious sniffing, went on again for a few feet, and finally stopped in front of the one door under which a tiny line of light showed.

Malone shut his eyes, counted to ten, opened them again, grasped the doorknob with a hand that trembled only a trifle, threw open the door, and walked in.

There was a little table, with a lamp on it. There was a benevolent-looking white-haired man sitting on one side of it. But Malone was looking at the other side of the table. And so was Hercules.

"Well for the love of Mike," Jake said, looking up from his game of checkers. "It's about time you got here. Where the hell have you been?"

Malone looked at him for a good thirty seconds and said nothing.

Jake blinked. "Where did you pick up the pooch?"

Malone shut the door. "Turn off that light, or else pull down the blind," he said. There was an edge to his voice. "And don't call Hercules a pooch."

The white-haired man rose, pulled down the blinds, and sat down again. Hercules walked over and rested one paw on his knee.

"How did you get here?" Malone managed to ask at last.

Jake scowled. "Don't you know? Didn't you get my message?"

Malone rolled his eyes upward and talked vehemently for twenty seconds about matters that concerned no one but Jake.

"But," Jake said, "but—" He caught his breath. "Wait a minute."

"I'm waiting," Malone said acidly.

The white-haired man looked up at him amiably. "I assume you're Mr. Malone. I'm Dr. Goudge."

Automatically Malone said, "I'm pleased to meet you," and held out his hand. In the same instant, the flesh froze on his bones, not all in one piece, but in little hunks. As though things weren't bad enough now, he and Jake were shut in the same room with a madman. He repeated, "I'm *pleased* to *meet* you," with a heartiness that would have done grace to a political convention, and almost shook the white-haired man's arm off.

"Look here," Jake said, "didn't you get a message from me?"

Malone shook his head. "Not unless you mean the necktie you dropped on the stairs."

"What stairs? Oh. I remember. That necktie." Jake frowned again. "He came and woke me up and told me about the Citizens' Committee, and helped me get out of the hotel without being seen, and told me where to go up the road to where a car would pick me up. It was a hell of a long walk. And he told me he'd tell you and Helene where I was, and all about it, and how to find me."

"Yes, yes, yes," Malone howled, "but—"

"And a car picked me up," Jake went on doggedly, "and brought me out here, and Dr. Goudge has been making me very comfortable—he's head of the place here, you know—"

"He's—" Malone stopped. "You're—head of the —county asylum—doctor?"

Dr. Goudge nodded, a hint of surprise on his face. "I've been head of it since 1937. Why?"

"Nothing," Malone said. He had an idea it wouldn't

be tactful to add, "I'd thought you were an inmate here."

What had been said? Florence Peveley: "He's been in the county asylum for the last four years." And Dr. Spain: "Wish old Doc Goudge weren't out in the asylum." Nobody'd mentioned in what capacity Dr. Goudge had been there.

But it was damned reassuring to know that there were three sane men in that room to cope with whatever might come. Not counting Hercules.

"He—"

Malone wheeled around suddenly to face Jake. It was the one thing he needed to know. "Jake. You said—*he* woke you up, *he* sent you here—who do you mean by—"

Jake had started to answer when the rock came through the window, with an ear-shattering sound of crashing glass. A yell from outside followed it.

"Don't move," Malone said very quietly.

"Come out, or we'll blow you out," bellowed another voice from outside.

Malone turned to the doctor. "How about this building. Is it full of people?"

Doc Goudge shook his head. "It was condemned two years ago. That's why it only has an oil lamp; there's no wiring. There's just the janitor has a room down at the end of the—"

There was a drunken howl from outside, its words had something to do with rape and murder.

"The quickest way out," Doc Goudge said, halfway to the door, "is through the old bridge to the next building on the second—"

There was a frantic howl from Hercules as the tar-

soaked torch came hurtling in through the windows.
Jake dived for Malone, throwing him and the old
doctor toward the door, just as the table, with its
oil lamp, overturned. Hercules leaped over them in
the same instant that the whole room seemed to
burst into flames.

"You can't get out that way," Doc Goudge yelled.
Malone spun around in his dive down the long hall,
grabbed Jake by the arm in the same instant, just as
the old doctor threw open a door. There was a little
balcony outside it. Through a cloud of smoke Malone
saw Hercules dive past them, over the balcony's railing, and into the darkness; in the same instant he
saw that the old building had been constructed on a
hill and that the balcony hung a good twelve feet
above the ground. The wall behind them was beginning to burn. Below, the mob was waiting for Jake.

"Jump!" he screamed. "Never mind them. I'll tell
them—"

Jake jumped. In the next breath Malone caught
the old doctor around the waist and lifted him up to
the balcony rail.

In the moment that he poised there, a car, headlights and spotlights on, and horn going full blast,
came screeching around the curve by the gate and
stopped not fifty feet from the blazing building. He
took a tighter grip on Doc Goudge.

Both front doors of the car opened simultaneously.
From one side the red-haired Florence Peveley dived
out and ran in the direction of the crowd. The girl
who appeared from the other door was Helene.

Malone took a breath, shut his eyes, and jumped.

Chapter Thirty-One

THERE were men in nightshirts and overalls pouring water and dirt on the flames behind him. There was Hercules licking his face, there was Jake and Helene, and Florence Peveley, and a mob of men standing in the glare of the flames.

John J. Malone struggled to his feet. For just an instant there was a whirligig of starred sky, black trees, white faces, and blazing timbers. His hands and face stung sharply, the breaths that he drew came painfully.

He looked at Jake's face, it was black and singed, and he realized that they must have leaped through the flames.

"That's the guy," a voice screamed. "The red-haired one."

Malone roared, "Just—a—minute!" The crowd of men suddenly hushed.

It was a hair's breadth, Malone thought, like the last sixty seconds before the jury went out. The mob inspired by the Citizens' Committee had been momentarily taken aback, but, he knew, only momentarily. Until Jerry Luckstone and the sheriff came, there was only himself to stand between Jake and the mob. And his throat hurt.

The fire was dying down a little. Malone struck a

pose and instinctively reached for a cigar. He had none. He addressed the mob.

"Has anybody out there got a cigar?"

There was an instant's pause, then a faint ripple of laughter. Someone in the middle of the crowd pushed forward and tossed something at Malone.

"Here y'are!"

"Thanks," Malone said, catching it neatly. He paused for a deliberate length of time, biting off the end of the cigar, lighting it, and throwing the match away, always acutely conscious of Helene's dead-white face and of Jake holding tight to her arm. It was a two-for-a-nickel cigar, and it tasted terrible.

He puffed at it, re-posed himself, looked out over the crowd, and spoke in a low-pitched, passionate voice.

"Listen, all you guys out there, who've got wives and kids. Do you want to go home and pat those little kids on the head with hands"—his voice dropped a good half octave—"stained with the blood"—he paused—"of an innocent man!"

There was silence, and a faint, subdued crackling of flames.

That's the stuff, he told himself, pour it out to them as if they were a Cook County jury. That's what they are, they're a jury. Pour it out. He felt a strange, uncomfortable tingling all over, the stinging burns on his face and hands seemed to have eased a little, and he wondered if he were dying. The mob had begun to murmur again, a few of its leaders had stepped up a few feet closer. Malone tried to stand so that he would be between the men and Helene.

He spoke quietly and persuasively. "There must be a hundred of you out there. A thousand dollars divided up between you would come to about ten bucks apiece." He gathered in all the breath he could stand and let it out in a last, frantic appeal to the jury. "Do you want to go to your grave with the blood of an innocent man on your hands, for a lousy ten bucks apiece?"

In the same instant Hercules, somewhere in the bushes beyond, sent up a heart-rending howl.

An uneasy, frightened movement began in the crowd, slowly men began pulling away in little groups and starting for their cars. A piece of loose tinder in the burning building behind Malone suddenly blazed up and sent an unearthly light over the scene, in the same instant Hercules let loose with another dreadful howl, and the movement toward the parked cars became a panicked rout.

Malone spun around and threw the cigar into the smoldering flames. There wasn't much difference, after all, between a lynch mob and a jury in the criminal court. You could convince 'em, or you could reason with 'em, or you could pray with 'em, but the simplest thing of all to do was to scare 'em. He wished he could take Hercules into a courtroom with him sometime.

Helene said, "Malone, how did you get out here?"

He looked at her. Her lovely silver-gilt hair was loose and flying in all directions, her face was smudged with smoke. Jake, beside her, had lost most of his eyebrows and a little of his skin. And Florence Peveley's red hair, in the immediate background, looked like a Fourth of July sparkler just about to expire.

"For that matter," he said to Helene crossly, "how did you get here?" A fire came into his eyes that wasn't a reflection of the half-burned building. "I thought I put you to sleep."

"Malone, forgive me. I poured that drink on the carpet when you weren't looking. I had to know what was going on. Then Flo—Florence Peveley—came. She'd heard about the mob. Her gardener was part of it and he'd been tipped off as to where it was going. So we got in her car and came out here—"

Malone said in a cracked, terrible voice. "I just need to know one thing. Who tipped off Flo Peveley's gardener? Who told this mob to come out here?" He gasped for breath. "And Jake. Jake, who warned you? Because—"

He was interrupted again. Another car screamed into the driveway, this one was blazing with official-looking lights, and its siren sounded a low whine as it came to a stop. From somewhere out of sight Hercules answered the whine, as Jerry Luckstone, Sheriff Kling, and the deputy sheriff climbed out of the front seat. Ed Skindingsrude, Mr. Goudge, and Phil Smith, the latter still holding his head very straight above the bandages, came out of the back seat and followed the sheriff up to where Malone was standing.

"They were in Marv's office," Jerry explained, "and they came along with us." His face was pale. "My God, Jake Justus! Are you all right?"

"Obviously, no," Jake said between scorched lips.

"We've had a little trouble here," Malone said acidly.

There were questions to be asked, and answers to be given. But before anyone could say a word, an ominous roar and crackling sounded from the building behind them. A sheet of flame shot from one window, darted to the next, and then burst out on the floor above.

"Look out below!" Malone yelled, "it's breaking out on the other story!"

There were shouts, there was confusion, a great rushing back and forth of men with buckets, and a smothering outpouring of smoke. Someone took Malone by the arm and dragged him backwards; he saw the flames receding from his sight, shut his eyes, and let himself be propelled over the lawn. A door was opened and strong hands helped him through it and into a chair.

"It's under control," a voice said from somewhere, "and the fire department is on the way out."

"Give him a drink," another voice said.

Malone opened his eyes and saw a glass being filled from a bottle of Dollar Gin. He wondered if the fire wouldn't have been easier to survive.

"Take this," Helene said firmly. He took it, blinked a few times, and looked around the room.

Everyone was there, Jake and Helene, holding tight to each other's hands, Flo Peveley, her red hair flying in all directions, Jerry Luckstone, pale and worried, the sheriff and Joe Ryan, his deputy, Doc Goudge, who wasn't a madman but was head of the county asylum, Philomen Ma. Smith, Mr. Goudge, and Ed Skindingsrude. A cold, wet nose pushed its way into his hand. It was Hercules.

"Malone, listen," Helene's voice begged. "Remember. The other story. Do you know now what you meant?"

Malone closed his eyes and nodded. He thought he knew what he meant, but he wasn't sure.

"The other story," Jake repeated urgently. "Pay

attention, damn you. Where another person might have said 'the other floor,' you said 'the other story.' You said it once before, and you said it was important."

"It was important," Malone said, nodding. The effort hurt his head. "Because I meant the other story of the courthouse." He opened his eyes. All he could see was a circle of white faces around him. In a minute he would have to point to one of those faces. And he knew, now, which one it was. "I meant"—it was painful, forming the words through those blistered lips—"the man who shot Senator Peveley, and blew up the bank, and strangled Cora Belle, was not on the second story of the courthouse." He gasped at the air. "He was on the other story. The first story."

A voice said, "He's out of his head. He's delirious."

"I am not," Malone said. "None of the people we listed as being on the second story of the courthouse shot Senator Peveley. The man who did shoot him was supposedly downstairs." He gasped again. Someone poured another drink of Dollar Gin down his throat. "He knew the Senator was coming to the courthouse at that hour, he went upstairs and concealed himself in the broom closet, he waited until the Senator started down the little staircase and shot him in the back, he closed the door of the closet and waited until everyone else had gone down the stairs, and then," he tried to draw a breath; it stuck in his throat.

"Malone, go on," Helene said.

"Then," the little lawyer whispered, "he went through the courtroom and down the big, main staircase and joined the crowd in the hall, as though he'd just come from his own office. I know it. The murderer could never have come out of that closet and down the little staircase without being observed by the people standing in the hall around the Senator's body. It had to be like that. There was no other way."

He realized dimly that Helene was shaking him. "Malone. Who was it? What was his name?"

Somehow he managed to form the words. "Don't you know? It's a matter of simple arithmetic. There's only one person it could be."

He knew, as he said them, that those were the last words he would speak above a whisper for a long time, maybe hours.

But at the same time, he knew that he didn't need to speak. The faces around him weren't looking at him now.

"That's right," Jerry Luckstone was saying, in a curiously strained voice. "There's just one person who was in the bank that day who was on the first floor of the courthouse, not the second, when Senator Peveley was shot."

Malone grabbed at the young district attorney's arm, shook it to attract attention, and went through a series of complicated gestures. Jerry Luckstone nodded in agreement.

"He put the bomb in that package of school-fund records Ellen McGowan brought to the bank. Because he wanted to make sure they were destroyed." He looked back at Malone, who made more gestures. "He strangled Cora Belle because she knew where Harold McGowan was buried. He cut Ellen McGowan's throat because she was about to tell—" he stopped and pointed.

Alvin Goudge had decided to make a break for it. He didn't get far.

It wasn't the sheriff or his deputy who stopped him. It was Hercules who leaped on his chest, at exactly the same moment that Doc Goudge stepped in front of the door, yanked a blackjack from his pocket, and brought it down neatly over his skull.

There was a moment of complete, deathlike silence in the room. Malone looked around at Jake and Helene holding hands, at Florence Peveley, her friendly, homely face smudged with smoke, at Jerry Luckstone, Ed Skindingsrude, and Philomen Ma. Smith, all three of them pale and shocked, at the red-necked sheriff and his open-mouthed deputy, and at the white-haired old Doc Goudge, standing with a blackjack in his hand, over the unconscious form of his brother. Then he closed his eyes for a minute.

"I always thought he'd turn out this way," Doc Goudge said very quietly. "There's always been a bad streak in the family, and it came out in Alvin. But I never knew anything about what he was doing." Malone's ears caught the soft sighing of a long, indrawn breath. "When he asked me to have a car pick up Mr. Justus, here, at Grove's Culvert, and to hide him out here, I thought he was telling me the truth, that Mr. Justus was the victim of unfortunate circumstantial evidence and that the vigilantes were after him. I didn't know what he intended to do."

"But what did he intend to do?" Sheriff Kling cried. "What was the idea?" He paused, scowled. "I see he was the murderer but I don't know why he was, I see he got Mr. Justus out here but I don't know why he did it. I see he was back of organizing the Citizens' Committee, but—"

Suddenly there was a chorus of questions, not only from the sheriff but from all the corners of the room. Why did he do it? What was the reason? How about Ellen McGowan? How did Malone know? What was the idea, what was the idea, what was the—

Helene pulled her hand out of Jake's and sprang in front of the little lawyer just as Hercules moved in from the other side.

"Leave him alone, can't you? Damn it, he's been blown up in a bombing, he's been pulled out of a river, he's helped open up a grave, he's been in a fire and jumped out of a window. He'll explain everything, but for the love of mud, give him time." She wheeled to face Doc Goudge. Her voice broke a little. "Look at him. Half the skin is off his face and he can hardly talk. Do something about it, can't you, don't let him just sit here and be bothered by a lot of"— she looked around the room—"damn-fool incompetents!"

Hercules put his front paws up on Malone's shoulder and licked gently at his left ear.

"We've got to tell something to the people still hanging around outside," Sheriff Kling said anxiously.

"Tell them we've got the murderer and we're taking him to jail," Jerry Luckstone said.

There was a little commotion in the room. Philomen Ma. Smith was standing before Malone, his face very grave.

"They made me secretary treasurer of the Citizens' Committee," he said slowly. "I thought it was a respectable civic organization. Instead I find I have been the front man for a lynch mob."

Malone's eyes popped open. He wondered where

the classical scholar had picked up the term "front man."

"I made a terrible mistake," the white-haired man went on.

Jake cleared his throat. "We lament the mistakes of a good man, and do not begin to detest him until he affects to renounce his principles," he quoted. *"Bartlett's."* He added, "I guess we both got the same book."

Philomen Ma. Smith smiled at him gratefully.

"Mistake or no mistake," Malone whispered, "you've still got that reward money, haven't you?" He saw Philomen Ma. Smith nod and managed a last breath. "You can deliver it to me at the General Andrew Jackson House." He closed his eyes.

"I'll deliver it in person," the white-haired man said. He paused. "But the reward of a thing well done is to have done it. Emerson."

Chapter Thirty-Two

"NOTHING wrong with him," Doc Spain said. "Got a little skin and hair burned off, but that's nothing." He plastered something oily and unpleasant-tasting on Malone's under lip. "Probably have a terrible hangover in the morning. Tell him nothing'll cure it except time." He began plastering Malone's forehead. "I remember a fella once out in Jay Creek got drunk and set a hayrick afire—"

Malone groaned. "I don't care how bad I'm going to feel tomorrow," he said unhappily, "I feel worse now."

There were only five people, beside himself and Doc Spain, in the little room, but it seemed unbearably crowded. Malone wished they would all go away and let him suffer. But Jake and Helene sat side by side on the window sill, Philomen Ma. Smith occupied the one chair, and Jerry Luckstone and Ed Skindingsrude lounged against the wall.

The lawyer sighed. "It won't hurt me to talk now, doc, will it?" he asked hopefully.

"Not a bit," Doc Spain said heartily, too heartily.

Malone picked a cigar off the bed table and began unwrapping it. "It's a long story," he said, "and I've got to invent it as I go along. But, Jerry, you'd better take notes on it so you can check it with Goudge's confession. Where his confession disagrees with what

I guess at, you can be sure he's not telling the truth."

He lighted the cigar and puffed at it for a moment.

"It all has to do with money," Malone said. "Seventy-six thousand dollars, to be exact. Lord only knows what he did with his share of it, but he got it."

Jerry Luckstone stirred uneasily. "You mean that's where the rest of the money went?"

"Where else could it go?" Malone asked. "Ellen McGowan never spent a penny of what she stole on herself. Not one single penny went into her stomach or on her back or for anything in the world that was any good to her." He paused for a moment; there was a sore place in his mind, and he wished he hadn't touched on it.

"Her father was short twenty thousand dollars in his accounts when he died," Malone said, "but Ellen McGowan embezzled seventy-six thousand dollars. The difference had to go somewhere. And where would it go, except to the man who had stumbled on the juggling of accounts, the county treasurer; the man who didn't make his discovery public but checked up on Ellen McGowan's story that her father had gone to California and found that he had never been there at all, who checked up on the state of the old man's health"—he paused and turned to Dr. Spain—"am I right about that?"

The doctor nodded. "He came to me once and asked just how bad Hal McGowan's heart condition had been. Just kind, friendly anxiety. I told him."

"There you are," Malone said. "I told you I was inventing this as I went along, but that much is corroborated. Well, anyway, Alvin Goudge was a damned smart guy. His whole family must have been smart, or they wouldn't have had so much insanity in it.

He added up the juggling of the school funds, the information from California, the condition of Mr. McGowan's heart, and the story of Luke McGowan laying a concrete floor in the McGowan basement, and came to the same conclusion I did about what had happened. Only he went to Ellen McGowan and said, 'I know the whole story, and you're in a position to do a lot more juggling of accounts, so kick in.'" Malone paused and added quietly, "Maybe he didn't phrase it exactly that way."

"You mean," Jerry Luckstone said, "you mean that he blackmailed her?"

"That's the word for it," Malone said, between parched lips, "and don't look so shocked. It's going on all over the world, all the time. Anyway, Ellen McGowan kicked in, over a period of four years, to the tune of the difference between twenty thousand dollars and seventy-six thousand." He wished his cigar didn't taste of medicine. "She didn't want to do it, but she didn't want the world to know her father was buried under her basement floor and had died owing the county a pile of money."

"Senator Peveley," Phil Smith began, a little uneasily.

"Don't start with Senator Peveley, start with Cora Belle," Malone said. "She was another wise baby who tumbled to the whole story. Luke McGowan blabbed as much as he knew to her, and she guessed the rest. With the result that she called in Senator Peveley, president of the Farmers' Bank, and told him what to look for and where to look."

The little lawyer closed his eyes for a moment. "Henry Peveley said his brother went around angry for a week, and that he was angry on the day he died.

That was the reason. He went to the county treasurer's office and demanded the books and records of the school funds. Goudge probably stalled him, but the Senator got away with one book of records. Goudge could see what was coming. So he provided himself with a key to the little broom closet and a gun."

Ed Skindingsrude said, "But how did he know that the Senator was coming up to the courtroom just at that time?"

"Ellen McGowan tipped him off," Malone said dreamily. "Either in person or by phone. She told him 'the jig's up,' or however a well-bred lady would put it. The Senator would come over, he'd look for Jerry Luckstone first—since he needed the district attorney to lay his case before—then he'd go downstairs to fetch Goudge and the evidence. So Goudge waltzed upstairs and parked himself in the closet and waited for the Senator to start down the stairs, and when he did," Malone paused for dramatic effect, "Goudge shot him dead."

There was a faint movement in the room. The little lawyer lay back against the pillows for a moment, feeling inordinately pleased with himself. "The rest, you know. He had to destroy the school-fund records, so he made himself a little bomb and planted it in them. He waited till he got to the bank to set it off, so that there would be a number of other likely suspects for the crime. You'll recall he was walking away from the bomb as fast as he decently could when it went off.

"But there was still Cora Belle," he went on. "She was always a danger, because she knew the truth. And she was especially dangerous because she hated everyone in town like poison and was looking for nothing better than to stir up new trouble. So he called on her early yesterday morning—had it only been twenty-four hours ago?—"he must have been there before at odd hours, since she let him in without any protest, and he strangled her.

"But," he said, "when Ellen McGowan was confronted with the evidence at the bank, she broke down and told the whole story. She was on the point of telling more. He wasn't prepared for that. But the luckiest thing in the world for him happened just then. His daughter jumped into the river."

"She did jump?" Helene wanted to know.

Malone nodded. "And I found out why Tom Burrows didn't jump in to save her." He paused. "He can't swim."

After a moment he continued, "Ellen McGowan had fainted across the desk. All Goudge had to do was take advantage of the excitement and the confusion, slip back into the bank, cut her throat, and slip away again, to reappear later at the door of the bank and be terribly shocked by it all. He probably used a pocket-knife, you can check up on that. He wasn't prepared for this murder; he had to use the first thing that came to hand.

"Then," he said, "if anyone asked embarrassing questions about why he wasn't panting on the river-bank when his own child was being dragged up on shore, he'd covered himself by proclaiming, 'Gentlemen, I have no daughter.' "

Helene sniffed. "I knew a line as corny as that had something phony about it."

There was a little silence, before Malone spoke again. "That's probably the way he'll dictate it to your stenographer in the morning. If he leaves any-

thing out, just refer to your notes. I think that's all."
He closed his eyes and wished he could die and was
glad he was alive, all at the same time.

"No it isn't all," Jake said suddenly. "What was
the idea of this guy coming up and dragging me out
of bed, and telling me all hell-fire and damnation
were after me, and hustling me down the stairs, and
having me park all day out in the county insane
asylum, of all the damn places in the world?" He
paused and added, "Not that the food isn't better
than in the General Andrew Jackson House."

"And what about the Citizens' Committee?" Ed
Skindingsrude asked. "What was the idea of that?"

Malone groaned. "You people are more trouble.
Can anybody here give me a drink?" There was a
pleasant, gurgling sound, and someone held a glass
to his lips. He drank, closing his eyes, and sat up in
bed.

He realized suddenly that Doc Spain had put him
to bed stripped to the skin, and hastily pulled a sheet
over his chest. "It's like this," he said. "All of a sudden
Mr. Goudge discovered he'd left out one important
element. There had to be somebody who'd committed
these murders. Town feeling was running pretty
high. Any moment some smart guy like John J. Malone from Chicago might happen onto the truth. So
he organized the Citizens' Committee. Public feeling
did the rest. Then he planted Jake out at the County
Farm, where he knew his brother would take care of
him, and went around quietly buying drinks for a
lot of excited young punks and tipping them off to
the fact that Jake was hidden out there." He paused.

Helene was holding Jake's hand, tight.

"He was a darned ingenious guy," Malone said, "and perhaps the oddest thing about him was his variety of methods. Usually when somebody commits a series of murders, he does 'em all the same way. But this guy picked five different methods. Murder by gun, murder by bombing, murder by strangulation, murder by knife, and murder by mob."

He closed his eyes. "If anybody has any other questions, write me a letter."

It was silent in the room. A pleasant peace and coolness began to flow over his body. Everything is all right now, he told himself. Jake is alive, and back with Helene. Jerry Luckstone is going to marry Arlene Goudge in the morning. Florence Peveley would inherit all her old man's dough, and probably end up buying dinners for hungry artists on Chicago's near-north side, and telling them about her neuroses. Tom Burrows had beaten the visiting press on the identity of the murderer, by the happy accident of being the sole occupant of the General Andrew Jackson bar when the news broke; he would be busy spending his space-rate check for the next six months. Sheriff Kling would get all the credit for having run down the killer, and would be re-elected next November.

It was all very perfect and very wonderful, Malone sighed. He felt unhappy. He wished everybody would go away and leave him alone.

Buttonholes had come and taken Hercules home. In fact, he'd come and taken Hercules home several times. The bloodhound showed a proclivity for returning to the General Andrew Jackson House and Malone.

"Well," Phil Smith said, "I guess there's only one

thing that remains to be done." He drew a checkbook out of his pocket. "As treasurer of the Citizens' Committee." He began filling it in.

"It's John J. Malone," the little lawyer told him.

"Do you mind telling me what the middle J. stands for?" Phil Smith asked, signing the check.

"Joseph," Malone said. "John Joseph Malone."

He took the green paper oblong, said, "Thanks." It was signed "Philomen Ma. Smith." "Do you mind telling me what the Ma. stands for?"

"Not at all," Phil Smith said. "It's Philomen May-All-Your-Enemies-Be-Confounded Smith."

Helene looked at Jake, and Jake looked at Helene. Nobody said anything except Malone. He said, "Oh."

Jake and Helene were the last to tiptoe out of the room, turning out the light as they went. Malone tucked the check under his pillow, shut his eyes, and pretended that he was going to sleep.

There was a gray, wispy light beginning to show at the window. Malone stretched, yawned, closed and opened his eyes half a dozen times. It was no use.

There was that sound coming in through the window, the nasty, obnoxious, altogether objectionable kind of sound. He was able to recognize it now. The birds in the trees outside had observed the coming of dawn. They were only fairly well started, when the town clock came in as accompaniment for the chorus.

The little lawyer groaned, turned over, and buried his face in the pillow. If he could only hear one, honest-to-goodness elevated train again!

Chapter Thirty-Three

THE robin's-egg-blue convertible pushed its nose over one more hill. Ahead, checkers of green and beige fields, and patches of dark green woods, flickered and danced in the late summer heat. The white cement road ran across a little plain and pointed toward a hill.

"It's damned hot," Helene said, swinging the car expertly around a red gasoline truck.

Jake said, "In another hour you'll be back in the city and you can cool off."

"We came to the country to get cool," she reminded him, "and for peace and quiet and a nice long rest."

"We'll go back to Chicago, catch up on our sleep, and try again," Jake told her.

Malone sighed and said nothing. Ever since they'd left Jackson, Wisconsin, a deep melancholy had been growing on him. By now, two hours later, he was completely steeped in gloom.

He wondered why it was. Maybe he'd actually come to like the country and was regretting leaving it. It didn't seem reasonable, but it could be true.

"You'll feel better when you've had a night's sleep," Jake said to him consolingly.

From the top of the hill they had just reached, a small village could be seen nestling in the valley below, just a few roofs and spires, and the tops of the great shadowy elm trees, and a faint, soft haze hovering over all.

"There's peace for you," Jake said, "peace and quiet. I bet nothing has happened there for a hundred years."

Helene snorted.

"That little white house, set back from the road," Jake began.

"And right now," Helene said, "in that little white house Papa is probably in the basement murdering Mamma with an ax, and baby has cyanide on his bib. Don't talk peace and quiet to me until we get on Sheridan Road!"

Malone was still silent. He remembered, with what was almost a homesick pang, romping in that marvelous moonlit meadow with Hercules.

Dusk was beginning to fall as they neared the city. They had just entered the first suburban subdivision when Helene slowed down suddenly.

"Jake, what's that noise?"

Jake listened, and didn't know. Helene drove along slowly for half a mile, all three of them listening intently. Malone heard it too, a curious, muffled sound that he couldn't identify.

"It's something wrong with the motor," Helene declared. She parked the convertible by the side of the road and they piled out to investigate.

"There it is again," Jake said.

"And it doesn't come from the motor," she announced. "It comes from the trunk compartment."

Jake pried it open hastily and began pulling out suitcases. From behind them emerged a dusty, half-smothered, and very worried Hercules.

"I'll be damned," Helene said. "A stowaway!"

Hercules sat down and panted at them, thumping his tail on the ground and sending up great clouds of dust.

"He must have sneaked in while we were putting in the suitcases," Jake said gloomily. "Now we'll have to drive all the way back to Jackson."

"Oh no," Malone said. "Oh no we won't." He got back in the car and motioned to Hercules. The big dog bounded in, sat down on Malone's lap, and began to wash his ear. "We're going to Chicago." He added, "I'll square it somehow with Buttonholes."

"You could probably be sued," Helene said, starting the car, "for alienation of affections."

Malone said nothing. For the first time in hours, he was happy again. It was a wonderful world.

Suddenly there was a neon sign, then the first streetcar at Howard Street, and then the first taxis. There was traffic all around them now, cars and busses and cabs, fire sirens screaming and police cars going past with ominous moans.

It was just as they drove under the elevated that Malone snuggled back against the seat cushion and closed his eyes. Two seconds later he was sound asleep, a seraphic smile on his face.

"What do you suppose he's dreaming about?" Helene asked.

"Who? Malone, or Hercules?"

She looked down at the sleeping pair and shook her head.

"I wonder how that dog found his way into the car," she mused.

Jake took her one free hand in his and looked at her tenderly.

"Love," he said, "will always find a way."